The Crimson Edge Volume Two

The
Crimson
Edge

Older Women Writing

Volume Two

Edited by Sondra Zeidenstein

Chicory Blue Press, Goshen, Connecticut

Chicory Blue Press
Goshen, Connecticut 06756
© 2000 Sondra Zeidenstein. All rights reserved.
Printed in the United States of America

Book Designer: Virginia Anstett

Cover painting, *Café Fortune Teller*, 1933, by Mary Hoover Aiken.
Collection of the Telfair Museum of Art, Savannah, Georgia. Gift of
Friends of Mary Hoover Aiken.

Library of Congress Cataloging-in-Publication Data

The crimson edge : older women writing / edited by Sondra Zeidenstein.
        p.   cm.
    ISBN 1-887344-06-3
      1. Aged, Writings of the, American. 2. Aged women – United
States – Literary collections. 3. Aged women – United States –
Biography. 4. American literature – Women authors. I. Zeidenstein,
Sondra. II. Series.
PS508.A44C75   1996
810.8'09285'082 – dc20   95-36364
                                           CIP

Table of Contents

Joan Swift

Introduction

The Crimson Edge: Older Women Writing, Volume Two is an anthology of fiction, poetry and memoir by seven women writers past the age of 60. The authors range in age from 65 to 83, their average age about 70. All of them have been writing for many years, some since girlhood. For one of them, this is her first literary publication; for another, her second after a gap of fifty years. The cultural backgrounds of these writers are varied. They are Irish-American, African-American, Chinese-American, Jewish-American, Native American. One was born into a Mennonite community. Another is of unbroken French Huguenot ancestry. They live in New York, Missouri, Louisiana, California and the state of Washington. Clearly, their shared background – America for most of the years of the 20th century – touched them differently. What they have in common is that they are older women writing strong, gifted prose and poetry.

Why an anthology of older women writers? I can give no more honest answer than to say I publish older women because I need company. I have always depended on literature to understand myself, always believed that how we imagine our lives, how we make meaning of living, comes largely from literature. I learned philosophy and ethics from Camus, feminism from Lessing and de Beauvoir, my sense of life's nobility and tragedy from Shakespeare, of its romance from Keats, of sex from Whitman – with variations from Erica Jong and Kate Millett, to mention a few. I am still acutely aware of how skewed my understanding of myself was in the years of growing up, entering womanhood, married life, motherhood when there weren't many writers in whose work the texture of my life, my feelings, my side of the story had been transformed by the imagination. I tried to make sense of my life through the imaginings of men – Hemingway, Miller, for example – and didn't do a very good job.

The older I get – I'm 67 – the more I find myself seeking older women writers to tell me about myself. At this stage of my journey through life, I feel alone, again in a largely unimagined world. I can't get enough of the recent work of Stanley Kunitz, Alan Ginsburg, Hayden Carruth, Edward Field – amazing old men of long perspective, deep vision – but I long for the vision of women. There is only one Denise Levertov (no more), one Marguerite Duras (no more), one May Sarton (no more), one Gwendolyn Brooks, one Ruth Stone. I need to read what is written from the perspective of older women so I can imagine myself part of a varied, vital community, not as an anonymous, marginalized, stereotyped "senior."

But there are not enough of us. From the point of view of age and gender, we are the most underrepresented among published writers; older women writers from minority cultures are even scarcer. I publish older women writers because we are in short supply.

I chose these seven writers because of their art and originality. My editorial biases remain the same ones they were in the first volume. I look for an authentic voice; organic and resonant shaping of material; energy, as if the writing has been a matter of urgency; accessibility that is not simpleness but an expression of the writer's imperative to be understood, to share deep feeling. What Tema Nason, a fiction writer in the first volume, says about what she wants her own work to accomplish holds true for me as an editor. "There's a lot of fiction [and poetry] that's very good and very skillful, entertaining, interesting, but it doesn't move you. I want my work to move people, to touch them where they live, to connect with them."

Four of the seven writers are poets. Joan Swift's poems stem from her rape almost thirty years ago and its consequences for her, for a second victim and for the rapist. Written over a span of years, but recently edited to tell their "story," they provide a body of unflinching poems about justice and injustice.

Florence Weinberger's poems look, through the lens of her Jewishness, at four generations – from her parents to her grandchildren – that span more than a century. In poems that move from the Bronx, back to Eastern Europe, to the Holocaust (her husband was a survivor), to the American West, history and the intimately personal are inseparable.

Nellie Wong's poems are personal and political. The immediate and everyday – a secretary's fingers on the keyboard, a San Francisco streetcar's roar, an allergic reaction – evoke compassion and an unself-conscious desire for social justice that seem as necessary and natural as appetite or breath.

Carol Lee Sanchez's many-sectioned *she) poems* ride on compelling rhythms, as if just above the many-aspectedness of a woman's life. Details distilled from experience track this shape-shifting, reveal its progress toward meaning, reveal it *as* meaning.

Three of the writers contribute stories and memoir. Barbara Moore Balzer's story is about a woman driving her family belongings home from summer vacation on the day her oldest son is beginning college. On a whim, she returns, for the first time, to the cemetery where she buried a premature baby sixteen years before. Her quest to find the road, the cemetery, the grave marker, is a Joycean journey exploring memories of earlier deaths, especially her young mother's, and the way death informs our life.

Eileen Tobin's memoir is also informed by death, in this case the loss of a loving father early in her life. At a distance of more than seventy years, Tobin releases her material as if from fists clenched to hold treasures safe from dissipation. The reclamation of memories of her father and how his death affected her life sparkles with immediacy.

Pearl Garrett Crayton's stories seem to come from a lost paradise, a place very much like the world she grew up in – a sharecropper's plantation in Louisiana. This imperfect world, where African-Americans worked land owned by "the man," is transformed by imagination into a bayou Eden, with all the gritty and luscious failings of the human condition after the fall, but where, poignantly, humans retain the touch of the divine.

Each author's creative work is followed by an Afterword in which she "talks" about what is currently on her mind as an artist. Each Afterword sheds light on the author's work and writing life. Cumulatively, they suggest both the dilemmas older women writers have in common and their sense of authority and commitment to the work, their joy in it.

What is it about the work of these seven writers that has to do with being older? Their work, in style and content, is varied. None of them is writing specifically about being old. Yet each takes the long view, a perspective that suggests how life *looks* to the old. Being old means being layered – in time and setting, historical events, politics, technology, ideas. All of our past, the political and the personal, is alive in us. Our changing perspective is hard to pinpoint in the writing, but not in the living. It is something like the difference in experience between taking our newborn grandchild into our arms and, long ago, holding our own first child.

In the preface to *A Wider Giving: Women Writing after a Long Silence*, thirteen years ago, I used a particular metaphor to capture my experience of this changing perspective. Being old, I wrote, "is like the way hills flatten and sea spreads out as you climb toward a village at the top of a mountain, the heightened experience of sounds and smells in steps taken more slowly, the evocation of deeper memories with sharper elements." Now I would extend the metaphor to include being able to see how the cove I've started from is related to the next cove over that I'm just beginning to catch sight of, the connection of one place to another, how patterns emerge – and change. How everything changes. Yet how bright the daisy is at one's foot, how the butterfly rummages in it!

Soon one in four of our population will be over 65, I read recently, in an article that offered this information as a warning, as of some catastrophe coming to our nation – an onslaught of wrinkled anonymity, to be ministered to, a burden. I can't stand thinking of myself that way. When I talked, several years ago, about subtitling the first volume of this anthology "Old Women Writing," a friend who was 82 recoiled in horror. "Oh no, Sondra," she said, raising her hands over her head, one of them with a delicious nut brownie in it. "Old – the word makes me see snaggletoothed, wrinkled visages, makes me think hag." "That's ageist," I said smugly, 63 then, chewing the luscious white icing off my carrot cake. "You've internalized the prejudice against women's aging that dominates our culture," I argued. Nevertheless, I decided to use the mild word, older.

Of course age changes us. Like adolescents, we old women share a lot of changes in common, especially the weathering of accumulated years on our bones and skin; we have no trouble recognizing each other. But age does not take away our uniqueness, though every voice of our culture would insist that it does, would pin the seeming sameness of age to our consciousness and unconsciousness until we cringe from being seen as one of *them*.

What we all need, I believe, is to re-imagine ourselves in all our individuality and authenticity. To do that, we need more women writers of the long view and passionate immediacy like these in *The Crimson Edge*. They show us what age really looks like: that we are varied, that the accumulation of years leads to unique expression, that we are meaning full. We need more old women writers to help extend and people the territory literature claims for the imagination, to remedy the break that now exists in the continuity of imagined life.

I believe even more, now, what I wrote to introduce the first volume: that strong writing by older women will make the contemporary world a new and richer place, as a blaze of intense color, lighting the horizon, *the crimson edge*, reconfigures the sky.

Sondra Zeidenstein
Goshen, Connecticut
September 1999

Barbara Moore Balzer

For Ruth Moore and David Balzer, their lives a legacy of pioneer courage and faith.

Transition

Reality consists of a multiplicity of things. But one is not a number; the first number is two, and with it multiplicity and reality begin. C. G. Jung, *Mysterium Coniunctionis*

She still wavered as she approached the intersection of the two routes. To turn off onto the eastbound artery would lock her day into at least an extra hour of driving. She had traced the route on a map in the service station while she had been waiting there for the strange noise in the engine of her car to be checked out. That was when the idea had first occurred to her. It felt right, yet she was afraid of it. To act upon it would provide an alternative way of marking the transition from silent, introverted summer to the collective life that would thrust itself upon her as inevitably as would the soggy polluted air of the city at the end of this day.

She dreaded its coming: the phone's strident ringing, the month's accumulation of mail bringing with it the predictable anguish of decisions that could no longer be relegated to a future time – to the fall. The predictable reminders of family life: bills to be paid and dental appointments to be made, repairs and music lessons to be scheduled, houseplants to be carried in from the yard, the refrigerator to be cleaned and restocked. The contents of the children's drawers and closets to be sorted through and passed on. And the beginning of a school year! A new group of twenty-odd charges to be her responsibility until next summer. Their lives to be enmeshed with hers for ten relentless months until lengthening days brought temporary reprieve, bought with the deposit of another layer of reports in her file drawer: accounts of shared experiences, sparrings, friendships, antagonisms, academic accomplishments, plays conceived and trips taken, paintings produced and clay molded, social venturings and private strugglings – stranded, as if by the murky receding waters of a prolonged seasonal flood, on the banks of a river meant to be more tame.

Some of the children, indeed most of them, would become forever part of her. She would dream about one or another of them years later, identified, as they inevitably were, with one or another of her inner children. Their struggles would inevitably touch something deep within her, remind her of the way she had once been or of the way she was still. Taking them on – the mere thought of it – was the largest part of the burden of each fall.

So reluctant was she to take leave of summer that she had toyed with the idea of returning to the summer house and going for a last solitary swim. But the mood was wrong. The car was packed. The last roll of dust was wiped up from the floor of the rented house. Its doors were locked. Summer was behind her. Her books and papers, emblems of its freedom, were inaccessible in the tightly packed car – fitted, as the irregular spaces permitted, among the accouterments of her family's life: the children's hiking boots and knapsacks and flashlights, the piles of towels and sheets and blankets packed to conform to whatever crannies were still unfilled, squeezed into the few inches under the driver's seat next to the dog's dish and the bag of vegetables harvested yesterday from the garden, piled onto the bucket seat next to her, stacked on the meager floor space in the rear. The poor dog! She had had to ease his tail in before she'd gently closed the rear door. He sat awkwardly on the back seat. There was no room for him to lie down. The packed car, its weight on her mind, symbolized transition. She could not go back. The next step was unpacking at the other end. Unencumbered solitude was dispelled far away. For all of her having left the house so neat, she felt the more that her life was a clutter. The packed car symbolized the process of trying to condense two households into one, trying to combine desire for freedom with realization of obligation in one span of time.

Deadline! Summer running out. If it weren't for the

smaller deadlines of life, how could one contend with the
final deadline? The packing for the move to another place.
The confronting of the scraps, the unfinished business,
of a segment of one's life! The encroachment of the debris
of years lived. What to do with it all?

But she could postpone the unpacking. She thought, as
she surveyed her state of mind approaching the intersection,
of all the procrastination in her personality. She thought of
her younger self, of the time she had almost let herself drown
in the swirling currents of the Mississippi River to avoid facing the end of summer and something that her seven-year-old
self had surely known at the time: that her mother's life was
ebbing; that the end of that summer was to mean the end of
childhood. She thought of a snatch of clumsy poetry (she
remembered it still) she'd once scrawled in a notebook as the
rocking clacking train, carrying her back to college on a
bright fall day, had crossed a bridge over the Mississippi near
the site of her mother's grave:

> That part of the fall was over
> When the sides of the bluffs,
> Sun-warmed with color,
> Lived gay their last.

> You were laid to rest
> In black ground
> And needles of the spruce
> Dripped ice tears upon you.

And another line: *There is nothing beautiful about even a moss-
covered grave.* (She could not remember the occasion that
had prompted her writing of it.)

This day, in a sense, marked a double transition. It was
also the day of her oldest son's journey to college. Her
husband had left early that morning in the rented car, its
trunk crammed with their son's Kelty pack, guitar and
records (how different the style of luggage that travels to
college in the seventies!) to get him to registration by

nine in the morning. The younger children had elected to accompany their brother in that car and had braved the chilly September dew, yawning, groping their ways through the pre-dawn fog.

She'd felt a little left out as the car pulled away, and the familiar feeling was, as always, a dilemma to her. She knew she was an introvert by inclination, and must remind herself that her wish to be part of the socialization of family it had been her desire to create had, at its heart, envy of something she'd never had, and, as its appendage, wonder at the spontaneous ease and joy of communication that had developed among her issue. She was the only one locked out. Her temperament cut her off; the way she was. Born? Become? The question remained. Her desire, the occasional fulfillment of which brought her deepest contentment, was for communication with a closest someone. And for a while, that closest someone had been her firstborn son.

She remembered the first time she'd been given his tiny body, just emerged from hers, to hold on her chest; how she'd looked into his face – still wet, ancient-looking, eyes pinched closed – and had been witness to his first yawn, a miraculous moment in her consciousness. The miracle was that this tiny mouth contained a tongue! The glimpse of that tongue put her in touch with the unblemished perfection of new creation, with all the promise of communication, of speech that would occur between them some day, of the passing on of human knowledge, of continuity in the generations of mankind. The thought of it still filled her with awe.

In that moment of new life had come the healing of her prematurely severed bond between mother and child that had been her lot earlier. When she was seven, her mother had said, "Goodnight" (her tongue had spoken the word), the last time she had been ushered in to visit in the downstairs bedroom in her childhood home. That word, the last she had heard from her mother's lips, had been the definitive lie. It had meant "Good-bye." It would have been kinder to say it outright.

Years later her father had said, on his deathbed, "I wish I could talk to you more." That was a statement of human truth – probably a great struggle for one as reticent as her father to get out. She was grateful that he'd given expression to it.

Her baby's tongue. It embodied her experience of the miracle of birth. A few minutes after she'd glimpsed it, the doctor had dialed a number on the wall phone and handed her the receiver so that she could tell her husband of their son and then her father of his namesake grandson.

How many times since then she had thought, in the presence of her husband, her older son, her younger children, "I wish I could talk to you more." The excuses she'd made for herself: Too tired. Too complex to try to say. Too heavy a trip to lay on one so young. Too upsetting. Too angry a statement to utter aloud. Too wretched a feeling to give expression to. Too much resentment showing through. All the excuses flooded through her mind now, accompanied by the thoughts she was always thinking: Am I proceeding prudently through my time on earth? Am I dealing consciously with my options?

She recalled the records she'd kept of their first son's words. In each of them a cosmos was distilled. Mommy. Daddy. Ouhouse (*our* house, which engendered many aspects: family, security, togetherness, home). Park (which meant outdoors, freedom, sun and wind on face, rustling leaves, discovery, quick motion).

She remembered a golden moment. Her son had just turned eleven. They had hiked to a mountain top, cooked supper there, and were lying in sleeping bags on a bed of thick moss under brilliant stars. He had said to her, "You know, some of my friends can't talk to their parents. I can't imagine not being able to talk to you and Dad." She had held back the words she might have said, given this opening. She, his mother, protecting him. It would not have been appropriate (she'd thought then; she thought still) for her to tell him how it was with her. So she had lain awake much of that long, cold, crisp night warding off evil spirits while he slept the sleep of the innocent.

So thinking, she approached the intersection. She made the turn. The die was cast. Almost immediately, she began worrying about time. Now that she was past fifty, procrastination was not as simple as it had been at seven. Once she pulled over to the side of the road to verify route numbers on the road map. The first section of the eastbound route was a superhighway, a part of it on a long bridge over a gorge. Then there would be a turn south, onto a narrower road. To be going south would mean once more heading in the right direction, in the direction of unpacking the car and shouldering the responsibilities of fall. The smaller road would be passing a great reservoir.

Once she was on it, she slowed her pace. The reservoir was surrounded by majestic stands of white pine. She caught a glimpse of the water. The scent of pine woods contributed to the slackening of her pace. Breathing in the woods always did that for her. Just that summer she'd thumbed through a book written by a Gypsy woman. The author, writing of bringing up her own children, had said, "Take an angry child out into the air (especially if it is raining) to bring him back to reason."

Now the road wound in deep shade through woods which had been recently logged. A section of old stone wall had been bulldozed down. The sight of the destruction offended her. She thought of that time – sixteen years ago it had been – she was trying to contact. She had not known then how attached she could be to a stone wall, how important, how beautiful, old stone walls were to be to her. What a different person she had been then. That was before she had taken to rambling in the woods, before she had developed her passion for running streams, before she'd realized how important a relationship to wilderness was to her. Yet she was confident that there was sufficient continuity of being in a personality that the germ of her love had always been there. She thought of old stone walls she had happened upon hiking with her children. How tranquil, how familiar they'd always seemed, evidence of long-ago occupation of the land. As she drove on, she was glad of the presence of the walls and of the lazy stream that meandered toward the reservoir. It came to her that she wanted to photograph them. She fought the temptation. Another photograph to cling to? The resurrection of a memory only to preserve it? Yet the procrastinating side of herself prevailed. It said, as it had so many times in the past: "I can't deal with throwing that out today. I'll try tomorrow when I have more energy." It said to her, "You won't ever come here again. Memories are so difficult to pin down. You need proof that this place exists."

She had examined in some detail the genesis of her need to hang onto physical evidence. Stored somewhere among those fluid memories (and she was sure it had happened although there was no photograph of it) was one of her younger brother saying to her one night as she'd leaned over his bed, "I'm crying because I can't remember what our mother looked like." That moment had etched itself deeply into her consciousness. Of course she had no photograph, either, of the moment when he'd run into the downstairs bedroom the morning after their mother had died. She, the older child, had been told of the death upon wakening that morning. He had spent the night at a neighbor's and had somehow escaped them to run home to show his mother the stones he had in his hand. The neighborhood women were airing the room and stripping the bed. They stopped in their work and stood staring at him, the little blond boy at the moment of the shattering of his innocence, as he demanded: "Where's my mother? Where is she?" She had stood there transfixed by the horror of it. And not one of them could say a word. Nor could she. But at that moment she left childhood and became his mother, her own mother, mother of the family, of the world around her. No photograph, but it was all there. Why, then, did she want a photograph of a stone wall? To tie past and present, childhood and motherhood, together?

The cramped dog leaped out when she opened the car door. He knew much of stone walls and rambling in the country with her. She held his collar, kept him near, focused the camera and pressed the shutter. She was obsessed with the idea of proving the existence of this place. Just as she was dragging the dog back to the car, she saw a small toad. It hopped once, then nestled into the leaves. She cupped her hand over it, secured it, felt it struggling. She scooped some moist dirt and leaves into the plastic bag in which she'd carried the camera. One part of her deplored taking the toad from its home. The part that prevailed said: "It's only temporary. I'll keep it a few weeks in my classroom. Then I can return it to my land in Vermont near the stone wall there. Maybe I'll keep seeing it as I did the red eft. It will be a link between my land and this place."

A shaft of sunlight fell on the toad's small form on the palm of her hand. She was struck by the symmetry of its pattern. She noticed the flatness about its nose, its angular boniness, the perfection of its tiny form as it sat in her hand. A faint sound escaped it. Its eyes glittered gold in the sun. "Golden Eyes," she thought. "A toad has a jewel in its head…." Where had she heard that? Yes, it was a medieval legend. She thought of a toad she'd once brought to her class, a creature she'd found on a weekend hike. The children had named it, Golden Eyes. It had grown fat on the worms they'd fed it during the weeks it had spent with them. They had sketched it, observed its habits, and then, as a group, they'd journeyed to the woods to let it go.

She put the toad into the bag that would be its temporary habitat and folded the plastic over several times. Once they were in the car together, it would be necessary to protect the toad from the dog. She thought of a cigar box that held a borrowed staple gun. She rummaged in the pile of objects on the middle seat, unearthed it and put the bag gently inside. To further distance it from the dog, she put the box on the floor of the car under the driver's seat.

When she saw the sign announcing that she was crossing

the town line, her pulse quickened. Now she would be entering territory she had seen before. She strained forward toward the windshield, drinking in each detail. She reflected upon the mysterious processes of remembering and forgetting. Could it be? Had she really ever been here before? Was there any landmark she could remember? On the two previous occasions on which she had entered this town, she had approached it from the south. Now, coming from the north, it seemed to her that the cemetery would be on the left side of the road. But could she even be sure of that? How could one, as an adult, having an adult's awareness of the significance of an event so important, not have had total recall? Yet it came as a shock to her when the cemetery came into view (and it *was* to the left) that it was surrounded by a stone wall. Another detail she had not registered sixteen years previously was that the cemetery had three entrance gates and a group of venerable family vaults cut into a gentle hillside. She had no memory at all of an area of graves surely dating from the Revolutionary War, crumbling headstones leaning askew. No plastic flowers here, no flags; merely a moldering into the earth of the two-hundred-years-ago past.

Now that she was here, now that there were suddenly three driveways to choose from, how would she find it, the place she was looking for? How would she find a tiny flat stone set even with the earth in a cemetery vacant of live persons this early September day? Especially when what was etched into her memory was a scene on the day she had arrived there to the startling presence of the black car of the undertaker, its trunk gaping open, and a small white coffin laid on the ground between the grave and the mound of yellowish earth. The scene photographed by her mind's eye came rushing back: A midsummer's day. Sun. The minister (she couldn't remember his face). He had come to visit her in the hospital, puzzled by her, a stranger to him. Puzzled, she was sure, by the words she had written down and wanted him to read. The undertaker. She'd seen him only once – on this occasion. She had no memory of him at all. Just that the trunk of his car had been open. That was where the coffin had been carried. Coffin. The hard jouncing cradle for new life, newly dead.

She wondered whose hands had touched her baby. A nurse's? The undertaker's. She had wanted him to be wrapped in the quilt that her mother's hands had once fashioned for her. She'd wanted him to wear the sweater she had begun knitting for him. That was how the generations were meant to connect in the miracle of new life.

She thought of her earlier self on that day. Sixteen years younger she had been, and wearing a white dress, a dress borrowed from the one acquaintance she'd felt close to in the city they'd lived in just those three summer months. She remembered she'd worn her newly washed hair hanging loose down her back. They had seemed symbols of youth: her white dress and her long hair. Saying to the world: "I can't be a mother. I'll be a child. Maybe that will give me a new start." Her body had ached with the fullness of her breasts and the emptiness of her womb. Her throat had ached with tears she could not cry.

The doctor had not, of course, been at the cemetery. However, she remembered him better than either the minister or the undertaker. She remembered his grip on her hand after he'd arrived too late for the baby's abrupt birth in a corridor outside the delivery room. The baby had already been carried away to an incubator. Its feeble muffled cry was still ringing loudly in her ears. She'd asked him then: "Is there any hope?" That was when he'd gripped her hand. She had noted his rough, ungraceful face, his awkward bed-side manner, those three days she'd been his patient in the hospital, hoping to forestall premature labor. It was in his hand grip that she'd felt a profound in-touchness. He, in all his gracelessness, had become the one she remembered with the most affection and respect. He had been the one to contact the minister, once she had asked for one. He had intervened to banish from her presence the tactless woman pediatrician with all her useless description of the dying baby's coloring and her suggestions about the theoretical benefits of a post-mortem.

Memories flooded in upon her, more vivid than a photograph blown up ten times life size. But how would she find the small stone she had had set here? Where had that spot been? Her memory was of a site near the back of the cemetery, farthest from the main road. But the three driveways interjected confusion. Having crept the car silently over all three, she was at a loss to know how she would find the place without the landmarks of open trunk and fresh loose earth. Maybe it would come to her if she got out of the car and walked. She stopped the car in a shady place so that the dog would not suffer when it was parked. He tried to push past her as she opened the door. She held him firmly, pushed his chest back. "Stay!" she commanded, startled at the volume of her voice in the silence. She opened the front window a crack to give him air. He was panting and his eyes were alight. He cocked his head to one side in the familiar posture of curiosity. His eyes followed her.

Here she was, wandering in an unfamiliar territory. The names on the tombstones were Yankee names. The dates spanned a hundred and fifty years, even in the part of the cemetery that was obviously newest, away from the tombs and the earliest graves. All was alien, in keeping with her impressions about that summer sixteen years ago.

She thought of the cemeteries that were familiar to her. She thought of herself as a child, sitting with her maternal grandmother under the spruce tree that drooped its branches over her mother's grave. Of looking up at the bluffs and being conscious that somewhere at the back of that cemetery the land dropped down to the river winding below. She thought of walking to that cemetery with her grandmother, along the ties of the spur track which perilously straddled a backwater slough on a trestle. She thought about driving there with her father/son and her brother/son to lay wildflowers on the grave. Of her father's saying: "Your mother loved wildflowers the best." She thought of the lump in her throat that always choked back speech when she was there with her father. She thought of the steadiness in her grandmother's voice and how that steadiness called forth a steadiness in her response.

She thought of the cemetery in her hometown on the prairies, of the large stone with her family name on it standing among the graves of three generations of her father's family: great grandparents, grandparents, siblings of her father. She thought of the small grave of her father's sister who had died as a child. All those family members, lying adjacent to each other, fitted snugly, neatly into the family plot. With her father's grave, the newest of them all, the space was almost filled. There were only two grave sites left now, for the two remaining siblings of her father.

She thought of walking in that cemetery with her small daughter the last time she'd visited the prairie town. And of the lines she'd written the following December:

On the Names of the Dead, in My Address File

There they are,
Names. On index cards.
On tombstones.
In my consciousness.
In my memory.

I stroll among them
Reverently.
My small daughter at my side.
Each one once a life.

As little aware as she
Of time's passing.
As reluctant to look upon
The final evidence
(Beyond all doubt!)
Since it first impressed itself upon me
(And I her age!).

And my organism recoiled with horror,
Then put up its guard, saying:
I look no more. I feel no more.
I think no more.
I throw myself into eternal youth,
Denial that this will ever happen
To me.

Ever since she had been (or was she yet?) out of the grip
of the stifling prairie town, she had categorized her aunts
and uncles, her father's siblings and their spouses, according
to which of them had chosen to be buried in the dark loam
of the prairie. The classification had begun with her mother,
although it had not started until twenty-five years after her
mother's death, when she had been standing, with her
husband and her father, beside the now sunken grave in the
shadow of the bluffs along the river. Her husband had asked
in his direct way: "Why wasn't she buried in the cemetery
at home?" And her father had replied, with greater force
than was usually at his command: "She wanted it this way.
She said: 'Bury me by the river.'" At that moment the classification had started in her mind. She had known from that
moment that she would take the route of her mother. No
containment by the boundaries of the family plot for her.

That tour of the small town cemetery with her daughter
had started as a walk together into the country on a summer
day and had become an eerie journey into childhood memories, spurred by the realization, gradual in coming, sudden
in crystallization, that those beings who had been important
to her, had surrounded her in childhood, had been trans-
ported to the cemetery of the town, were buried there, still
members of a community, the community related to her,
the first community she had known.

There they all were, their names now inscribed on tombstones: those of the generations ahead of her, beings who
had populated her childhood. Her favorite great uncles. The
town constable. The great aunt who, at the age of eighty-two,
blind in one eye, had knit with fine white thread a pair of

gloves for her high school graduation. The doctor who
had attended her birth and his successor who had given her
allergy shots. The grandmother of a close friend (she
remembered her caged canary, the sugar cookies she baked,
the dill seeds in her garden). The owner of the gas station
who had been killed in a grotesque accident when a tire
he had been inflating had exploded. The owner of the furniture store from whom she had bought a vase with money
she'd saved. Another friend's uncle, the mail carrier.
Another accident: a Chevy van, parked too near a mail pick-
up hook, side-swiped by a train. The young minister whose
slow suffering death had shaken the town sometime in her
adolescence. She remembered the occasion of his first
sermon in the town. She remembered the Good Friday he
had died. The farmer's wife who had once given her a kitten,
and who had braided six rugs for her wedding present.
The saloon keeper. The banker whose heart had failed one
morning in the lobby of his bank. The seamstress who had
made over a cousin's winter coat to fit her. A farmer whose
house had been borne away by a tornado. She remembered
seeing straw driven by the wind's force into the trunk of a
boxelder tree (still standing!) that had flanked its doorstep.
A high school classmate. The date on his tombstone the
year after their graduation. Pronounced images of alternative fates. The life of a small town transfixed. A huge com-
posite photograph.

With such intimate knowledge of lives and deaths of the
occupants of the cemetery in her hometown, with such
long familiarity with a grave by a river, it was no wonder she
had not wanted her baby buried in the cemetery of a city
in which she had lived a brief temporary two months of her
life. When the doctor had told her of a section in the cemetery for dead infants, she had flinched. Her baby, anonymous infant, to be buried there, unrelated to the fabric of
society? How regimented! She could not accept it. It had
come to her then that she must arrange for the burial in the
cemetery of a town nearby, the one town in New England

which connected with family, with childhood. As a four-year-old, with her parents and baby brother, she had attended a family gathering in the parsonage of that town, then occupied by an uncle and his family. She wondered: had the word *cemetery* even been in her vocabulary when she was four?

And now she was walking quietly among the graves in that cemetery, stopping to read headstones. Her eyes were drawn to all small graves. She read every child's name and computed its age. *Hiram Jones.* Three years, ten months and seven days. The sun was high in the sky now. Clouds, setting off bright September blue, were drifting lazily among tree-tops already tinged with the gold of early autumn. "Foolish journey!" she thought. "This is taking too long. The children will be concerned about me." Yet she stayed, searching, trying to reconstruct the site of the grave. She remembered the cemetery as having been more overgrown, but much smaller. What had been a comfortably shabby town for the dead had turned into a large well-groomed city.

She made several false starts toward the car, each time stopping, distracted by some other vista that seemed familiar. She drove the lengths of the three driveways again and navigated all possible passages between them before she finally quit the premises.

"I'll drive into the town, to the church," she thought. "I'll see if I can resurrect any memories of my four-year-old self." Here she had a photograph to go by, a photograph she had seen of herself as a little round-cheeked girl, tam on her head, bangs almost hiding her eyes, sitting on the parsonage steps next to her mother's knees. As she nervously picked up speed on the blacktop road to the village, a thought crossed her mind: maybe there are two cemeteries; maybe I visited the wrong one.

The town was obviously a mill town, a fact she'd had no basis for comprehending when she was four, and had not really taken in when she'd passed through the town sixteen years previously. Maybe there *were* two cemeteries – one for immigrant mill workers and another for Yankee mill owners.

She thought of stopping in the town library to ask, but it appeared closed. So was the church. She stood on tiptoe to try to peer into a corner of a stained glass window. She tried the side door. She realized for the first time that the town was named after the man who was, by the description on the cornerstone, the chief patron of the church that her uncle had served. The streets of the town were bare of children; school must have started…there was no other cemetery.

And still she could not quite make herself abandon her search. Instead of heading further south, she swung north again, wondering how one would locate cemetery records. She was shy of stopping to ask. Her search seemed too private, too personal, too inconsequential. She drove back to the cemetery, through the first of its gates again, reaching back with her right hand to cup it over the dog's muzzle, to soothe him, to comfort herself. She parked, alighted from the car, began systematically covering the ground from driveway to driveway. "If I had all day," she thought, "I might cover the whole cemetery this way. But even then I might miss it."

A car drove up slowly, behind her own. A woman older than she got out with a trowel and a pot of sedum. The older woman knew where she was going. She tried to appear equally purposeful. Standing there awkwardly, she heard the sound of another motor straining. A dark green pick-up truck pulled into sight and down the slight incline to where she was standing near her car. Its driver, a kindly faced, white haired man said, "Can I help you?"

Words did not come easily. They never had to her. More-over, she had been silent since early morning. She said: "I'm looking for a grave. It would have a very small stone. It says: God is Present."

There! The words were out. The secret she had carried in her heart for sixteen years had been spoken, was known to another human being. Except for the gentleness she read in his face, she could not have done it. If he had not spoken first, she could not have managed the words. She searched his leathery brown face for a response.

"Goddard, you say? The Goddards are right over there. See that tall stone?"

"No" – her voice strained – "the stone I'm looking for doesn't have a name on it. The stone is very small. It says: God is Present."

Recognition crossed his face then. "I *have* seen that stone. I know that stone…seen it in my mowing. Now let me think where it would be…you see (apologetically) I haven't had this job very long…If I had my records with me…Tell you what. I'll go get them."

"I don't want to put you out. How far is it? Could I follow you and come back on my own?"

"No," he said, "they're just in my house in town. It's only a few minutes. I'll be right back." He glanced at the license plate of her car. "You've come a long way."

She was alone again. "What am I doing here?" she asked herself yet another time. "I didn't once hold this child in my arms; yet I mourn him sixteen years later. Sixteen years – and my arms and my womb still feel empty…his hands never grasped the beads on the toy my other children called *Clack Clack.*…"

Why should she think of that toy now? She didn't know. It had something to do with the spherical shape of wooden beads sliding on a dowel. It was somehow connected with the fact that the toy was made of unfinished wood and was the right size for a baby's hand to hold. It had something to do with the patina it had acquired through repeated handlings and mouthings of three babies. It was a toy she had not given away; she was keeping it to be passed on to another generation of babies.

Even after sixteen years, it all seemed wrong. He had never sucked the milk that had flowed out of her, engorged her breasts. Muscles of her body had pushed him into the world before he was ready for it, in spite of her struggle against it. Birth should not be into death. Other babies grew up to ramble in the woods, to climb mountains, to walk by the sea. To grasp objects, to reason, to hear music, to find friends.

She wanted to give her baby something. Part of it was self-conscious, now that she had an audience. The man would be watching her. She must make a gesture. A flower? Could she pick a flower and put it on the grave of a child she'd never taught about flowers?

She thought of the Jewish custom – she'd learned of it only recently – of placing a small stone on a grave at each yearly visit by a close family member. A token that the mourner had been there, in person, to visit.

She'd picked a small handful of flowers by the time the truck had returned. She thought, in her self-consciousness, "I must be as alien and confusing to him as I was to the minister."

The worn record book, looking as if it must go back a hundred years, lay beside him on the seat of the cab, with a roll of dingy maps, marked in pencil. She told him her last name and he thumbed through the book. He announced, "I've found it. Here it is. It's under Williams for some reason. That would be over here in Section E31." He consulted the map and led the way.

Williams was the name on a large polished stone under a pin oak. Yes, it was at the back of the cemetery, farthest from the main road. She wondered: Why Williams, but was afraid to ask, reluctant to stand there for the painful conjecture about the circumstances of her baby's having been buried next to someone named Williams. She'd seen penciled on the map a section labeled The Town Poor. But that was not it. The Williams stone was a substantial one.

But where was the stone she searched for? The caretaker found it first. It was flush with the ground and was almost overgrown by grass. Only a flash of a lighter hue showed between the creeping strands. The man was on his knees, tearing away at the grass, freeing the stone. She bent down and ran her hand over the surface. She was startled. She'd forgotten that she'd asked for the words to be carved in Gothic lettering. Why? Again, she could only guess at reasons. To match the lettering on her mother's grave stone, she guessed. She associated Gothic lettering in other mysterious ways with her mother. Her train of association went something like this: An English name. An English teacher. Chaucer. Old English. New England ancestry. Her mother's grandfather had indeed traveled to a frontier river town from Yankee Massachusetts. And here, come full circle, was the grave of a great-great-grandson with another name – with no name at all! – buried in Massachusetts under a stone with Gothic lettering on it.

She knew immediately why the Gothic carving had startled her, however. It was because the words on the stone had been excerpted from a more complex Latin declaration: *Vocatus atque non vocatus Deus aderit*. The visual image of those words had superseded and enhanced her original memory of the stone she had seen, some years later, a photograph of the stone lintel of Jung's house: VOCATVS ATQVE NON VOCATVS…carved in Latin letters.

She had chosen the words, the cryptic pronouncement of the oracle at Delphi when consulted to predict the outcome of a battle, to sum up an experience. (Would it ever be summed up?) She knew nothing of Latin tenses, little of ancient history. The words spoke to her of the battle of mortal flesh and mortal will (*her* flesh; *her* will) against a force which had bested them…She noticed that moss had filled in the letter *n*.

There were tears on her cheeks. The caretaker noticed them and said with an almost forced heartiness out of keeping with his underlying humility and tact: "The grass needs to be trimmed. I'll come by here with my clippers this afternoon." Then, after a pause, "If you want, I could raise that stone a little bit for you. It would be no trouble. I did one just last week for that lady over there – Mrs. Hawkes."

"Oh, no, no – I like it this way." That was true. Leveling with the ground meant assimilation. Her voice came out muffled through tears. Tears at the man's kindness. Tears at the awkwardness of the human situation between man and woman, between generations. Tears at the mutuality of the experience of grief, of terror, at death. Or maybe it wasn't mutual in this instance. He seemed so at home in this cemetery, so accepting of the naturalness of a community of the dead. Still the mother, she wanted to say something to put him at his ease.

"I've been thinking while I've been here. I remember the cemetery being much more overgrown years ago."

There was a barely perceptible easing in his face. He said seriously, "I try to keep it up. I've only been on this job two years. We moved here, my wife and I, after my retirement. It's a kind of a part-time job for me. My real job is restoring old houses. I…well, but you don't know the town, do you?… I bought the old tavern. It has three fireplaces you can practically stand in. I've been scraping down all the wood myself…refinishing the details on the stairs. You wouldn't believe how these old houses are constructed."

A point of contact in life; a welcome, affectless communication about material reality. There they stood, facing each other over a grave.

She said, "I can appreciate that. One of my great grandfathers was a carpenter. He built the house I grew up in. He built the family cradle." (There it was! Affect creeps in after all, she thought.) "My father's generation used it, and my generation, and I used it for my babies."

Words released, they rushed out. "I've always wanted to work with wood. That was something girls didn't do when I was growing up. I'm making up for it now. I've been building a shelter on a piece of land I have in Vermont."

His eyes brightened. "Vermont. That's where my family first settled. I only moved to Massachusetts as a young man."

She asked, "May I know your name?"

He replied, "Oh, it's Heuziger – a German name."

Associations again. They sped through her mind. I could prolong this conversation. Talk of family genealogy. Of common German ancestry. Of ethnic settlements in Vermont. But what point in it? Why am I here?

Panic about time gripped her. Summer was in this place.

The cleaving to childhood and the introversion it nourished. But she must go on to what awaited her at the end of the day. She pressed her lips together, composed herself, offered her hand. "I thank you for helping me."

He lowered his eyes. "I was glad to…Well, I'll leave you." He started away.

She said again after him, "Thank you so much."

He turned around. "If you ever need to find it again, that little shed over there could be your landmark. They're not likely to move it."

Then he walked to the shed, pulled open its door, and rolled out a power mower.

His presence lingered. She would have wanted, if she could have chosen, to have paid this visit privately. Then symbiotic relationship between mother and child could have been preserved forever. It would be as if the baby had never been born but remained, in her perception, in memory cells of her brain, forever part of her, never having entered the consciousness of anyone else.

The caretaker was far in the background now, starting the motor of the mower, guiding it up over the rise. She knelt down and brushed the dust and grass off the stone. She was faintly glad of the moss growing in the letter *n*… assimilated…reclaimed by nature…"a moss-covered grave"… "nothing beautiful…."

What to do with this spot, with the reality of a grave, with this moment, now that it had arrived, now that she had brought it about? What to do with the piece of herself buried here? With the smoldering memories her seeking had disturbed, fanned into illuminating flame?

The clear specifics: A birth into death. A white coffin instead of a family cradle lovingly wrought by an ancestor to comfort a growing baby wrapped in garments quilted and knitted and stitched by welcoming mothers and grandmothers and aunts. She felt part of every mother who had ever lost a child, of every child who had ever lost a mother. Of *Hiram Jones*. Of *Leonard Reid, Son of Thomas and Elizabeth,*

Died July 22, 1811. Three years, eleven months, sixteen days.

> "Tho in the dust I lay my head
> Yet gracious God thou wilt not leave
> My soul forever in the dust
> Nor loose thy children in the grave."

(God is Present!)

And it was no help. The emptiness was still there.

She laid her bunch of wildflowers on the stone. She searched in the driveway for a pebble to signify: I, the chief mourner, was here in person. She stood a long time lost in thought. The mowing machine was far away now. She scrutinized every detail of the scene. It suddenly became important to her which trees were shading the grave of the little boy who had never learned about trees, which family names besides Williams were neighbors of her orphaned child in this city of the dead.

She went back to the car and got her camera. She snapped close-ups and distance shots. She abandoned herself to making permanent the memory of a lost child. She thought, with some anger, "I've been told that my whole life has been spent in arrested mourning. So be it. There *is no* assimilation. Moss fills in the letter *n*; my mother's grave is a depression in the earth after forty-odd years. The stones of the Revolutionary War soldiers lean and totter and crumble and molder into the ground. And there is no resolution. If a telephoto lens existed that could encompass this scene from two hundred years hence, the grief would still remain, distilled into moss and lichen on stone weathered by rains and snows and winds. In subtle muted grays and mauves it might be subdued, but it is not vanquished...."

She thought of the moment just before her father's coffin had been lowered into the earth of the prairie. The local undertaker had offered her a rose from the bouquet that had blanketed the lid. She had spurned his offer impassively. That was one local custom she, now departed from the prairie, would not be party to. A flower as a souvenir? A dried flower to keep? Death was not flowers; death was earth. Ashes to ashes; dust to dust.

Still thinking of that moment at her father's funeral, she stooped down and picked up two of the flowers from the tiny bouquet she'd placed on the stone. She pressed them into one of the books lying on the car seat next to her.

She drove the car slowly as a hearse up the incline. She waved to the caretaker and headed south on the asphalt road, lost in thought: My baby boy. My boy no longer a baby. My children. The orphaned child in me.

Longing for the return of lost innocence. Contemplating the mother-child bond, the tie so fundamental that the very word *mother* posits the birth of, the existence (somewhere!) of a child.

Part of her original planning for this day of transition had been a short detour – no more than a mile or two – off the main highway to glimpse the campus her oldest son was to move onto this day. She had no thought of contacting him. Her good-byes to him had already been said. Not once, not definitively, but many times in many ways: as he had defied her, wrangled with her, in early adolescence; as she had at first tried to intervene and then, wiser, left him to fight his own battles in conflicts with his father; as he first touchingly committed himself to a girl and was rejected by her; as he had come down the aisle, as was tradition in his high school graduation ceremony, arm in arm with a girl unknown to her. To her, the pairing had been an impersonal symbol: rising generation of male and female, linked together automatically, automatic foils for each other, whose mature accomplishments she could, from her vantage point, only imagine. She merely wanted – or was this a mother's rationalization? – to get an impression of his new surroundings, of the people who would be his new companions.

Signs pointed to the exit closest to the university and indicated the way from there. She found it readily. It was a young campus: acres of newly constructed roadways, lavish buildings, ramps, walkways, parking lots. She missed the presence of old trees. She searched the faces of students going purposefully about their business.

The cramped dog was panting down her neck. He was her last child. Communication between them was wordless – by smell, touch, tone of voice – akin to communication between mother and infant. The warm wetness of a crying infant communicating in the darkness of night to a mother ministering to its needs. The smell of milk and sweat between them; the feeling of mutual nourishment. No words involved, so no misunderstanding, no resentment, no bitterness. No overlay of memory to contend with, so no implied accusations, no functioning out of guilt. The dog's unawareness of the reason for his discomfort reminded her of something she'd almost forgotten: another day sixteen years ago. The car had been packed that time, too. They had been leaving the area for good. She had wanted to detour – another procrastination! – to the cemetery, just, she'd told her husband, to see that the stone had been set in place. Their two-year-old son, now eighteen and spending his first day on a college campus, had (like the dog) pulled eagerly toward the car door as they'd entered the gate. "Park?" he had said.

So lost in thought was she that she missed the turn back onto the limited access highway. Searching for an alternative entrance, she meandered from route to route through the megalopolis. That morning's early rising hour was telling on her. She fought drowsiness. Her shoulders ached. Nearing the city now, the muggy air trapped exhaust fumes and industrial smoke. The highways became trails of red tail lights threading through dingy sameness. Neon gaudiness. Exxon stations. Burger Kings. She began to wish that she had not sought to prolong transition. Four and a half hours in a packed car is enough; seven hours is too much. She should never have sought after either lost child.

Twilight was deep as she pulled into the driveway of her own home. She fumbled in her handbag for the door key, gathered up first the cigar box that had been at her feet. The dog leaped over her arm to be first out of the car.

"Well," said her husband, "you must have gotten a late start! Were they able to fix the car? What was it delayed you? Did you decide to go back to the house after the repair shop?"

She pressed the children into unloading the car and she put the cigar box on the dining room table. She poured out the contents of the plastic bag into her hand. Moist dirt…leaves…no toad. She lifted the staple gun. The toad was not there. Her husband overheard her calling down to the children, "Be on the lookout for a little toad loose in the car."

He was annoyed. "Why did you have to bring a toad back? Can't you leave little animals in the country where they're happy? I don't want a toad hopping at me when I drive. Damn!"

After the children were in bed, she made yet another trip to the car with a flashlight. She felt in the crevice of the back seat. She unearthed a sock under the front seat, but that was all.

Four weeks later, on a Saturday morning, she found the toad. She had gotten as far, in her fall projects, as reorganizing the children's boots on the landing of the basement stairway. She was wiping up curls of dust and dog hair from the floor under the rack on which the winter jackets were hung. There was its dried black body, its eyes golden no longer, its desiccated toes long and delicate as a child's fingers. She picked it up gently, looked at its stark outline against the palm of her hand. She caught her breath. She swallowed a lump in her throat, but tears did not come. She thought: My body forced it out…out of its element. She thought of the breaking of waters, of the dryness of death. Of moss growing in the letter *n*. Of cloud spangled grass on a September day. Of the quietness in that place of death. Of the movement in life.

Afterword

From the vantage point of my seventy-two years, I see myself as still in conflict about what it is proper to express in print to an unseen and unknown audience. In relation to what I have written, I am grateful for conflict, for it is conflict that generates the need to try to express what meaning the twists and turns of fate have constellated in body and soul in the span of a single life. I hope to go on writing if fate is kind enough to permit me the time. I intend to go on trying to clarify (for myself if to no other) what has been revealed to me thus far.

Despite assurances by those who have read my work, friends who know me best, and the Jungian analyst whose commitment to working toward consciousness set my footsteps on this way, that what I have set down is of value to others, I must still deal with the voices in my head that whisper to me that "some secrets should be taken to the grave." I have long realized that searching out, understanding and expressing as much of my "truth" as I can is of paramount importance to me. In a novella of mine, *Bluegrass*, I write about the struggles, doubts and misgivings of a woman aspiring to write of her life. My own struggling with that central character, over the three years it took me to set down a first draft, established clearly for me that expressing hitherto "secret" areas requires the most courage.

Yet it is a grave – my mother's – and the fact of her death a month away from my eighth birthday, that plummeted me into a private and introspective inner world which still feels to me the safest place. Part of my introversion and my secrecy was a search for my mother – who she had been and who I, child of this unknown female person, was to be.

I was born in – but not into – a small farming community of Mennonites in southwestern Minnesota. My father had married an outsider, brought up on the Mississippi River across the state. My mother, who had earned her way to college by teaching in one room rural schools, continued, after her marriage, to teach English and act as high school principal in my father's home community. She also started the public library, a community chorus, a drama group and a women's club. She had cancer surgery in 1924, two years after her marriage. I was born in 1926 and my brother in 1929. Our mother died in 1934. Our father never remarried. My brother and I grew up in the household of our Mennonite grandfather. He, a patriarch of the community, sat at the head of the table. Our father's ten year younger sister became the woman of the household.

I have few memories of the years my mother was alive. With her death, I blocked out most of my memories of her, and of the state of affairs in our household before she was taken from it. She was not talked about in the house. People of the town remembered her kindly as a wonderful teacher and friend. They spoke to me about her. But it was obvious to me that she had been an outsider. I clung to a few dim memories of times before her death: visits in our home from her family and her good friends from the Minneapolis high school in which she had taught for five years. Since no one in the house ever spoke of these times (conversation was sparse at best), these memories were not reinforced and I began to doubt them.

I do remember, from my first years, my parents taking turns reading aloud to each other and to my brother and me. I remember my mother and father singing together to us, and teaching us poetry. I remember the closeness of these times. The loss of my mother was a wound to the family that deprived me of a father as well. My father and brother shared a bedroom, and my father read aloud to him. They talked at night. I had no access to these times. I read to myself all the 398's in the short shelf of fairy tales in the public library. For me there was no enlivening conversation, no interesting discussion at home or at school.

In the small, isolated village, the public school curriculum and the morals of the teachers were closely monitored by the conservative churches. For a couple of years, a movie house struggled to keep afloat, but succumbed to the opposition in the religious community. The residents of the town were enclosed in an environment regulated by the church. Plain dress. Female modesty. Men and women separated from each other, sitting on opposite sides of the aisle in the plain churches, sitting in separate rooms, eating in shifts at the large family gatherings – men first according to age, then women. Children last.

For four summers after my mother's death, my brother and I went to stay with our maternal grandmother in the river town, Wabasha, during the months that school was not in session. With her, I could have easy conversations, even standing at my mother's grave. Here, talk of my mother was not taboo. It was easy for my grandmother to talk about my mother's childhood. My mother's sister and two brothers were often part of the scene. Participating in this unconstrained family atmosphere, my voice began to re-emerge, to be able to frame questions.

From my grandmother's house, we could hear the sounds of the river. My grandmother would get us out of bed to watch any exciting event. Barefoot and in our pajamas, we would go down to the river to watch paddlewheel steamboats signaling to each other, passing at night. I read an Oz book a day from the public library. I learned to play cards. Had my grandmother lived on, I would have learned much more. But she died when I was eleven, and there was little contact with the Moore family from then on.

My grandmother's unanticipated death coincided with the end of sixth grade. Children had been separated by gender in Sunday School classes from the beginning. Now the sexes were also separated in school for gym classes and for mandated vocational training: home economics for girls and agriculture or manual training for boys.

When war started in the 40's (the community was opposed

to involvement in war, of course), I discovered how to use the short wave band on the radio in our living room. I listened by myself to overseas propaganda broadcasts and was excited to have this access to places far away. Had there been an imaginative teacher in elementary school, no better way could have been devised to make the far off world real, but there was no discussion of the war in school. Questioning was looked upon as dangerous.

I was editor of the school paper in seventh and eight grades and also in high school. I wrote an editorial advocating that students in our public high school be allowed to mix with young people in nearby towns after basketball games played elsewhere in the county. My daring effort produced no changes.

My mother's college literature books were on shelves in my childhood home, but I never touched them. Was it a reverence for her memory, a fear of disturbing anything she had touched, a fear of being overwhelmed by a sense of what I had lost? For whatever reason, I was afraid to approach the books. Certainly the English teachers I had in high school were not inspiring and provided no bridge to the study of literature. They followed the prescribed state curriculum. They taught parts of speech and diagramming sentences (which I loved!). There were no discussions based on the short stories that were perfunctory required reading. Creative writing was not part of the curriculum.

The year I was to graduate from high school, an uncle, who'd been on the faculty of Carleton College, suggested that I might be interested in investigating Antioch College. I was immediately attracted by the ideas set forth in the brochure and did not apply elsewhere. I had scant basis for evaluating a college. Though I did not know it at the time, I wanted to get far away from the community that had enclosed me.

When the Antioch catalogue arrived, I pored over its pages: the menu of a great feast. Freedom! – the possibility of freedom from dull constraint and the tension of keeping passive silence. I journeyed to Ohio by daycoach, changing trains in Chicago, glimpsing steel mills and industry – sparks and flames shooting into the sky, yellow smoke, and then, as daylight came, the red earth of southern Ohio – all a dramatic contrast to the familiar black loam of the prairie. I shyly and tentatively made friends with females my own age who were as turned on as I to the riches of learning.

I discovered in my new friends a kinship I had never before experienced. I learned from my peers. I picked up new vocabulary, new ideas. I carefully observed the way my assigned roommate held a cigarette in her stained, nail-bitten fingers, the way the Black town kids jitterbugged to the juke box in the cafeteria. I was determined to make the most of every moment. I had a lot of catching up to do.

On co-op jobs I met older mentors. In several progressive schools at which I held jobs, I met gifted and dedicated devotees of the early progressive education movement – extraordinary people, disciples of exciting, meaningful learning, inspiring me in environments that turned me on, opening windows and worlds. Several of them became life-long friends.

From the rich menu in the college catalogue, I selected and squeezed in an extra elective course each division. Because my two closest friends were lit majors, and because now, belatedly, I wanted to learn more about my mother's field, I elected a course in Shakespearean tragedy taught by Vivian Bresnehen. She was magnificent – and offered me, at last, a bridge into the study of literature. In my senior year, I elected to take her course, Essay and Article Writing. For the final paper in that course, I wrote a trilogy of biographical essays on three of my Mennonite great-uncles. The essays were praised by the members of the small writing seminar and by Miss Bresnehen. That same year I needed to take a tutorial science course in atomic physics to round out my science requirement. In 1948, atomic physics had just emerged on the scene. The physics professor gave me a syllabus to read, and, knowing that I would possibly teach high school science, asked me to write a series of articles at high school level, telling the story of the splitting of the atom. He submitted my project for publication and the articles were published in ten installments in a magazine called *School Science and Mathematics.*

Not surprisingly, despite the fact that I had taken a combination of courses that certified me to teach science and literature, I found my way into progressive independent elementary schools. In my first post-college job, I taught fourth grade and eighth grade English in an independent school in Rochester, New York. The assistant principal at Fieldston Lower School in New York City, a dynamic woman of great depth, came to Rochester to observe me and my teaching for a day and recommended me to teach at the Fieldston Lower School. I spent forty-four years associated there.

During my first year in New York City, I met the man who became my husband three years later. He was born in Berlin. At age eleven, in 1939, he was removed to England on a Kindertransport and, in 1945, at the end of the war and ready for college, had come to the United States. When we met, he was working for a documentary film company and writing plays by night. Each of us had grown up in a family very torn apart. Each of us was clearly searching for a family we did not have.

In 1956, the woman educator who had hired me, now become a friend, gave me as a gift a series of four lectures on human relationships delivered by an older woman analyst, one of a trio of women doctors who had worked with C.C. Jung in Zurich and pioneered his work in America. I ordered for myself the next lecture series given by Dr. Esther Harding, another of the trio. Attracted by what I saw in her face and in her bearing, and yearning to know more about the deeper dimension that she both described and exemplified, I asked my friend how I might get a referral to a Jungian analyst. I was ripe for the experience, but, of course, I had no idea of the hold Jungian analysis would come to have on me. In a

continuation of the kindness of fate, I began working with
Dr. Edward Edinger.

Part of the discipline of commencing a Jungian analysis
is to write an autobiographical statement. Though I was
not yet thirty, mine was complex. Another requirement was
to keep a written record of one's dreams and one's analytic
hours. It was analysis – my involvement in the process and
the notebooks I kept – that first set my feet on the path
to writing. I had always been interested in my dreams. They
were intricate and vivid. Monitoring them, and being
required to describe what I had dreamed, fostered an ability
to describe precisely the dream landscapes and situations
in which I found myself.

I was a teacher of eight-year-olds when I began analysis.
In one early session, I spoke of my amazement that third
graders talked in such detail about their mothers while I
remembered almost nothing about my mother. My analyst's
reply was: "I'm sure it's here somewhere." Even now, at
seventy-two, I observe in myself my reluctance to touch anything that my mother once touched for fear that it will
crumble and that I will lose it completely.

Within the first month of my analytic work, my dreams
began to refer to my mother's death. I'd never really dealt
with it – just accepted passively, in the tradition of stoic
faith of the community that had surrounded me, that it was
God's will, that one did not question the will of God.

It was in 1964, thirty years after my mother's death, that
I was able to contact and express the grief I had suppressed.
By this time, I was a mother of two sons: a five-year-old
and an infant. Because of material in a dream, I knew it was
time for me to let grief touch me. In an evening after the
boys were asleep, I opened my notebook and started to write
a piece about my state. I titled it: Variations on a Theme.
I wrote a section in the voice of each member of the broken
family: my father's voice describing his lonely burden of
knowing (months before she knew it) that my mother was
dying; my own voice describing my anger at having been

talked down to; my younger brother's voice describing
finding her bed empty when he came into her room to show
her the pretty stones he had just found. I wrote on in what
I imagined was my mother's voice, what she must have
felt when she realized in her last hours that she was dying.
I wrote all night. Thirty years after my mother's death, now a
mother myself, the tears I had not been able to cry came
out. I was afraid, as my weeping went on, that I would not be
able to resume my normal role the next day. Yet I couldn't
stop. Near dawn I wrote in the voice of my adult self as a
mother. I walked into my sons' rooms, stood looking at their
sleeping forms and wrote an ending.

I told my analyst in our next hour about the experience
of my tears. He asked me to read him the piece I'd written.
At first I told him that I couldn't. The following week I
did manage to read aloud the words that had come out of
me. It was the first time I'd let anyone see me cry. This was
the beginning of freer writing in the notebooks in which
I kept my dreams and my thoughts. I wrote poetry from time
to time, drew pictures, painted, wrote down the melodies
which came to me when I improvised on piano or flute.

I was busy during those years. A third child, a daughter,
was born two years after my second son who had been born
neurologically impaired. Until she was five and he seven, I
taught only two days a week. I taught a course in folklore
and mythology by telling stories to classes at third, fourth
and fifth grade levels. I supplemented my income by tutor-
ing learning disabled children ten to fifteen additional
hours a week.

Clinic workups diagnosing and evaluating my son's
condition and progress went on for several years. Research-
ing programs, schools, therapies consumed my days. I
worked with other mothers of exceptional children to start
the first Exceptional Child PTA in the local public schools.
During the twelve years that my son was funded by the
school district, I co-edited *Exceptional News*, a six-page news-
letter with a circulation of a thousand which went to families

and care providers of exceptional children. When my daughter was five and could attend a full day kindergarten, I was asked to consider resuming full time teaching. I taught full time until my retirement four years ago. I was never bored and was, in fact, energized by developing my own curricula, by speaking at educational conferences and to college classes and parent bodies. I was disheartened many times by what seemed the insurmountable problems of my own exceptional child and others, yet moved by and grateful for the learnings imparted by their presence among us.

An unusual physical occurrence prompted me to start writing my first story. At the end of a summer in Vermont where we had rented the same old farmhouse for several years, I had a bout of diarrhea which, however, did not run its course and stop. When I returned to my teaching job in September, my doctor began an investigation of my condition. I got through days and nights by taking paregoric. By the end of November, when all the outpatient tests had been done, I was hospitalized for five days. While I was being put through inpatient testing, I began making notes for a story about what had been taking place in my inner life around the time the malady began. The hospitalization did not shed any light on a cause or a cure, but the notes, when I wrote them into a first draft of a story some months later, turned into the story, *Transition*, about a woman (myself) searching for the grave of her infant who had lived twelve hours and then died.

I was then having only occasional sessions with my analyst. I made an appointment to see him and brought with me a typed first draft of the story. The writing of that story did not make a dent on my relentless disorder, but in the writing, I had contacted and expressed something deep inside myself. When my analyst returned the story, he said, "You must go on writing. I understood you more fully through your writing." He posed some pertinent questions about what might come as a sequel, and set me to the task of writing at least fifteen minutes a day. He was well aware of the shape of my life: teaching full time, mother of three children – one requiring my driving him to speech therapy and other weekly appointments. He knew I was always driving the VW bug with one eye on the dashboard clock.

"And hold yourself to that regime," he said. He knew that my early life in a patriarchal community had instilled in me that a wife must defer to her husband's work, that a wife is a silent partner. He knew that my job contributed significantly to the family income. His reading of *Transition* had revealed how deeply engrained was my bent to fill the void left by my mother's death by mothering everything around me. The earliest draft of *Transition* had a line near the end: "It doesn't matter who leaves first, mother or child, the theme is the same."

My malady, as I'd begun to call it, went on for many more months. I could not take any more paregoric, but the doctors put me on a non-narcotic medication so that I could continue teaching. My internist, concerned for me, told me that improvement would come only gradually, if at all. However, in setting down a section of a second story, *Change of Life*, I was restored to a semblance of normalcy in a single day. For a time, small fluctuations in my physical condition occurred, but I never relapsed. When I thought about it, I realized I could pinpoint the theme that had effected the "cure." The lines from the story which made the change brought up my relationship to my own femaleness – motherhood and the difficulties in communication between male and female being aspects of it.

I adhered to my analyst's prescription, faithfully spending at least fifteen minutes a day writing, and, when I could and was deeply drawn into a theme, a day of a weekend. Once I discovered it, I loved Eudora Welty's writing. Her short novel, *The Optimist's Daughter*, moved me to tears when it was first published in *The New Yorker*. I remember having read somewhere that Welty spreads out fragments – bits and pieces that have come to her – on a big surface and connects them. I proceed in a similar way. I categorize a developing story into the emerging themes, sort my fragments, on a big surface, into related piles. If one writes every day, a theme comes up and recurs augmented, sometimes – quite often, in fact –, by the comment of a dream. Eventually, themes attach to other themes and the essence of the story is revealed. I include dreams in my work because they are as vivid to me as actual happenings in the physical world. I write about my dreams because I can't ignore them. My stance is that it is dangerous to ignore dreams: the objective messages from the unconscious.

The summer I was writing notes, i.e. fragments, for *Bluegrass*, I was living by myself in the rented house in Vermont for the summer. Our younger children were away at teen camp, our older son was off earning money for his last year in college and my husband was involved in the making of a film. There were some intervals of several consecutive depressed days when I couldn't write at all. Near the end of that summer, paragraphs and pages came at me in a rush. I would wake in the mornings, let the dog out, make tea, prop myself up in bed and just write through the afternoon. September came, and the return to the obligations of my job and my household in the city – husband, children, appointments, ongoing reality of living. Almost gratefully, I gave up the burst of expression – for I had been in conflict about it.

The following summer, with the start on *Bluegrass* still pending, and now luring me back into it, the aunt who had been the female presence in the household of my childhood was in a coma following surgery in the small town hospital in Minnesota. My dreams barraged me with comments I felt I must heed and unravel. I laid *Bluegrass* aside to concern myself with writing about the personal decisions I could not evade: the question about whether I should journey to Minnesota before my aunt's death to involve myself with her more closely. I wrote of my ongoing situation day by day over months of difficult indecisiveness, while my unconscious was occupied with the family and community which had shaped me. Within three months after my aunt's death – nine months after my agony and hers had begun –, I had finished a draft of a long piece I titled *The Severing*. I had needed, myself, whatever insights my writing about the situation could clarify and put into perspective about the mysterious currents set up between men and women in my childhood community.

My earliest thinking about *Bluegrass* and *The Severing* alternated back and forth over five summers. My thinking about one piece fed the other and vice versa. Both are concerned with death and with complex relationships (*always* complex!) between the sexes. Both involved my own concern with the central female character's daring to express, tentatively, but in writing, difficult conflicts about her right to do so.

In the last few years, with increasing frequency, terminal illnesses and deaths have impacted upon me, as those women who have been closest to me and whose lives have meant the most to me (i.e. those women who have always been substitute mother figures for me) have died. In my most recent writing, some of which is in a folder titled "Summer Dream Poetry" and some in a folder, "Over Seventy," the constant theme of death makes its presence felt in a different way. As dear friends are widowed or their husbands become widowers, contrasts and distinguishing features between male and female stand out in ever sharpened relief: the searching of one for completion and of the other for containment. As I feel for the struggles of our now grown children, motherhood over forty years takes on another aspect. In a story, *Grapevine*, I have written a phrase describing a mother as "connecting generations through her body." Now over seventy, I, still a mother, always a mother, am coming to realize that my body is connecting birth and death.

Nellie Wong

Dedicated to the memory of Karen Brodine, comrade, sister-poet and friend, who never stopped believing in the power of the working class and who pushed and encouraged me to write deeply from my working life.

Toss Up

You call me into the hall,
standard procedure for a conference
between a supervisor and a secretary.

You ask:
If we had a fight,
whose side would you be on?

His, because he is Chinese
or mine
because I am a woman?

World Traveler

The *Oakland Tribune* spreads across her wooden desk.
She inhales its words, sweetmeat for her eyes.

She is lost in a world of newsprint, fingers
each word whether rough or smooth.

This girl wants to learn, this girl wants
to read, live, travel the world over.

She wants to leave home, wants to roam
in Paris, Shanghai, the Himalayas.

Anywhere except within the four walls
of Wah Que Chinese School in Oakland Chinatown.

A Secretary's Song

She places her fingers on the keyboard.
As she begins to type, music ripples
beneath her skin. Hairs on her arms rise.
As she types, poetry flows
from her fingertips.

Stolen Moments

I type memos, add figures, sort mail.
I try to hang on to the pressures at hand,
to the work before me at my desk.
But my mind's hands claw words from
newspaper headlines, radio commercials,
hallway conversations, bulletin boards.
And it's no magic then
those hands store language
sacks of long grain rice
in the bins of my body.

After reading at a benefit
for battered women and children,
a woman said she appreciated
my saying that I stole from my job
in order to write.

In reply I laughed and said
I only made it up,
that is I stole things from my job
but not erasers, magic tape or Ko-Rec-Type,
but moments, I stole moments
that no job can steal from you.

So that is what working at a job is,
bartering my labor for moments,
swallowed in wrist movements,
raised eyebrows, tired eyes,
before I, a working, ambidextrous thief,
get caught as the clock strikes five.

In Search of Song

The *N-Judah* roars by, such a rattle on the tracks
as jazz syncopates in my ears as I look, search
for music, music, songs to call my very own.

That piano has wings, yes, and my fingers fly
unsure of their dance steps listening
to the piano keys and even the ringing
of my workmate's telephone.

An administrative assistant is moving
to Albuquerque, New Mexico. The party floats
in Millberry Union, platters of chimichangas
and bowls of strawberries, pineapple and cantaloupe
take center stage as laughter freezes, caught
like moonlight on an uncharted galaxy.

And while sun shines over the Golden Gate Bridge
emptiness pervades the words of farewell
amid administrators and staff sipping mineral water
and plastic glasses filled with Chardonnay.

Lumps of emptiness resonate mournful tunes
while workers ponder their next paychecks,
whether they'll pale or disappear
in desks and computers that won't be there.

Behind each celebration the noise, the unsaid.
Beyond our sight, women in black march silently
to save a shelter in the Tenderloin
as Black & White Ball revelers drink and dance
until 3:00 a.m. on the asphalt streets.

Sing to Me

Sing to me, love,
play that melody
that lingers on my fingers

Let those piano keys fly
Sit proud in that tuxedo
musician of my youthful dreams

Woody Allen's angst
amid Manhattan skyscrapers
and Italian restaurants
need not occupy
this resonant heart

Just sing to me, play,
play across the landscape
of songs that mourn, that lift
the Broadway of a once young girl's dreams

Shower me, maestro, fill my ears
with notes that dance, that swim
upstream, like brilliant carp
in a Chinese pond

from afar in the land
of my ancestors
where farmers till the soil
and the water buffalo raises
its head at American visitors

where tiny Chinese cousins speak
my native tongue, saying
they will never be able
to fly to America
because it's much too far

and I, the prodigal daughter,
stand near the graves
of my parents on a hilltop
in Oakland not far
from my sister
and brothers-in-law

with flowers in these aging hands
with petals falling like rain
remembering, living
the woman that I am now.

Eyebrows, Wings

I see a woman's eyebrows and they catch me
boats turned upside down.
And I say to myself: how sad, how sad.
And why, how sad, how sad?

Is the woman's face a pinch?
Is her forehead a mountain?
Are her eyes whirlpools?
And is she drowning?

She rushes by me, a breeze.
I pass and my neck cranes.
Those charcoal lines, those downward curves.
Does she ride away under her own strokes?
Does she pull away from the hair I don't see?
Does she dream of foreign ports or sail home
into the islands of my curious eyes?
Should she erase them and begin again,
let the hair grow
whisper of new sprouts?

I am a poet walking on Front Street.
I am a secretary among hundreds
rushing to hamburgers, petrale, wine.
And this woman, are her eyebrows wings?
Are her cheeks peaches or persimmons?
Are her eyes iridescent, tiny bubbles, the Aegean Sea?

The newspaper headlines escape me, her vanishing
figure. Front Street, to Davis, around California
we scurry in leaps over lines and cracks.
Some toes pinched in spiked heels still.
The sun breaks, I swallow a sandwich.
And to that woman I want to say:

Baby, what long way have we come,
what long way have we come?

Eulogy for a Tie

A tie lies on the pavement
    shredded of remorse.
Its lifeless body twists,
    its cotton batting innards
    bursting through the seams.
It no longer knows
    the breath of a man
    though the paisley pattern
    is still intact.
Woe, woe.
A tie has died.
A tie has lost its tiemanity
    while street art thrives.

Imagining Lice

Once in a class I wrote about a beggar squatting
on the Zocalo in Mexico City. I described the man
as picking lice from his head. And though I said
I saw the man from a distance, actually across
the street, my professor asked: "How could you see
that they were lice in his head?"

I said I didn't know but only imagined that it was
lice or maggots or ticks or whatever species
might prefer to congregate on a man's balding head.

Then it seemed impossible that I saw lice
on the beggar's scalp. The imagining of lice loomed
in my own head, of course. Since then I've wondered
if I should actually see things with my own eyes
before I write them down.

Journal Entry

November 26, 1992

After midnight, my sister's name, Gee Ling Oy, in calligraphy, Flo Oy Wong, stands out, black on white paper, the front cover of a catalog of her art exhibit at Mills college in Oakland.

The calligraphy is stark. Reminiscent of childhood, bold, full of strength, flooding me with memories. Not memory lane, but a journey, a wide open window to Flo's life, her creative abilities as an artist and activist. My baby sister. And we are now women in our 50's, alive, fighting back.

The calligrapher is an artist. The strokes of the calligraphy compel the naked eye, draw it close to the heart. The calligraphy is forceful, not forced. Yet it follows a human being's creative talent, the first Chinese writer, the first Chinese calligrapher, whoever he or she may be. There is wonderful movement. In "Ling" there is the symbol of person, the human being is in control. The person dances over earth, covers the land and the oceans where stories stream forth.

In "Oy" I see a woman dancing. Her legs move so quickly I cannot figure out what kind of dancing it is. Nevertheless, a woman is dancing under a symbol for "heart." "Oy" is also my name except that I am Lai Oy, Beautiful Love.

Our surname, Gee, is a fierce and proud warrior whose birth as a peasant offers us our humble beginnings. It is a tower of strength, of courage, of feistiness and unfathomable power. I may be struck down for making this up. But then I have an audacious spirit. The warrior circles his lance. He stands tall, facing adversity and oppression. The straightness of his body tells him that with courage, with the eyes of a hawk, he will see beyond his own existence, that he can make a future for his people, women, men, children, all.

On a snow-white field, a woman is a warrior for the love of earth and the people. To be Chinese American is black on white embodied in thousands and thousands of women and men whose ancestry is Chinese, whose lives and blood intertwine, who have not always loved one another just because they share Chinese blood.

Reading the catalog inspires my pen. For many months after the massacre at Tiananmen Square in June 1989, I was at such a loss. The words to express my grief froze my pen. The hours of watching young Chinese women and men being killed on the TV screen outraged me. Had the Chinese government gone crazy? Were the men in power not fathers, brothers to those youth they killed?

My poems would not come. The words hid themselves in my eyes, in my naked body, defenseless, helpless, unarmed. Yet from those days, I, like Flo, did not sit still. Passivity did not hold me captive. As a member of the Freedom Socialist Party, I took part in the demonstration in San Francisco. Thousands of us, mostly Chinese and Chinese Americans, marched and protested, from the Chinese Consulate to Portsmouth Square in San Francisco's Chinatown. I can still hear the anger, the collective grief, the outrage that covered the city. Almost a Chinese city with so many people of Chinese ancestry gathered to express their outrage and anger at the Chinese government which ordered the deaths of youth fighting for democracy. Our party's analysis was my expression. The pain I felt was not personal. It was collective. Our response became public through forums and writings and internal discussions.

I spoke at the Bay Area FSP's forum on China at Ohana Cultural Center in Oakland, along with two Chinese students from UC Berkeley and Stanford. I was the Chinese American and a woman, seizing within me all the power of the party, we, the Trotskyists, women and men, Chinese and non-Chinese.

As a poet and writer, I do not own the words that I use, the words that I spoke on behalf of the FSP. The speech was difficult to write. I worried about what I would say, in my own words, to clearly state the party's analysis. Didn't want to be rhetorical. Afraid of taking a lead. Yet I knew then that I must and I did. Comrade Henry wrote a document. We consulted and spoke. I did not want to read from a long, prepared text so I had turned to mind-mapping what I needed to say. And it worked!

It was white on black, light against dark. It was beauty of dialogue and analysis, a fusion of many brains at work, the heart of a feminist party, the tautness of our center. Our revolutionary spirit sprung forth.

When I think about the poems that didn't come, I realize that my poet-life does not necessarily mean that poems can blossom at will. I took in the images I saw on the TV screen. I gathered the newspapers and magazines as if I were a maniac. I drowned myself in the sea of words that fed my hunger to understand why Chinese youth were being killed.

The patriarchs in the Chinese government. I shall never forgive them. It's not an issue of morality. The lives they took told the world who was boss! The young Chinese people died for a principle, for democracy, a voice in how their lives should be, could be.

I had walked on Tiananmen Square in 1983. On a hot summer night, in June, I walked and walked with my Chinese host, a woman who taught English literature. I breathed in the history of the square. I wanted to live the lives of all the martyrs and heroes of the 1949 revolution. The history of China! How could I learn and study it all?

I dream a red dream. As Roque Dalton, the revolutionary poet of El Salvador, wrote: "One day communism will be an aspirin the size of the sun."

I take a big leap. My head itches. Black on white, white on black. Silence the morning after Thanksgiving. Against my bedspread of white and pink Japanese wildflowers, I write, not knowing where the pen will lead me. A white hair falls on my turquoise terry robe.

Haikus for Tiananmen Square

Tiananmen Square
hunger strikers sleep, awaken
calls: democracy!

Young students' bodies
crowd together, lie on the
square, so hungry

Tiananmen Square
Banners unfurl, calligraphy
wave this spring in May

Free speech flowers
on Tiananmen Square, calling
for a better system

Tiananmen Square
Women's arms, legs, bodies, mouths
push back young soldiers

Workers on motor
cycles, ride from town to town
spread words, freedom

Tiananmen Square
breathes with life, martial law
defied with protests

Soldier disemboweled
workers rage, tyranny will
die, people will win

What do you think you
are, soldier, are you king and
not of the people?

Man in a white shirt
defies a parade of five
tanks, life in his hands

Tiananmen Square
where students, workers, youth
collide with bullets

Shanghai, three workers
shot in the back of the head
martyrs for freedom

A woman turned her
brother in, student who worked
for democracy

Supreme Commander
of Tiananmen Square Chai Ling
defend comrades' lives

Goddess stands tall
in Tiananmen Square, her Chinese
eyes blaze for freedom

Heads, eyes, arms, hands, legs
disappear from Tiananmen
Square, their spirits live

Cabbages and homes
for all the people in China
people everywhere

Facing death, singing
the International, song
for workers' freedom

Bodies cremated
how many women, how many
men died for freedom?

The dead on the Gate
of Heavenly Peace, we give
you flowers, our hearts

Flying

Holding my arms out like the wings of a bird
I walk the crack, a straight line, on the sidewalk
heel to toe, heel to toe.
Obedience, now, is a virtue.
The early morning air engulfs me
the moon is hiding
from my brown eyes
filled with intention
staying calm on this flight
on Guerrero Street.

Pivoting, still walking
heel to toe, heel to toe.
Another order assails my ears
no turning up my hearing aid now
no, no movement that would provoke
a bash on the head, verbal abuse,
or handcuffs around my wrists.

A captive student in jail on the street
being told not to fly, don't be a bird, I think,
his badge shining in my eyes
as he barks just follow my instructions
just do exactly as I do.
Cooperating is my forte
right, left, right, left, left.
He thinks that I will make a mistake.
He thinks that I will not know
the difference between left and right
that my manner breathes intoxication, resistance.

Yes, intoxicated with desire
for democracy in a socialist China

intoxicated for a woman's right to choose
intoxicated with the strength of woman warriors
intoxicated for the right
to speak a native language in the workplace
intoxicated for freedom, roofs
over the heads of the homeless

I fly, yet keep my hands at my side
my eyes straight ahead, devouring his silver badge
knowing that a woman alone on the street
is deep, a targeted enemy, a bull's eye.

A man walks by, watches my movements, watches
my left hand touch the tip of my nose
right hand touch the tip of my nose
left, right, left, right, left, left.
Meanwhile the other cop yells
don't you move until we tell you to.
Undaunted, I reply: You don't have to yell.
I like talking back.

Yes, left, left, the glass is half-full
the night is a friend
with no comrades in sight
intoxication is breath
restless sleep, wakeful,
a ribbon of red riding night-dreams.

The immediate goal is to fly
feel safe in my own room
surrounded by pictures of family
wondering how it happened
being stopped for running a flashing red
light, flashes of imprisonment,
concrete walls, flashes of lights
this danger hovers over me

as I jump into my car
encountering another police car
at the next intersection
hoping they will not notice this woman
flashing red, flashing left, left
intent as a signal, sober as landscape,
flying with immense desire
for freedom, for freedom,
flying, flying
home.

When You Think of a Spa

Your mind floats
to a resort with mineral springs
You see your body
on a treadmill,
a woman attendant near by
ready to hand you
a lush cotton towel

You lie on a slant board,
your eyes closed
as visions gleam
of palm trees
and white-sand beaches
near baskets of oranges
and pitchers
of iced herbal tea

You flash forward
to us, Asian women who
recently immigrated to
the United States

We, yes, worked
at the Bangkok Spa
in Houston
where Apollo 13 astronauts
once tumbled back to earth,
where scientists huddle
about the next space launch

but you can't leave us,
one of us is 15 years old,
kept locked behind padlocked doors
and locked burglar bars

for our crime
of being female,
dispensable as rag dolls,
compelled to have sex
with five to eight men
per day, per day
for 45 minutes each

and you, in the spa,
toweling off after
a swim in the pool,
head off to a shower,
then a hot tub

as we sweated
from noon to five a.m.
daily, daily
and received none
of the $120 fee charged
each of our customers

Ah, the Bangkok Spa
where our women's activities
were conducted by
our own female compatriots
smiling as they collected money
for the labor of our bodies
who forbade us to leave
to use the telephone
to write letters

To these United States
we fled for our freedom
one of us paid
$34,000 to be smuggled
here to work
as a prostitute
thinking that
in three weeks

I would earn enough
obstinate as I am
believing
in the industry
of rich Americans
to pay off my debt
in three weeks
and freedom
would be mine
in this the land
of the free

If one of our fathers
would pay $10,000
to the head
of the prostitution ring,
one of us would be
set free
if not, one of us
would be sent
to San Francisco
where I would be required
to have sex with more
than 500 men

We are your eyesores
the unwanted,
illegal immigrants

You don't see our faces,
our female bodies
having sex

Your government
will deport us
back, back
to Thailand
to Vietnam
where mango trees bloom

What other spas exist
in the honeycomb
of your mind
what other resorts
will rise
for the entertainment
of men at our expense
though you know not
our Thai and Vietnamese names?

When you think of a spa,
remember the Bangkok Spa
remember us
as we are shipped
back to work
to pay off our debts
in the land of mango trees

Reaction

No, it cannot be the fish,
not my beloved rock cod
smothered with tomatoes and green peppers

nor can it be the honey and lemon dressing
atop my jicama and honeydew melon
so sweet, so soul satisfying

No, no, it cannot be the brown rice
with sauteed mushrooms
the butter having melted,
making it all the more palatable

nor can it be the steamed artichokes,
my beloved artichokes, each leaf tender,
sensitizing the mouth

It cannot be the weather,
not hot, yet cloudy and windy,
nor the garbage piling against
the wall of the stairs
of my Victorian flat

No, no, this reaction
is temporary, is ephemeral
this swelling of the skin
red and splotchy, angry
as a burning field of rice crops
napalmed, hands and arms flying
into midair, as cries in the night
haunt the memory, the vision
of people being machine-gunned down
like lambs led to slaughter

No, no this reaction
is not the same as war
as genocide, as hatred of dark skin
of another people's culture
another way of life

This reaction, this foe,
this allergy I cannot separate
from my body aching for relief,
from the terrible itching,
from people standing in line in soup kitchens
for handouts of governmental cheese,
from a homeless couple lying in a storefront
moving their bodies to keep warm
on the street which is their home
for another spring night

Waiting for Tomatoes

You and I head up to the counter.
We order dinner. We order
huge platters of beef over rice and green salad.
It is not beef under snow.
It is beef over rice and green salad.
The counter is crowded with other people.
No one knows whose turn is next.
Everyone knows hunger, everyone wants to be up front.
Suddenly a small man with a gun shouts:
"Back up, back up!"
The crowd moves backwards, makes room
for the small man waving his gun.
We rush up again to the counter.
We do not know if the small man with the gun is crushed.
We rush up again. Our priority is hunger.
The restaurant is actually a street,
a street between the counter and the kitchen,
a restaurant we have never seen before.
Strangers walk down the street of this restaurant.
The food looks appetizing, it smells of garlic.
Our nostrils flare, inhale the odors.
They are escapes through tunnels in the dark.
The waitress appears, says she has to get tomatoes.
We look at the counter. The counter is full with bowls
of tomatoes and onions, but the waitress says
she has to get tomatoes.
We look at the counter. We wait patiently.
We eye baked apples big as grapefruits.
We eye cinnamon rolls bigger than all of our hands.
A waiter, no, a chef comes to serve us.
We tell him we are waiting for tomatoes.
He understands we are waiting for the tomatoes

the waitress has gone to fetch.
Where is the waitress?
Why has she been gone so long?
The waitress is buying tomatoes down another street.
She only buys tomatoes when she has to.
Finally our food is ready.
We carry out huge platters to another room on the street.
People are eating in silence.
The room has no candles, no electricity.
The room floats on the dock by the water.
You and I lower ourselves into our chairs.
Flowers have been carved on the seats of our chairs.
We are happy to eat our dinner.
At last you and I begin to eat in the dark.

Eggyolk Melody

You can have the "Realm of the Senses,"
"Last Tango in Paris," or even
"Belle Epoque."

Just give me a bag of buttered popcorn,
five rows from the front.
Just let me sink into a chair,
curl my feet up into a ball

and watch two lovers sharing
an eggyolk between them,
back and forth
back and forth

until the gangster's girlfriend
reaches orgasm because the yolk broke
in her mouth

Just give me "Tampopo," a film
about making the best noodles
in town, letting the whole body
of a fresh chicken dip

in a cauldron of water
laced with green onions

Just let me boil,
a chicken in hot water

Just let me be

Elegy for Dennis

Farewell, dear Dennis,
long-time *Oaklun ngin*
you who bowled
in the Oakland Chinese Bowling League
making spare after spare
strike after strike
at the Broadway Bowl
laughing with Leslie
and your other teammates
making every move count
as you all swoop down
to Chinatown for *sieu yeah*
devouring those bowls
of *cha siu* noodles
and *op gahng yee foo won ton*

you who played tennis
whacking that ball over the net
sweating in the hot sun
pausing to gulp some water
take a deep breath
before you're on the court again
winning victory after victory

how we'll miss you, sweet friend,
companion to Leslie
and friend to Noel, Erin and Dana,
remembering your relish for *La Bohème*
and *Aida* and exercise and how your love
for Sam made him laugh and scream
as you tickled him and threw him high
in the air, promising to take him fishing

and playing games
at the Festival of the Lake

how your and Leslie's house
at 690 Spruce Street
will miss you, your movie poster
of *The Maltese Falcon*

your magazines
and newspapers piled atop
the dining table,
boxes of jello and pudding,
empty boxes, paper bags
and pop-top cans in your kitchen
all reflected a beam
shining through the window
of your 50 years

your life glimpsed in pages
of your datebook calendar
of visits to the doctor
beginnings of opera classes
flea market swaps
your Ma's treks to China and back
nieces' and nephews' birthdays
nights of restless sleep
continuous coughing
your optimism noted
in your fine hand
that you were doing better
after your heart attack

Dear Dennis, you'll not roam far
from our hearts as we dream
for you on your journey
to another part of Oakland
as we burn paper money and incense
and provide for you *bock tit gai,*
steamed long grain rice,

Texas Patna, of course,
and white wine
that you'll swim, picnic
and fish, that you'll take
photographs of sunrises and waterfalls
and pools of golden carp
laughing as you climb mountains
and explore this universe
with your beloved Leslie
on a hillside overlooking Oakland
finding your place
among the glittering stars

for Dennis Jow, beloved brother-in-law and friend

Launching 62

Latino chefs in white coats and chef's hats
puffed like pastry rush, filling orders
of po' boy sandwiches of soft-shell crab,
blackened red snapper, deep frying
potatoes, flames reaching a foot high
as cream becomes sauce
while Spanish dots the landscape
of oysters being shucked,
phones ringing, customers hugging
Michael, the pony-tailed chef
and I, launch my sixty-second year
on a stool at the counter of
PJ's Oyster Bar as Dylan, Spanish and Irish,
pony-tailed, treats me
to a glass of Chardonnay
with "Here you are, m'lady"

and my birthday rolls off in my favorite venue
watching cooks work, the kitchen assistant
in a red baseball cap chops vegetables
such fireworks in the flames engulfing
three and four pans as cauldrons
of broth boil and boil as I scan headlines
that two Clinton aides resign
to protest the new welfare law

as I try to undream the vision
of millions of children standing
in bread lines, in cheese lines
your children and mine
of every hue and background
because welfare is being ended
"as we know it"

and immigrants, legal
or undocumented, their skin
itches, raises a crescendo
of shame, shame
to the Democratic president

who, with a stroke of a pen,
imbeds in our consciousness
our real lives
that states can do it now
that states can collect block grants
dole out crumbs embellished
in the name of democracy
as we know it
'cause money shrinks
'cause capital shrinks
'cause the economy dilapidates,
shrivels, shreds the hopes
of the poor, single mothers
on welfare, youth battling
on the streets wondering
what America has become

as many of us rally, discontented
with the content of our character
when the homeless Black woman
asks, three times consecutively,
for some small change
failing to remember
my Chinese face
as I walk on Valencia
but when she remembers
that I already gave,
she thanks me and God

and the white homeless woman,
disheveled, hair stringy, toothless,
too poor to own dentures,
sways to and fro

outside the taqueria
hoping a customer's change
will drop into her palms,
hoping someone will buy
the *Street Sheet* crumpled
in her hands

while Jessie, my Black homeless friend,
waves his *Street Sheet* at me, assuming
that a dollar bill will fly from my wallet
as he chants his sweet refrain
"if you can, if you can"

and I think of Sam, the jazz aficionado
who sold *Chronicles* and *Examiners*
at the corner of Valencia and 16th
who's flown to jazz heaven
and I think of Sam, my father,
who's drying Chinese mushrooms
with the love of his life, my mother,
and I think of Sam, my nephew,
his penchant for Wu-Kong,
the Monkey King, and X-men
clash across this keyboard

as I sing this ancient song, yet new
and warm while the U.S. is preparing
bigger air strikes on targets in Iraq
and the headline crows
that a missile is fired unsuccessfully
at American jets on patrol
over a protected zone
and the U.S. seeks to end
direct aid for the Kurds

and no matter what this launch
brings, someone's brother,
someone's sister,
someone's child

will haunt the hallowed ground
for food and medicine
for the hate that is still to come
embodied in F-117's targeting Baghdad,
gathering worldwide forces
of those of us against the embargo

of resistance for peace and jobs
as we will know it
and we will know it

Afterword

Writing. The scratching of my pen on paper. Fingers tapping
the keys of the computer keyboard. Writing is my life. My
life is writing. But that's not all that counts now that I'm 62
years old. The lovely, musical part of this journey, as my hair
turns white, is that I'm alive and kicking, alive and a revolutionary feminist who works, writes and organizes in the movements for radical social change. To be specific, I'm the San
Francisco Bay Area Organizer for the Freedom Socialist Party.
I'm also active in Radical Women, an international socialist
feminist organization committed to building women's leader-
ship so that one fine gorgeous day we'll all be able to eat,
work and create on a higher scale of human potential.

I began writing in my mid-30's. My baby sister, Flo, a
wonderful creative artist, was the one who told me I should
take up writing. Why, I had asked. And she said, "Because
you're funny. There's something you should develop, Nell,
because your newsletters to the family are funny. You ought
to check it out by taking a writing class." So, what the heck, I
told myself, I was single and still wondering if I'd ever marry.
I signed up for a writing class at Oakland Adult Evening
School, just five blocks from where I lived with my mother.
And there in class, I began to write fiction.

From there, my teacher, Kathy Manoogian, who wondered
why I was taking her fiction writing class semester after
semester, urged me to attend San Francisco State University.
Kathy had wanted to tutor me, but at a secretary's low
wages I could not afford to spend ten dollars an hour. I had
looked at her offer only from an economic point of view, and
sought no help from anyone to see if it were possible for
me to be tutored. Kathy recognized my budding talent, but I
had resigned myself to "fate." I was not moved to move.

I thought I was old when I began studying as a freshman

at San Francisco State University. I thought that the younger students would teach me a lot. After all, they had benefited from the Third World strikes to make Ethnic and Women's Studies a part of the curriculum. They would show me the way, I told myself, a full-time secretary who knew only the business of working. How innocent, how deprived, how hungry I felt. But my balloon popped. I discovered that with my work experience, I, along with the re-entry women that I had met, was able to offer my classmates the experience that I had gained as a working woman. And that, indeed, my maturity was not a detriment but an asset.

Attending San Francisco State University as a grown working woman excited me. I was eager to learn. I was "only a secretary" in those distant days. But in fact my having worked since I was seventeen hadn't limited me after all. I had learned about racism and sexism on the job as a secretary. At Bethlehem Steel Corporation where I had toiled as an executive secretary for eighteen and a half years, I had been demoted because I was planning to have children and my boss hadn't wanted to be inconvenienced should I become pregnant.

One of my first classes was taught by an Asian-American woman who identified herself as a Marxist! She talked about triple oppression, about our economic status as women, as workers, as women of color. I knew that I had to catch up, but with what, I didn't know. I only knew that my feet were finally planted on a ground that was a campus, a place that I put on a pedestal because my insignificant self finally had lifted her feet toward higher education, toward a discovery of myself and others that I hadn't imagined.

The 1970's were central to my waking, writing and activist life. I wrote a paper on the poet Sylvia Plath, "earning" a "C" grade for my writing skills because I used clichés. The clichés, my professor had told me, were banal. I recall that I apologized for being a working woman, but, of course, I learned to write papers. Plath's poetry nudged me. This dead poet's work had something to say to me, a Chinese-American woman, a long-time worker, a first-born daughter of Cantonese immigrants, who was "only a secretary." Plath's imagery worked for me. She spoke as a woman – which I identified with, although I was Chinese American. I liked the feistiness that exploded in her work. At that time I was unaware of the writings by women of color, but I was "hooked." Women's poetry became a bridge to my then unarticulated life.

In another class, I kept a journal on Shakespeare. Shakespeare! How could I ever understand Shakespeare? I certainly didn't understand *Midsummer Night's Dream.* When my sisters and their husbands and I had gone to see Shakespeare's *Midsummer Night's Dream,* I had poked my college-educated younger sister all evening long. "Flo," I asked, "what are they talking about? I don't understand." Flo shushed me and explained to me later on what had ensued on stage. But I did begin to understand Shakespeare and my journal writings on his plays revealed that I had a sensibility and a feminist one at that. How thrilled I was to receive an "A" in that class. A fellow student told me she had never read anything like my journal musings on the role of women in Shakespeare's works.

* * *

I must mention my late comrade, sister and friend, Karen Brodine, who died of breast cancer in 1987. I met Karen at San Francisco State, and it was Karen, one of the finest poets I've ever had the beauty of knowing, who urged me to write about my working life. "Why?" I had asked. And she responded, "Because we spend so much of our lives at work. You've got to do it, you have lots of material." She even suggested that I put together a manuscript for Kelsey Street Press, which became my first published book, *Dreams in Harrison Railroad Park.* Never would I have thought of putting a manuscript together. My poems were, after all, in those days, just "stuff I was writing." It was precisely because of Karen's support and encouragement that I wrote poems such as "Toss Up" and "A Secretary's Song" which are part of this book. Now I have many work poems scattered in different anthologies.

I see now how I had put myself down. I had put my life as a secretary down because in those heady days of my awakening feminism, I was told by the media and society in general that being a secretary didn't amount to much. Women worked as secretaries because they had to earn their own living. Or because they were too poor to go to the university. Or because that's what women did. Who was I to think that I could go to a university and become something else? My vision had been narrow, my life so contained.

Today, after writing for the last twenty years, I often ask myself whether I am a writer, a poet. My waking life is rich and full. I work full time at the University of California, San Francisco, as a Senior Affirmative Action Analyst. As a socialist feminist activist organizer, my weeks and months are full of organizing, attending meetings, doing administrative work, attending union and coalition meetings, speaking at community forums, reading my poetry. I often wish I had eight more lives so I could tend to my writing.

I keep a journal which is a very dear friend. I send out a few poems and see them published. I also receive my share of rejections, which is part of a writer's life. I read into the night and still manage to get up and go to work. Somehow I find that creative balance, often losing myself in novels, collections of poetry and nonfiction writings and still managing to steal moments to write those poems and stories that are stored inside me. I dream that one day I'll write that novel. I dream that one day I'll write that musical, a Chinese-American musical with Asian-American actors, singers and dancers and if I were younger, I'd probably assign myself a role! I dream that one day I'll finish that play and invite all my friends and relatives to the opening when I'm eighty years old. I'm very proud that two of my poems are enshrined, one in granite and one in bronze, on the streets of San Francisco as part of its Art-in-Transit and Waterfront Transportation Projects. And I feel just ornery enough to never quit writing even though I must steal precious moments to put the words down.

One of my heroines is the late writer, Ding Ling, of China. I had the good fortune to meet her when I traveled in 1983 to China with the first group of American women writers, hosted by the Chinese Writers Association. I had the chance, in that vast country, to stand on the soil of the village where my father was born. At a sumptuous banquet held in Beijing, Ding Ling protested being labeled a feminist, saying that she was a simple country woman who just wrote. But I knew better. The translations of her works in English, much about the conditions of Chinese women, have inspired me for almost two decades. Her short story, *When I Was in Cloud Village,* should be known by everyone who loves literature.

I don't know what I would do if I didn't write. If I didn't turn to my journal in the evening. If I didn't turn to my books piled high on my bedroom table. If I didn't eavesdrop on conversations I hear on the bus or streetcar. If I didn't pay attention to the murmurings coming from deep inside my heart. Once I wrote that I liked to put my mouth on paper. After all, a long life of silences had to erupt somehow in song, in puns, in jokes, in words that grew into phrases, stanzas, sentences, paragraphs, into those stories that Salman Rushdie has written about in his beautiful, joyful novel *Haroun the Sea of Stories,* which is one of the books I'd take with me to a desert island.

The silences I experienced as a girl and young woman affected me deeply. I rarely kicked and screamed. I found it difficult to defend myself. I felt censored and oftentimes deeply wounded because of my hearing impairment, as well as a skin condition known as atopic dermatitis that I'd suffered since I was a baby. I admired my younger brother Bill because he was always able to argue. He and my brother-in-law Ed used to argue at the dinner table. I sat back and listened. I didn't know how to argue. I felt then that it was "fate" that girls didn't speak out and that I would never learn to be argumentative. Indeed, it seemed easier to be passive and not ever assert myself.

Now, in my 60's, I have more to do than ever. The writing is there, waiting to surface. In a poem of mine, I wrote, "Just give me a memory, paper and a pen." That memory comes not just from me as an individual, but from the deeds of unsung heroines and heroes, my peasant and farmer ancestors, my working sisters and brothers in the strawberry fields, in the fish-packing plants, in restaurants and hotels, in the offices where their fingers on computer keyboards can shut this country down.

My activist life is intertwined with my writing life. My poems feed my activism and my activism feeds my poetry. When I'm moved, nothing can stop me. I often find joy in small things that I notice, such as seeing a man's tie crumpled on the street in front of my office, which inspired my poem, "Eulogy for a Tie." "Flying" blossomed from my having run a red light after I had a few beers following a public forum where Chinese dissidents spoke in San Francisco after the Tiananmen Square massacre in Beijing in 1989.

My inspiration to write comes from those working people whose beauty is as constant as struggle, as luminous as fighting for higher wages, employer provided health care and child care, who realize that change will come about from their own hands. Writing is as necessary for me as breathing, as we fight to survive so that we may live robust and healthy, with the eradication of cancer, AIDS, brown lung disease, asbestosis, sickle-cell anemia, woman and child battering, racial hatred and violence. Being a worker-writer is what I am and will continue to be, working toward a society free of exploitation because we're immigrants, old, of color, with disability, women, poor. And that society – socialist and feminist – will let us thrive in the joy of unimagined beauty, in the bounty of our earth, in the creativity of our own making, in our own languages, with our own tongues.

Nellie Wong
February 1997

Joan Swift

For all the others...

Somewhere

she knows who she is, the one who creeps
through fescue and Highland Bent,
her whole body twisted, looking behind.
She has a name. Not like his. But a name.
There was a bass player in the bar,
a song, sips of Glenlivet, the man beside her
ordering more. Now he blots out the sky
and the mansion's windows when she tries
to look up. Think. Think.
She can remember. But there is only his hulk
like a black hole in the universe
sucking her in. Then her face in the televised
courtroom drowns in a blue sphere,
the one who disappears.

and somewhere

a woman in a Shaker rocker sings to her child.
Through the window comes summer
and behind it his swing over the sill.
He wears prison denim and the dirt
Work Release sent him to dig,
final earth, the terror
of leaving it huge so she dips to his well.
The child has to watch,
not that she will remember, dead ten years
later because her mother's unsinging voice
told the world and he came back with a knife.
This was the last lullaby:
"Don't kill us," she said.
But he did.

and somewhere

a girl who will never read Keats
or write her own name or touch a piano key
sighs to the moon outside her barred window.
In the hallway, titters and shushes
as the two blind boys grope for the doorknob.
The one matron sleeps.
When the girl cries out,
the inmates hear only an owl,
on the highway a screech of brakes.
The boys are all fingers, vines feeling
a trellis all the way up, then down
the way clematis grows on itself –
ankles, shoulder blades, breasts, knees,
thighs, nipples, pelvic bones, labia, lips.
They take turns holding her down, pushing in.
Whoever said "Women like touch,
men the visual" was wrong.
They were blind.
She still answers the moon.

1970

Your Hands

I was grass you fell upon
that morning, quick as a storm,
the black cloud of your hulk
in through the door and my neck
seized like an ancient town.
My throat full of its scream,

your hands taking the sound,
toppled quietly.
I know I'd have died right there
on that perfect marble floor
held in your hand and your hand
like a fish gone glassy of eye

sinking and floating up,
but then I became your moon,
the way you turned me around,
my mouth under your hand.
My light and my body spun
in that gravity, your grip,

and my light and my body went
before you like a candle
you carried down the hall,
though my light was almost spent.
And though I was stronger than wax
your hands were two black rocks.

Then I became your bow.
You bent me. Always your face
stayed on some other shore.
Behind me, dusky law,
you crooned in your thick voice
of snow-white women. My fear

and my guilt gave you a knife.
Blade silver, all that gleam
poised to enter my back,
it hovered, an old grief,
enormous in that room.
And I became your stick

for striking the wrong world.
Your cup, your loaf, your slave.
There was hate and there was love.
After, I had to kneel
facing the closed curtains,
trying to believe the sun

becoming their color. Sat
listening to the house.
Gone. But those two fierce hands
of yours, they stay like islands
still unmapped, the palm's fate
curving along my face.

My Scream

Did you know it went down inside
    like mercury vanishing
        into the cold bulb?

It froze like a fossil,
    first losing its voice
        then its skin and its skeleton

until nothing remained
    in the shivering air
        bright as an icicle.

It was winter.
    I knelt with my back
        to the cave's door.

Snow fell from my eyes.
    Rabbits hopped through the drifts.
        I was clothed altogether in frost.

Did you know it slept under my ribs,
    the sliver of my scream,
        that piercer, that nail?

The Phone Calls

I want to sleep a whole night
but your voice comes wearing its hood
and the quick dark shoes of three a.m.
to wake up the sky like lightning
swinging its whips.
Each night you arrive with your black dahlia.

You send hate, you send hate
like a vine up any wire.
Your words race from pole to pole
toward…toward…
do you know why it is me?

The walls of my room are no solace.
You writhe out of the plastic and into my brain
like smoke through a crevice.
Night is your pond to fish in.
Your bait is a bell tossed overboard.

Do you know the sea?
Sometimes it rages so its waves stand
up like trees.
Yet its bells ring for safety.
And its tongues like down on sand.

Exchange

I gave you my white neck.
Like a gift I gave you my throat.
You gave me your black hands
ripping the knot.

I gave you my blue eyes,
two cold and shrinking ponds.
Your gave me your fierce stare,
your black wands.

I gave you my pale carpet,
some door knobs and one white wall.
I gave you my bed as blue as where lilies
tremble.

And you gave me your history
there, that old black book,
turning the creamy pages
until you shook

me out, a pressed flower.
I gave you my stem and my leaf.
Black bee, you gave me your sting.
You gave me your life.

The Lineup

Each prisoner is so sad in the glare
I want to be his mother

tell him the white light will go down
and he will sleep soon.

No need to turn under eyes
to shuffle   poor soldiers   boys

in a play
to wear numbers   obey.

They have hands as limp as wet leaves
the long fingers of their lives

hanging. They cannot see
past the sharp edge nor hear me

breathe. O I would tell each one
he will wake whole again

in some utterly new place!
Trees without bars   sun a sweet juice

a green
field full of pardon.

The walls come in. I am
captured like him

locked in this world forever   unable to say   run

be free
I love you

having to accuse
and accuse.

Perjury

Semen was all that passed between us, I tell the court.
    Nothing else.
I catch in the snare of my throat
        the three strange words before they fly
from my mouth.

I am the only witness. I pull my raincoat
    tight around
        the two moons of perspiration
where they eclipse each other
                over my breasts.

Not saying the words I wish I'd never said erases them
    from the air.
        When the defense attorney kneels
before a chair, resting his elbows on the seat,
    and asks was I like that,

I stare at the soles of his shoes,
    their worn spots like maps of different countries.
I was not like that exactly. I was nearly naked.
              Forget the words.
    They mean I am guilty too.

The defense attorney asks wasn't
    my husband out of town that day
    and didn't I expect this caller?
            My skirt sticks to the chair.
Didn't I actually ask him in,

the man that I say strangled and then raped me?
    No. I pull at the skirt's blue cloth where
            my own sweat holds it to leather.
He was a stranger when his hands circled my throat.
    When he entered my body he was still

            a stranger.
But the words are secret. The words are shame.
      I keep them in my mouth
where they refuse to melt like the sweet things he thought
      they were, poor fool, treacles, Life Savers.

Although I do not know it now,
      it's death I court with this one
                 held breath.

1970-1983

We live in an occupied country, misunderstood;
justice will take us millions of intricate moves.

William Stafford

Testimony

March 17, 1970, when I lived in Oakland, California,
I was the victim of rape, hardly the St. Patrick's Day experience my Irish great-grandmother would have wanted for
me. The rapist was a Black man – I am white. He was one of
several men who had knocked on my door the previous
autumn when a storm, loud with wind and rain, blew a tree
down in our backyard. All of the men asked if they could
haul the tree away. Since it fell from a neighbor's yard, I sent
each of them next door.

Months passed. Then one morning as I was busy at that
most female of occupations, sewing, the power was shut off
for repairs. While I waited for the electricity to go on again,
I painted a windowsill. Painting required only a brush and
a can of paint; like stitching on my great-grandmother's
sewing machine where a foot pedal activated the needle,
the work was accomplished without the aid of circuits and
wires. I thought the doorbell's ring announced the mailman,
perhaps with a package, but it was one of the workmen
returning. He wore a dark blue watch cap and black shirt.
I had no time to ask what he wanted or even to scream when
he lunged through the door and grabbed my throat.

During the two months following the rape, I wrote the
preceding sequence of poems (with the exception of the
recently added "Perjury"). The poems are not all equally
good but as a sequence they served as therapy. In 1970
there were no rape hot-lines, no rape crisis centers, no orga-
nizations of women who had lived through the same experience to which I could turn for assurance, comfort, and
counseling. There was only the welter of my emotions – outrage, fear, guilt.

Outrage. I had two daughters, ages nine and fourteen.
What if he had raped one of them? Fear. How could I go

through the agonizing procedure of facing him in court, prosecuting him as I knew I must? Guilt. The guilt I felt was not only the female collective unconscious guilt which seems to grip all victims of rape, causing them to feel it is they who have committed some crime, but guilt for being responsible for the rapist's capture and thus for his life. Because after he had finished the act, for some reason I'll never understand, I told my rapist I loved him. And because he returned the next day and was arrested near my house by a plainclothes detective.

In this first early sequence of poems, I disguised the event in metaphors, showing mostly compassion and very little of the anger beneath. There was no trial, only a preliminary hearing in which I was the only witness. He was indicted by the judge and charged with burglary or, in other words, forced entry into the house, and forcible rape, then bound over to Superior Court. When the case came up for trial, the attorneys were selecting the jury while I stood outside the courtroom door, not knowing I shouldn't be there, that I should be waiting instead at home for a witness call. Suddenly the situation inside the courtroom changed. The prosecutor and defense attorney huddled over the plea bargain. The burglary charge was dropped, making it appear as if I had invited him into my house, and the defendant changed his plea to guilty . He was sentenced to five years in San Quentin for rape.

A few years later I moved to the state of Washington. One January afternoon in 1982 an Alameda County Deputy District Attorney tracked me down and requested my testimony at an upcoming Aggravated First Degree Murder trial he was prosecuting. The same man who raped me had just raped and murdered a woman named Joan Stewart who lived three blocks from the house where I had been attacked. Not only was her first name the same as mine and her last name similar, she was 43 years old, the same age I had been when I was raped, and the circumstances under which both crimes were committed bore a close resemblance. There was rain and a howling windstorm. Trees fell over power lines, causing a loss of electricity. (I am reminded that rape is not an act of lust but of the need to assert power.) He strangled both of us.

The trial did not get underway for a year and when it did, the judge ruled my testimony "prejudicial" and "irrelevant." I was allowed to tell what the defendent had done to me only during the penalty phase of the trial, the phase following the part of the trial in which he was convicted. Had the jurors not found him guilty, a verdict reached largely through convincing forensic and circumstantial evidence, they would never have known of his prior crimes.

However, until the prosecutor asked me to leave the courtroom because my presence might jeopardize the case, I sat in the audience for much of the testimony, my hair dyed red in an unconvincing attempt at disguise. Hearing the various witnesses speak and watching their behavior, I realized that, rather than the small world of which I had been the center in the 1970 sequence of poems, a complex story was unfolding, one that involved a number of people, including the murdered woman. Using the testimony I heard in the courtroom, information gleaned from reading numerous transcripts of the trial, and my own words as I spoke them on the witness stand, I wrote another sequence consisting of twelve poems, each one spoken from the point of view of a different witness. The defendant, who never testified, is revealed through the language of others. And the victim exists only in the form of Exhibits A, B, C, etc. and some photographs and slides.

It was for the victim that I now felt guilt. This time I seemed responsible not only for a life but for a death. Although the therapists available to me now have told me over and over that the rapist is responsible for his acts, somehow I have wronged another too.

> Sister victim, I could have told you storms
> aroused him, wind's way with branches, whole trunks
> of trees blocking the road, all the small streams

swollen and spilling out of their ferned banks.
You knew nothing of me and can't now, breath
stopped by the same hands that grabbed my throat.
Did he chant behind you? No, he filled your mouth
straightforward, then made his awful cut.
I want to think he killed you accidentally
but those words I whispered *I love*
you are rain darkening back as the next day
he did and the police were there. What of
our matching names? I have no blood sister
but your blood stains my breasts, my thighs, my hair.

For this reason, I gave – and give – my testimony. The
defendant was found guilty following the conviction phase of
the trial. Two penalty phases were held and both ended
in hung juries regarding the death penalty. The defendant
is serving a life sentence without possibility of parole in a
California prison.

Jury Deliberates Fate of Sex Slayer

After a week of testimony, jurors Monday afternoon began deliberating the question of whether Charles Jackson should die for the rape murder of an Oakland woman.

Alameda County prosecutor Rockne Harmon asked the eight men and four women who found Jackson guilty of murder earlier this month to "consider the horror of the circumstances" of the Jan. 5, 1982 slaying of teacher Joan Stewart on a lonely hillside near her Montclair home.

Pointing to photographs of the woman, whose throat was slashed after she was sexually assaulted, Harmon reminded jurors that Stewart's husband, five-year-old son, and students had suffered a great loss.

He asked the panel to reject defense pleas that Jackson be sentenced to state prison for life...Jackson's attorney, Bill Linehan, begged jurors to spare the 46-year-old handyman's life and return him to state prison where he has spent all but six months of the past 15 years for burglary, child molesting, and rape...Earlier during the penalty phase of the Alameda County Superior Court trial, a woman Jackson was convicted of raping more than 10 years ago described the terror of her assault.

Oakland Tribune
Tuesday, February 15, 1983

Ravine

Because he thinks she moves like water,
because water moves down from the clouds,
slides along oak leaves, twines three-ply
strings in clay runnels, because rain
has been falling for days and a gale
has swept a tree onto the street,
because he thinks she moves like water
and water has always run away,
he wants to hold it in his fingers,
because the storm moves in his whole body
and nothing can stop it, his hands
are around her throat as he drags her
into acacias and ferns, feels himself
slip inside her mouth because
he wants to keep floating forever,
and because she moves like water
he sinks his knife into the flesh
of her neck to make a red pool
he wants to bathe in again and again.

Coroner

I had to follow her blood to its worst destination.
She knew the way. I kept to shadows and bruises,
staying close to her jawbone, her blue lips,
the scrape on the right side of her abdomen.
There was a kind of trail, neither north nor south,
along her arms and thighs. I saw sunset's purple
and the green of marshes. I was a hunter.
But there was nothing in her vagina, an empty cache,
and the eyes that saw everything were cold and shut.

I sat a long time near the lake inside her mouth.
Semen glistened in the fluorescent light over the table.
Nothing moved. I slid my knife into her throat
the depth of the other blade because some memory
might seep from the artery he cut, because
I wanted her fractured larynx to speak again.
Now I can tell you she died twice, early and late.
I had a tape recorder with me and a map
of the human body. I was not lost. She was.

Her Husband

Once I thought I knew all about live oaks,
dead butterweed, black roots.
The murderer was winter but eventually
everything was saved.
Summers we spent among the resurrected.
I focused the Pentax.
She shaded *Sitka columbine* and *yarrow* with her hand.
All evening we catalogued wildflowers
and in the morning climbed higher
to find *Flett violet.*

Now I know a second nature,
camouflage of trees after a storm,
streetlights out,
one night superimposed on another like two negatives.
He waited behind branches,
his breathing so light it could have been
their sway.
I looked for something white, her umbrella
at the side of the road,
the bread she'd gone for.
I never slept.
In the morning I found her face down,
throat cut, blood slipped into the veins
of all those fallen leaves.

Sometimes I dream she still waits
under a right pine.
I'm holding a stalk of crimson *paintbrush.*
Her body is taking the color.

Victim

Then the last being fell away from my face into the blindness
of shadow.
On my tongue words took the shapes of semen.
I was bruised all over, but I opened my eyes one final time.
There were the ferns.
There was the oak tree dripping rain.
I confused the shine near my throat, its sharp edge,
with a difficult ridge in the Sierra, some escarpment...

And where is the tangible part of me?
Torn blue jeans and tangled white nylon underpants
in a brown paper bag.
The district attorney asks my husband to identify my green
down jacket, blood crusted at the neck.
Poor man. He touches the label.
He brushes his cheek with the back of his hand.
He steps down.

And I am long since gone into the sad prison of emulsion
and paper.
I stare forever from police photographs,
the struggle, the long cut,
not knowing why I am here.

Beside her Husband

We sit in the courtroom's semidark
as in a far northern dusk,
the sun poised endlessly on the rim
of the windowsill.
Over and over her body flashes to the screen.
She is lying face down under an oak,
one leg drawn slightly up
as if she might start to run again.
Or her left arm reaches out for leaves
or ferns or hands.
Someone has turned her over now
like a page in a book.
The knife cut is the color of plums,
blood darkening across her throat.
"How can you watch?" I whisper
when the camera shows the zipper torn
from her jeans,
her underwear twisted like a rope,
the thatch of pubic hair.

I remember once it was my body
the defendant fell on like a hawk,
and the brown mice of my fear.
I knelt. I wept.
I could not die bravely.

He answers, "I look at the floor."

Her Husband, to Himself

Cyanide and sulfuric acid: the smoke curls up
around his shackles, shrouds him for his grave.
His face vanishes in a green haze.

    During recess the bailiff chats with him.
    The beast smiles. Hands that let my wife's
    blood out of her throat are two dark rabbits
    in the hutch of his lap. He crosses one foot
    behind the other like a schoolboy.

In a room with several doors, the one in the floor
drops open. His neck snaps like a branch in a storm.
Four rifles aim at a white moon pinned to his chest
where his heart's last night is waiting. His flesh
singes with two thousand volts.

    His ears have another blackness. Into it,
    his attorneys whisper the pure light of the law.
    They have made him comb out his dreadlocks
    and shave his small goatee. He wears a maroon
    sweat shirt while my wife dresses in blue eternity.

Gary Gilmore, Jesse Bishop, Steven Judy,
John Spenkelink, Frank Coppola, Charlie Brooks.
The executioner always wears a hood.
Blood spurts where his testicles slice off.
Behind the eyeslits it is always me.

His Mother

I wrapped the baby in a rag and ran away,
a blade of moonlight through the door behind me.
The house was one long room – they called it
a shotgun house – and we were the bullets
waiting for our deaths inside.
One last time I turned to look at the boy
where he whimpered in his sleep,
the floor rubbing his welts.
The girl lay behind the stove like a pile of sticks.
Later I heard their daddy took the wheels
off his new wife's wheelchair.
Two thousand miles away under the California sun,
I thought of him drunk on antiseptic,
cutting the willow twigs, braiding a whip.

Soot poured down the aisles of the train.
Halfway back to Mississippi, I got off
where cactus was blooming and a moon sat
in the daylight sky like a vanilla cookie.
I bought the girl a dress, had it all wrapped up
in brown paper. The sawmill was whining in D'Lo
like it always did, but still I heard the boy
teasing his goat. Something else tied to a tree
whose leaves keep coming back!
He watched his sister's fingers slide
under the string until the dress floated up
all blue and white like a cloud in the sky.
"Mama, you takin' her away from here!" he said.
The girl looked pretty, the two of us
skipping ties on the railroad track.

I went back for him too.
I don't remember when.
The years all stack like wood behind the outhouse.
"This here you put in prison is only a child,"
I said. My firstborn, only boy, son of Charlie Red,

I took him last.

His Sister

At nineteen he was still signing his name
with an X.
The prison doors had already opened and shut
and opened again like eyes that don't forget.
I cupped his fingers under mine,
black skin to black skin.
Together we made the tall letters with shadows
and the round ones like tears.
On the dark path of his name there was no blood yet.

Then it was done. He looked down at the page
and saw his marks like bird tracks
in the mud beside the Okatoma.
"That's you," I said.
I wanted him to fly.
Again and again we traced his loops and hooks.

D'Lo, de l'Eau

He walked almost every day by water.
Below, the city on flatland lay stone on stone
to reach for heaven.
He was more near on the hill among dark pines,
the dog *Duchess* taking the little rain-created
torrents in great gulps.
That autumn,
prison was across the bay.
From across his lifetime came the slender song
of water
he took for solace between one unhappiness
and another.
He remembered his head on a woman's breast
in a town named for water.
He was born there.
He was borne away.

Another Witness

The prosecutor wants me to open
my memory like a trunk,
pull out the dress of India cotton,
green and yellow print
like a field of regimented flowers,
and slide its looseness over my head.
He wants the judge to see me wear
old bedroom slippers,
brush the color *mulberry*
on a windowsill,
the jury to hear a sewing machine begin
when the electricity comes on again.
A lineman touches wire to wire.
The doorbell rings.
The jury sees me running up the stairs –
I think the mailman has a gift.
                              But it's you,
thirteen years younger than you are now,
sitting between your two defense attorneys.
The floppy black felt hat you wore
that day you asked to haul
the tree a storm blew down
is gone. Twice gone.
I almost say *Hello*
but you're too quick.
You grab my throat.
The lost crystal world of the chandelier
sways above my head.
No one hears the scream
I swallow when your hand
shuts over my mouth.
The other grips my hands behind me.

119 | Joan Swift

                              And I am so light
with fear you push me down the hall easily,
so light I float above the bed.
You pull me to my knees,
mutter an incantation behind my back.
Two gloves fly over my head.
You lift my dress.
Something feathered, a wren or winter thrush,
stirs between my breasts.
                              Now I must say it.
The word *sodomy* forms on my tongue,
dissolves like a wafer, forms again
to hang over the court reporter's desk.
A juror coughs.
I say *no.*
Oddly, you obey.
I think you have a knife.
When you enter the other place
I feel tears start.
The whole courtroom is silent.
Beyond the windows, Lake Merritt
shines in the sun
and joggers color its shore.
But I run back through time
until my thighs are sticky with you.
Don't tell, you say.
Thirteen years later
                              seventy-five people
turn toward the witness stand.
They see your limp hands on the bed,
a shred of noon light.
I kiss one knuckle. I don't know why.
The skin is sad and black.
A vein splits into two separate rivers.
I love you, I say into that air
                              and this.

Your palms stroke my face,
vanish like birds into a tree.
Don't move, you say.
Surely the blade poises
over my back now.
I wait to die.
Don't move, you say again.
The door shuts
and you are here
listening to how I wash my legs and face.
I change my dress, put on another,
rose and blue.
Outside, the street is a ribbon
tied to anywhere.
I drive an hour. Two.
I drive all the way to a telephone booth,
a police station, a lineup,
to another district attorney.
I drive to a different state
and back again
                    while you break rock in prison.
"Is the man you describe in the courtroom today?"
  the prosecutor asks.
"Yes," I say.
"Will you point to him, please?"
  When we face each other
                    she becomes visible,
the woman you murder twelve years
after me.
Her name is the same as mine.
Rain nets the hills.
Wind hurls a tree to ground
and lines sag without power.
She walks near that house
I left years ago, white shutters
and bricks unchanged.

One of us must lift her now
from the wet grass,
sponge clean her bloody throat,
I who spoke love,
you who killed for that lie.

Detective

I was in plainclothes, driving a car marked only
by late winter's mud. I thought clues would be hiding
inside the raped woman's house, bruises on her throat
in thumb circles or a spot like a crusted-over moon
shining from her dress. But a black man paused
near her hedge, his dark cords and navy watch cap
such as she described. He was wearing gloves.

The story is old now, obscured by murders,
but if I had accelerated up the hill
into Monterey pines, I think his steps might have
turned to her door. Of course, I picked him up.
He sat in the rear seat behind the police car's
steel mesh like a zoo animal. His face turned stone.

What lay in the palm of one glove was lipstick,
hers, as the laboratory proved later.
The print was of a slightly open mouth, caught
before the scream. It slept there in the empty
shape of his hand, the kiss he'd always wished
to awaken, although fatal.

Prisoner

The water speaks in all its slippery tongues –
Melanie, Margaret, Melinda, Wanda, Tish.
San Quentin above shows a single cell of sky
through the open manhole. He doesn't look up,

wants only the sewer's dark where his feet
swing down the limbs of iron footholds.
This is how he is free with orders from Maintenance
and a wrench for the penstock valve. This is how

he stands on a riverbank again, the arch of tile
his old bridge over flood. He doesn't mind the smell.
The water runs down to its purification.
He tries to remember the body it resembles most.

And after...

Nightjar

Asleep in elephant grass,
precise cover, dark
feathers overlapping lighter
dark feathers,
waves of feathers
rippling river grass –
asleep in thatch and swamp deer
hoof prints,
you do not hear the crash
of elephant feet,
so deep your dream of beetles.
The sky is pewter over
rosewood trees.
Then the animal takes one
thundering step in the brush
and the driver astride
the elephant's neck
pushes his bare toes down
behind the elephant's right ear.
The howdah shakes. We lurch.
And the whole sky flows
with the thrashing of white
wing patches, a beating like drums
to keep your heart in the air
to another horizon.
Held down and raped, I never flew
that day his hands grabbed at my throat,
death-out-of-nowhere's hover.
You save your self's fierce dazzle.
I lay in my nest and never moved
from where I dreamed my life.

2.

I kneel again the way he made me kneel
at the end of the bed. A Bengal
tiger drags me to this window cut
in thatch for watching.
Moonlight that striped me running
through the forest goes away.
The tiger has a flood of lights
to gaze on blood, his straddle
over the water buffalo's flesh,
its roped left hoof. I did not die.
The only voice is your *chunk*
chunk chunk from where your
feathers fold near roots.
This place is called a blind.
One-note singer, chital-spotted
breath-catcher, I keep
a tiger always under my eyelids now.

Soul on Ice

In the cupboard behind the chipped cups
between *Becoming Orgasmic* and *Birds of Nepal*
in the garage where an oil slick shines under the car
I drive 27 years later –
among the jars of tarragon and basil
beneath sofa cushions
in the memory of the space between the original construction
and the added-on kitchen of my grandmother's house
where a rose bush inexplicably grew and I used to hide
whatever needed to be hidden
in piles of yellowing newspapers
in the dust under the beds of the daughters I saved
I search but the book isn't anywhere.
The cover was blue and white and black.
It lay on the glass-topped coffee table
then was a fanning of pages in the detective's hands
like the riffled landing and taking off of yellow-shafted
flickers on the lawn.
His mind flew between the black man who wrote the book
and the one who raped me.
It was only a book I was reading.
Did Eldridge Cleaver die?
What does this mean: life without the possibility of parole?

Paint

The raped woman with a paintbrush in her hand.
She has forgotten for a moment what she is painting,
the dripping color so like the breast feathers
of a purple finch. She breathes the origins
of the paint: vinyl polymer, quartz, silica from sand,
the water of a river. Pushing the wet hairs
flat against the rim, she watches as the paint runs
slowly down the side of the can, acquainting
the label with erasure. Here is the windowsill
emptied of its geraniums and iris.
Here is the wall, forgetful of its blossom.
She slides on her knees over hardwood to an oval
space of sun. There are endless ways to kiss.
She thinks how any minute he will come.

Flashback

This happens in dreams all the time:
the road is a river of sparkling fish
and one of them

eats you. With your right foot poised to push
hard on the accelerator, suddenly there is a mouth
behind you and a flare of bluish

lights crawls up and down your arms. The moon's old tooth
snags in the sky but you are only asleep.
Here is the truth:

I am the driver. Under the wings of pines I stop
while he moves through the shape of his own shadow,
dressed in black pants and his short-sleeved white summer cop

shirt, his arms bare and of a darkness I know,
behind him not the hall door kicked shut
but the crackle of a police radio.

Not a palm over my mouth, not
my scream smothered in fingers,
not the world ending in a shard of the chandelier, but

just this: his hands reaching in through the car's
open window, sweet night air, a hover of thumbs
close to my throat, how it lingers –

What does he want? My breath? The sums
of all my hidden parts again?
From somewhere under my ribs the thud of drums

begins. My eyes prowl his horizon.
There is the smell of grass as my teeth sink in.

Why She Wants to be Sand

Sand keeps the sun, each grain a tiny oven.
He will burn his feet on me.

Sand is the smallest particles of whatever minerals
churned for a million years in the sea.
He will bleed wherever he lies.

Sand takes the prints of fingers
and lets the surf lick them clean.
He will float away and drown.

Sand watches quick fish dart in their
yellow, green, plum, scarlet
under the blue lid of forgetfulness.

*Me desvincolo del mar
cuando vienen des aguas a mi.*

He will stay in the snail's house. Sand slips
on a new shape every time the sea changes tides.
He will not know me.

_____

James Wright's translation from the Spanish of César Vallejo:
"I am freed from the burdens of the sea
when the waters come toward me."

Afterword

I sat in the room just off the kitchen at 9 Superior Street, Rochester, New York, my feet not touching the floor, my face eye level with the old Royal Standard typewriter owned by a great aunt. One finger at a time, I jabbed at the keys, occasionally looking up at the white paper in the typewriter's roller. The room, used for storing dusty clutter not wanted in the main rooms of the small house, was referred to as "the cold room" and the door to it was kept closed so as not to allow any heat inside. Either it was summer or my mind's little frenzy was keeping me warm. I was five years old and writing a poem.

From that time on my mother thought of me as a writer of one sort or another. My father was a sports and human interest reporter for the *Rochester Journal American*. His mother, my grandmother, as well as his sister were both poets. Thus, as far as my mother was concerned, my vocation was foreordained. Off and on as the years passed and even as short a time as a decade ago, I wondered if I might not have made a better attorney. But I remind myself that attorneys have the law to worry about – jurisprudence, precedence, rigidities observed over centuries that refuse to be fractured.

Poetry has no boundaries. Even when I'm writing a poem in form, I'm not limited. I find the requirements of rhyme, of line and stanza length in the sonnet, for instance, one of my favorite forms, an invitation to free the imagination, to break through the dictates of the form to the wide open field of variation. Once I stood in front of a classroom full of students at the University of California, Davis, where I had been invited by my good friend, poet Sandra McPherson, to read and discuss some of our work. Sandra has a large collection of quilts made by African-American women whose originality in piecing the quilt tops, their startling use of color and wild variations on age-old designs, astonishes the eye. We hauled three or four of them in green trash bags over to the classroom where Sandra stick-pinned them to the wall for the students to see. There was no end to where the pattern could go – starfish spreading their arms forever across an expanse of purple sand, medallions uncentered to put the world a little off balance. And yet there were edges. An edge is something from which you can fall into the unexpected. Poetry is like that.

Although I've been making poems since I was five and publishing them since I was in my thirties, old acquaintances occasionally ask me, "Are you still writing?" Sometimes I feel overwhelmed by the numbers of poets in the country today, most of them producing very good poems. Maybe it's time to rest, time not to feel the need to re-create the world in words. But then I'll drive past a salt-water marsh and from the corner of my eye catch a glimpse of a great blue heron or the rain that splattered across my windshield will suddenly stop and in a single ray of sun I'll see an eagle perched on the branch of a fir tree or I'll be at a poetry reading and the words of the poet will start a flood of my own words surging through my head.

I'm most happy when I'm creating or re-creating some-thing. When my husband's parents died leaving behind a dilapidated cabin in a deep fir forest, it was I who insisted we keep it and started a project to remodel the entire structure, putting in a foundation, adding a small wing for a new curving stairway to replace the one with seven-inch treads and eleven-inch risers, knocking out interior walls for space. With the fireplace crumbling beside me, I find myself sitting beside it and starting a poem. In late spring I lie on the new cedar deck surrounding decay, look up at the stars in their circle of branches, find them all in their May places, and the images begin.

Writing is hard work but easier than not writing. Many times I write a poem to explain something to myself, to help me understand exactly what has happened. Making a poem can be a gesture towards control over the chaos of the exterior world. The poems in the first section of this book are that kind. After the initial shock had subsided, I remember the urgency I felt to begin writing about what had happened to me. I know this sounds strange, but I wanted to understand the rape by the only way I knew how to: writing poetry. I had to be alone. Since the freeway I lived near in Oakland was a constant roar, I first wrote in a friend's backyard, then took to Joaquin Miller Park where I slid the car into a space above the amphitheater ("Dedicated to California Writers") and while the dog ran free among eucalyptus and oaks, scribbled with a pen in a spiral notebook. I was unaware then that my experience didn't fit the statistics: most rapes occur between people who know each other, most rapes take place between couples of the same race.

Paradoxically, the poems have everything to do with white and black, and yet nothing to do with it. The high school I attended in Rochester during the early forties was 20% Black. I sat beside Black students in class, stood beside them in line during graduation, and when I went off to college at Duke, walked immediately to the back of a Durham, North Carolina bus where the Black passengers stared at me incredulously. So that fateful 1970 noon in California, when I opened the door to its insistent bell and saw the Black man who had asked for yard work a few months earlier, I started to smile. Was my first smile an invitation? Had he murdered before? Did I make him a murderer? Did others die because three words I spoke probably saved my life? I'll never know the answers to these questions but all these years later I can't forget the reason I have to ask them.

Every now and then something occurs that ignites another poem. *Soul on Ice* is the most recent: the memory of that book on my coffee table when the rape took place and later when the police arrived to investigate popped into my head at a book festival. When I searched for it at home, anxious to write from the unformed emotions I was feeling, the book had vanished in the accumulation of years. I suppose these out-of-the-blue connections will go on for the rest of my life, but with the poems in this book, I feel the story is complete. The poems are not only for those who like poetry but for all other victims of rape. They're for my rapist too.

As an undergraduate at Duke I studied creative writing with William Blackburn. Much later, a stranger in the middle of the country in Iowa, where I was alone all week with an infant daughter while my husband traveled the Midwest, I managed to get to Drake University for a creative writing class. But it wasn't until I attended Nelson Bentley's evening poetry writing workshop at the University of Washington that I began to take my own work seriously. When our second daughter was two years old, I enrolled in the English Department's graduate school. It was late 1962. The University of Washington at the time was one of the few schools offering an advanced degree in Creative Writing, now an M.F.A. The poet who taught "verse" writing was Theodore Roethke.

I was terrified. He chose his students from the list of those who signed up. Only ten or eleven would make it. I remember waiting for a phone call and when it didn't come, I despondently enrolled in a course in the metaphysical poets taught by a professor more formidable than Roethke. I wrote one wretched four-page paper for that class and then, wandering out of Parrington Hall at the end of the first miserable week, I ran into Theodore Roethke himself. "Where the hell have you been?" he asked. I learned then that he posted the names of his chosen class members on the door to the classroom and I hadn't known enough to look. That class turned out to be Roethke's last. He died the following summer, August 1963. From him I learned the taut elegance of three-beat, four-beat, and five-beat lines, the importance of hearing the poem. In his fervor to teach us "ear," he required that we memorize a poem each week, ready to recite it aloud in class. On Thursdays, it was not unusual to find eight or nine of us standing with our faces to the wall just inside Parrington, heads down, silently saying poems written by Stanley Kunitz or Louise Bogan.

I don't remember when I decided on the name under which I write. For four years after graduating from college, I worked as an advertising copywriter. It was the infancy of television, a medium where the creator of clever commercials is never identified. Swift is my husband's name. I was born Angevine, ninth generation descendant of French Huguenots who came to this country in 1699. My mother's parents emigrated from Sweden in the late 1800's. I tried Joan Angevine Swift for a while, then settled for the near anonymity of Joan Swift. I think now I never really believed I could write. If I failed, the name itself would efface me. It wasn't until the early seventies that I dared declare myself "writer" or "poet" when I filled out forms asking my occupation. Up until then, I was just "housewife." Poet friends such as Sandra McPherson, Gwen Head, and Madeline DeFrees have helped me re-vision myself.

Looking back I realize I was trying to conform to some image I carried in my unconscious of what an ideal wife and mother should be. My own mother began divorce proceedings against my father when I was six. Their marriage was marked by tumult – stormy arguments, stony silences. My father would sometimes stay away from home for days on end. I remember my mother cowering behind the hat tree in the hall while my father pummeled her. I remember her tears and blackened eyes. When I dared to open the door to my parents' bedroom one quiet Sunday morning, he threw back the blankets with a roar and hurled me down the stairs. Often my mother vanished, packing me off to the home of one of her sisters. I never knew where she went, what she was doing during those absences. Was she trying to keep me out of the line of fire? Was she hiding from my father? Was she hiding me? Such mysteries. Such violence.

During the two years it took for the divorce to be final,

my mother and I lived with her parents in the small coal mining town of Antrim, Pennsylvania. I often wonder what my hard-working grandmother thought when her youngest of four daughters moved back home with a six-year-old in tow. For decades my grandmother had risen at three a.m. to get my grandfather off to work in the mines, a five-mile walk down into the valley and then back up another steep hill before he was carried into the mine by a railed wagon. She tended to her five children, milked the cow, fed the pig. I remember her bending over the peonies in her summer garden, a bit of color and joy in what must have been a difficult life. And suddenly there I was, long after her own four girls and boy were grown – another little girl. My mother returned to the city with her divorce papers during the depths of the Depression and, a pioneer in the field of single divorced motherhood, worked at clerical jobs to raise me alone. To her credit, she kept close contact with my father's side of the family, although not with my father. She never married again.

"How can you stand up in front of so many people and read those poems?" she asked more than once before her death in 1991, referring to some in this book.

"I just pretend I'm someone else," I told her.

Pearl Garrett Crayton

To my father, Edwin Oliver Garrett, one of the greatest story-tellers who ever lived.

How Deep The Feeling Go

Most of my life I been scared to tell this. Maybe I oughta not tell it now. Lord knows I don't want folks to be going around looking for Malice like he some kinda desperado. They be seeing him in places he ain't never been. They be hating some poor innocent person thinking that's him. But we in the sixties now, and some folks who used to hate everybody who wasn't exactly like them done loosened up so much they eating at the same table with folks they done tried to lynch. But them same folks still might not be able to stomach Malice.

Not even here on Little River Lane where all the folks was living close like one big happy family, not even here where womens loved their children so much they been known to jump into the river when the water was high and save them from drowning, not even here where mens loved their families so much that they been known to stand with one shotgun trying to hold off the Ku Klux Klan and get killed trying to save their families, not even here in the days when this land was ruled by love did Malice find enough of it. Where else in the world is he gonna find it?

Just the same, I get the feeling sometimes that if I tell this tale I might get one other person to see what I seed in the boy. Maybe that'll put a little more love in this world for him. Lord knows he need it.

When we was growing up, Malice was my cousin Sam's best-best friend. He was good-looking, but not enough to brag about. What I liked best about him was how easy he borrowed the horses of folks who wasn't nowhere close by. Didn't make no difference how skittish a horse was, that boy could walk up and say a few words and do a little rubbing, and in no time he be trotting down the road on that horse.

Then after he break the horse in some and gentle him down, he'd let the rest of us ride.

One day we borrowed two of Old Man Ebby Jeems' horses and rode them double all the way down to The Point. And who did we run across but that old man right out there on the road we was riding on. He done gone riding in a car with somebody, and the car done had a flat, and there they is down on their knees fixing that flat.

By the time we seed him we was right on him – too late to run off.

"Them look like my horses" was the first thing he said to us.

Anybody with a dime's worth of sense know his own horses. Just the same Malice tried to out-slick the old man.

"You didn't tell us we could go riding on your horses, Mr. Ebby. And you know we don't steal." His voice had the ring of the gospel, and it could sweeten honey.

Lord have mercy! We done already borrowed every single horse on Little River Lane and Old River Road and over half the horses down in The Point. And can't nobody count the plums and peaches and pears and figs we done borrowed off folks trees all over that part of the country. Never asked nobody for nothing. Never paid nothing back. If that ain't stealing, what is?

Old Man Ebby done stood up and comed to the horses and looked them over real close. Then he shook his head.

"I could swear these here my horses," he said. "But I know everytime Malice sing in church he bring in the Holy Spirit like nobody else can ever do. Ain't nobody that close to The Lord gonna steal nothing."

I thought we done got outta the mess scotch free. But after we rode a mile or so more down the road, Malice said we gotta take them horses out to pasture and let them go back home.

"How we gonna get home?"

"Walk."

"All them many miles? No way!"

But we did. He talked us into it. That boy could talk his way outta Hell.

But when it comed time for him to talk his way into the hearts of those who supposed to been loving him alla his life, he didn't get nowhere.

Like most things that tear a person's heart out, it started off just as easy as cream. Me and him and Sam was fishing in the river one Saturday morning in October, setting quiet on the grass holding our cane poles waiting for a bite. Something struck Malice's line and sunk his stopper.

Up he jumped, and in no time he pulled in a great big old white perch.

While him and Sam was making miration over the catch, I seed blood on the boy's overalls.

"You done hurt yourself!" I hollered. "The seat of your pants covered with blood!"

Sam looked and hollered, "Lord have mercy! Man, you bleeding to death!"

He put his hand on his bottom and felt around and said, "That ain't nothing but my time of the month done come down again."

First time I ever heard anybody say mens have a time of the month, and I told him so.

He said his mama told him his daddy have one, and her daddy and all her brothers have one, too. Every month.

At that time I wasn't but twelve, so I had sense enough to know I hadn't heard everything. So I hushed.

But Sam said, "Rena told me her time of the month come outta her tootie hole. Boys ain't got no tootie hole."

"Yes, they do, too!" Malice hollered. Then he started crying.

Me, I didn't know what to tell him. Just the same I stood there looking at him crying, and all kinda feelings I ain't never had before was bumping into one another inside me trying to put on words and come outta me. But couldn't none of them find no words. And I got to hurting so much I could have cried, too. On account of one thing I did know from changing diapers on the babies in our family is that boys sure'nuff ain't got no tootie hole. Unless....

Sam up and said it. "You must be done turned into a morphadite!" *

That's the one thing alla us children was scared to death of. If what the bigger children done told us was true, when a girl sass grown folks and let other folks talk bad about her mama, she start growing a tee-wee and turn into a boy. When a boy be bad like that, he start growing a tootie hole and turn into a girl. That's how come some folks get to be morphadites.

I thought about that. I'd been around Malice all my life, and I'd been with him in just about every bit of devilment he ever did. So if he done already done enough bad to turn hisself into something so horrible, what about me?

"Man, you better go home and get outta them bloody clothes," Sam was telling him.

We walked all the way to his house along the edge of the river to stay out of sight so nobody would see how bloody Malice was.

Soon as I got back home I went to the toilet and checked myself to see if I had started growing a tee-wee. It didn't make me feel no better when I couldn't find no sign. I remembered how Malice was all right when we left home to go fishing, all right up until he caught that white perch. Then all of a sudden – blood! So I figured maybe a thing like that popped out on a person all at once.

This got stuck between my ears the way being scared can do sometimes. And it just kept on getting bigger and bigger as the day wore on. I couldn't hardly get nothing right that Mama told me to do.

Then, before I knowed what was happening, there was Malice standing before me all dressed up in my best Sunday dress and my one and only pair of Sunday shoes. Just looking at him was hard enough on my nerves. But when

*Colloquial word for *pseudohermaphrodite.*

he asked me how did I like wearing his bloody overalls, that knocked me plumb outta my mine. Because I looked at myself and seed that I had on boy clothes, shoes, cap and all.

I hollered.

Mama comed running.

Then here come Daddy holding the coal oil lamp.

That's the first I knowed it was nighttime.

Back when I was real little, Mama always put me in her bed between her and daddy everytime I woke up hollering from a bad dream. But after I got big all she did was leave a lamp burning in my room. But that night I woke up hollering again, so she sot up in a chair by my bed for the rest of the night.

Next morning I was puny, on account of I could almost feel a tee-wee getting ready to pop out on me. That took away my appetite.

Mama said I was coming down with something, maybe worms. She kept me home from church and gived me some asafetida and made me drink mint tea all day.

Come Monday I done perked up enough to go to school. But Malice didn't come. None that week. His two little sisters told us he was sick.

When he did come back the next week, he wasn't hisself no more. He never had been no big, husky-looking boy. Although he was two years older than me, he was about my size or maybe a couple pounds heavier. But it looked to me like he had started melting away. Just like a butterball in hot sun. And when we had recess, he sot on the church-house steps and watched the rest of us play.

I figured turning into a morphadite done made him sick, and it might be killing him. Lord, have mercy! Was that gonna happen to me, too?

After school let out, Malice didn't keep up with the other children walking home. So me and Sam lagged behind with him.

First pecan tree we comed to, he wanted to stop and pick. Back in them days children took their dinners to school in syrup buckets. Everybody had to wash out their bucket after they finished eating. So the three of us had clean buckets to pick up pecans in.

"I done already picked up two hundred pound grass sacks full of pecans while I was home sick," Malice told us. "This year I'm gonna have me a whole heap of Christmas money. I gonna buy presents for everybody I know."

Every year most of us children got out and picked up pecans and sold them for a nickle a pound to make spending money for Christmas. But all I had so far was a foot tub full. I'd made up my mind to buy Big Mama one of them big, pretty glass bowls with foots on it. That alone would take a hundred pound grass sack full of pecans to pay for. And I had a heap of other kinfolks I wanted to buy Christmas presents for. So I got to thinking about how far behind I was. I laid down my booksack and went to work.

Every day except Sunday after that the three of us picked up pecans. The man who did the buying comed around in a truck twice a month. In no time I made eighteen dollars and six bits. Sam had almost twice that much. And Malice had over three times that much. That boy might nigh melted hisself away hustling pecans.

Then his time of the month comed down on him again. In school. He stood up to read, and there it was. Blood all over the seat of his overalls.

The teacher took him in the back room of the church where the pastor and deacons always took care of business. Then she sent him home. She sent his two little sisters to walk with him to see after him on the way.

It was a whole week before Malice comed back to school. And me and Sam didn't run across him under the pecan trees. I figured he picked up all that he wanted to before we got out of school every day. Didn't neither one of us go to his house to see him. Looking back on that time now, I can't remember if we even talked about going to see him. All I remember is how shame I felt. As long as nobody else didn't know Malice done turned into a morphadite, it was all right to be friends with him. But after he showed hisself bloody before the whole school I was scared everybody might think I was like him. And I was scared, too, that maybe I might be.

Malice and his family lived on the end of the plantation closest to the churchhouse where we had our school. We lived on the other end. So walking to school that morning Malice first comed back, we didn't see him and his little sisters.

As soon as we got to school, I seed him standing off by hisself on the edge of the churchyard like he didn't want to be in nobody's way.

When school let out for morning recess, alla the girls in my grade went out together. Soon as our foots hit the ground that sassy little Catherine, who thought she was Shirley Temple, started saying mean things about how come Malice done turned into a morphadite.

Then Rena asked her, "Ain't you been sweet on Malice since way yonder last year? Don't you think kissing you is what turned him into a morphadite?"

The rest of us laughed.

Catherine had that kind of bright skin that turned red when she got mad. But I guess she figured wasn't none of us on her side, and we was too many for her to handle. So she runned over to where Malice was standing.

"Boy, I hear tell you in a family way," she told him in a voice loud enough for everybody to hear. "Who is your baby's daddy?"

Some of the children standing around in the church yard laughed at that.

Malice didn't say nothing. He turned away from Catherine and walked off.

She followed him, asking, "How many babies is you done had already, boy? Ain't you been drowning your babies in the river so wouldn't nobody know you had none?"

He kept on moving.

She kept following him.

Pretty soon some of the other boys and girls started

following him and poking fun at him, too. Every now and then one of them would run up behind him and push on him. But he didn't try to stand up for hisself.

We didn't have but one teacher for a whole churchhouse full of children from Little River Lane Plantation, The Rockford Place and The Fairlane Place. She had to keep a eye on alla us, but she couldn't be in but one place at a time. And that church yard was big.

If it hada been me, I woulda runned to the teacher to get them children offa my case. But, being a boy, I guess Malice thought he wasn't supposed to hide behind no woman's skirt tail. So he never once went nowhere close around the teacher. So he never once got no peace at recess. Not none that day.

Every word they said to him made me feel like they was kicking me in a spot on my body that was already sore. It was like I done finished turning into a morphadite myself, and it wasn't him they was treating so mean, but me. Just the same I didn't say nothing against it.

Didn't nobody say nothing against it. And didn't none of us tell the teacher what was going on.

As soon as we got a little ways out of sight of the teacher after school was out, Catherine went after Malice again.

"You so coward! You so weak! I bet any little bitty girl could whup you!" Then she slapped him.

Malice didn't say a word. And he didn't move. He didn't even cry.

Look to me like he thought he was the bottom of the ocean, and all that meanness everybody was heaping on him wasn't nothing but water, and he could hold as much of it as the Atlantic and the Pacific put together and not overflow.

But me, I done had all I could hold. I went up to Catherine and told her don't she hit Malice no more.

"Looka here, y'all!" she hollered. "This here the daddy of Malice's baby! She done comed to take up for him!"

I throwed down my dinner bucket and booksack and lit into her with fists flying.

Before the bigger children pulled us apart, we done tore each other's dresses and scratched each other's faces.

When I got home, Mama was knocked offa her foots. On account of I hadn't had no fights since I was about nine.

I told her how it happened.

"You can't be going around here fighting for other children," she told me. "How come that boy couldn't fight for hisself?"

Everybody on Little River Lane knowed that Malice never did fight nobody. Anytime somebody get mad at him, he'd talk his way outta that tight spot. So I didn't even try to answer Mama.

"You been telling me alla the time I oughta have feelings for other folks," I told her. "And you know for yourself how everybody going around talking about what done happened to Malice. Ain't I suppose to feel for him?"

Mama had a way of drinking in what I said with her eyes. She'd set them on me, and I could see my words flow straight into her eyeballs and go straight down to her heart and stir up her love for me.

"You right to feel for him, but you ain't got no business fighting for him," she said. "You ain't got no sisters or brothers to take up for you."

Her voice sounded kind of sad, like she thought this was her fault.

"Catherine got a house full of sisters and brothers. They might double-team you and hurt you real bad."

I knowed it wouldn't do no good to say nothing about that because they done already done the same thing to other children.

"Just about every child around here got sisters and brothers to help them fight but you," she went on. "So you try to stay outta fights. And you stay away from Malice, too, because he ain't gonna do nothing but get you into more fights."

"But he's Sam's best friend! If I stay away from him, I gotta stay away from my own flesh and blood cousin, too!"

"Sylvia ain't gonna let Sam play with that boy no more.

Ain't no telling which way he gonna turn, but whichever way
he do, he gonna be bad company."

Bad company? Sweet, smart and wonderful Malice? How
he gonna get to be bad company?

But Sam's mama was my mama's oldest sister, and she
didn't have half the tenderness in her that Mama had.
I figured she done turned Mama against the boy. Nothing I
said was gonna sway her.

Then it hit me so hard that words I hadn't even thought
up rushed outta my mouth.

"When I finish turning into a morphadite, everybody
gonna treat me mean like this! And ain't nobody gonna play
with me! I'd be better off dead!"

Mama frowned up her face the way she did when she
heard something she didn't believe. Then she told me, "You
can't turn into no morphadite. Don't nobody never turn
into no morphadite. They be born that way."

I told her what the bigger children told us about morphadites.

She told me there wasn't a bit of truth to none of it.

Then I remembered out loud, "Long time ago I heard
you and Aunt Sylvia talking about y'all's cousin who turned
into a bulldager after she moved to California. If somebody
can turn into a bulldager, can't somebody else turn into a
morphadite?"

"It don't happen that way."

"Then how it happen? How come folks be bulldagers and
morphadites?"

Mama gave me the same kind of look she used to give
me way back when I used to be little and used to ask her
things like, "How come I can't see the wind?"

She let what I asked run through her mind a while, then
she told me, "I don't know the answer to everything. I'm
learning things every day as I go along just like you doing."

That settled that. All these years Malice been thinking he
a boy, that blood been boiling inside him getting ready to
come out like it was doing now. How did I know what kind

of juices was boiling and churning inside me that might come out one day and turn me bottom-side up? I kept on being scared I was turning into a morphadite.

The next morning, me and Sam was walking to school with our cousin, Rena, and two of our friends, Booger and his sister, Noon.

Booger told us their mama and some other womens went to Malice's mama and told her she oughta send the boy off up North or to California or somewhere far, far away where don't nobody know what he is. On account of if he stay around here, ain't nobody never gonna marry him. Besides that, he gonna always cause trouble on the place.

Like it was his fault folks so hateful to him.

After while we seed Malice's little sisters standing on the side of the road like two fence posts. When we got closer, I seed they was both crying.

"Somebody, please!" the biggest one said with her mouth so full of crying that I couldn't hardly make out what she said. "Please talk my poor brother!" She done cried so hard she had to stop and catch her breath.

The littlest one stopped crying long enough to say, "My poor brother! Daddy done whupped him half to death to make him go to school!"

"But he still won't go!" the biggest one cut in. "Y'all please talk him into…."

She was crying so hard I couldn't make out nothing else she said.

I looked around for Malice. Not a sign of him did I see. "Where he at?" I asked.

"Down the riverbank," the littlest one answered, pointing her finger.

Sam told the other children to take the sisters on to school and tell the teacher what happened. And tell her we'd be on in a little while with Malice.

Finding the boy wasn't hard. He was setting on a stump close to the edge of the river. His booksack and dinner bucket was on the ground at his foots.

I was expecting to see him all scared up from the beating his sisters said their daddy laid on him. But he looked to me like he hadn't had a finger laid on him. He looked better than his sisters did because he didn't look like he'd done no crying. He looked like he wasn't never gonna cry no more. He looked like he done been hurt so bad, and he done held the pain inside hisself so long, he done forgot how to cry.

Sam jumped headlong into telling the boy how come he gotta go on to school so he could get his learning and make something outta hisself. All the stuff grown folks been telling us since we was in diapers. He didn't say nothing new.

Malice didn't even answer him. His face just got sadder.

Me, I didn't know what to tell the boy. After Sam had his say, I figured I had to say something just to show I ain't done gone deaf and dumb. So I asked him wasn't his daddy gonna whup him again if he didn't go to school.

"I'd rather take a whupping than have folks deviling me and hitting on me all day," he said.

Then Sam butted in and said, "My daddy told me a black man gotta learn how to stand up under hard words and keep his mouth shut. Don't make no difference how hard words get, they don't never draw no blood."

All of a sudden I seed all of yesterday, all them children poking fun at Malice, following him around the church yard, pushing him. And I knowed I just couldn't stand many more days like that.

"How come everybody gotta be so hateful to Malice?" I asked. "How come everybody can't let him be what he is in peace?"

Right away I could see on the boys' faces that I done asked another one of them questions that Mama wouldn't have no answer to.

After a while Malice said, "That's how come I know I can't stay around here no more. I'm going somewhere where folks gonna treat me right. And from now on I'm gonna be a girl."

Lord have mercy!

Look to me like my mind took off running. Maybe I could be friends with a morphadite, but ain't no way I'm gonna be friends with no sissy! I wanted to run away, too, but my foots done stopped working.

Me and Sam looked at one another, our eyes asking questions that didn't have no words.

Then all of a sudden, like my running away mind done runned slap dab into the trunk of a big tree, it hit me. This boy been having a time of the month for the longest. This boy is already a girl.

But Sam didn't see the same thing. So he jumped on Malice with all the vim he could muster.

"Man, you can't be no girl. Shucks, when we go fishing you always catch the most fish, and the biggest ones, too. And you can handle horses can't nobody else handle. And you can pick up more pecans than I can. Can't no girl do none o' them things."

"But I been feeling like I wanta be a girl for a long, long time."

"Man, all you have to do is go to the doctor and find out how come blood be coming outta you sometimes," Sam said. "I bet you the doctor gonna tell you that you sure 'nuff ain't no girl."

All this time Malice been setting on the stump. But now he stood up, and he pulled hisself up taller, like he was putting iron in his back so he could keep the stand he done took. And his face got darker, like all the meanness folks done heaped on him done turned it to iron, too.

But his voice wasn't like no iron when he spoke. It was quiet and tender, and the sound of it begged us to see this thing his way. "Y'all don't know how deep the feeling go."

The sound of his voice told me that he done fit against this thing too hard and too long already, and now he know the battle lost.

From the way Sam acted, he didn't even hear the boy. He dug back into everything he done heard for as far back as he could remember, and he dug up all the stuff he done figured out for hisself, cock-eyed and all, and he dumped alla this on Malice. He might nigh talked hisself sick.

Malice, he didn't say nothing.

Me neither.

After Sam talked hisself out, Malice started walking along the edge of the river going in the direction away from school.

I seed he didn't pick up his dinner bucket or his book-sack, so I figured he done made up his mind to run away from home.

I walked along behind him, and I could hear Sam's footsteps coming behind me. As we walked along, I seed that Malice done melted down so much he done got frail. Then look to me like he turned into a dried out cane fishing pole with nothing but air inside him. Not once in my life had I seed anybody so much all by hisself as that boy was. Children I knowed who lost their mamas or daddys always had big mamas and big papas and parrains and nen-nens and kinfolks or somebody to see after them and fend for them. And they had places to live.

Here this boy was walking ahead of me with nobody to turn to, nothing to lean on and nowhere to go. Still he was going out against a world he didn't know nothing about.

For a little while I had a notion to grab him and stop him and tell him to stop being. What's the use when didn't nobody care? But then I remembered that I might turn into the same thing that he was.

Lord have mercy! What chance would I have of making it all by myself? Same chance that this boy had.

I tried to remember how much grown folks say it cost to ride the bus all the way up North, and at the same time tried to remember if Malice done made that much money selling pecans. But look like something black and oozing like hot tar done dripped into my mind and messed it all up.

After a while a notion hit me, and I said, " Malice, you gonna need a heap of money to buy your bus ticket. I'll lend you some of my Christmas money to help you out some."

"I don't know if I'll be able to pay you back before Christmas," he answered.

"That's all right. Pay me back whenever you get on your foots. Every year my parrain give me Christmas money. And I ain't lending you alla what I got, just some of it."

"All right. But no more than half what you got. I don't want to ruin your Christmas."

I didn't tell him, but my Christmas was already ruined. We was close to my house, so I runned on ahead. As I was crossing the footwalk across the river in front of our house, I seed Sam running up the riverbank toward his house. We both knowed our mamas wasn't at home because every day they went to help take care of Mama Polly. She done comed down with the dropsy and sugar in her blood. All the cotton and corn had been picked, so our daddys was both out doing public work every day trying to make enough money for next year's crop.

Sometimes running get the blood all stirred up. That day it got mine going so it made my heart bigger and flung it wide open.

Soon as I got inside the house, I went straight to Mama's trunk. I'd found out a while back that she made a Christmas dress for me on Aunt Sylvia's sewing machine. Sam told me about it. One day when Mama was away from home, I dug down to the bottom of her trunk and found it all wrapped up in store-bought colored paper and tied with real cloth ribbons. The dress was fine sharkskin material, a pretty old rose color with little bitty violet flowers sprinkled all over it. For most of my life I'd wanted a dress made princess style. This one was.

That day I'm talking about, I took the dress outta the trunk and hugged it. Then I seed how Malice was gonna look wearing it. He had the kind of coal-black, silky, curly hair that growed fast. So I knowed in no time he'd have great big plats on his head to tie the ribbons on.

I wanted to keep my pretty dress because it was the prettiest one I'd ever had. Didn't make no sense for me to give it to nobody. But the harder I hugged that dress and the more I wanted to keep it, the worst I felt.

I knowed poor Malice didn't have nothing and no way to get nothing and nobody else in this whole wide world to help him but me.

After while I picked up the only duffle bag that we owned and put the dress in it. That made me feel just a itsy bitsy bit better. Then I went into my room and got three of my school dresses and put them in the bag. Then I put in some of my socks. Then I put in the only pair of Sunday shoes that I had. Then I got the leather billfolder that my parrain bought me for my birthday and put it in the duffel bag. In it was every cent of the money I'd made picking up pecans.

By then I knowed I done lost my mind. What I was doing didn't make me feel good, but it sure did stop me from feeling so bad.

When I got back to the riverside, Sam had already comed back with a pillow case and his Christmas money for Malice. He told the boy he was giving him his best khaki pants and shirt in the pillow case.

Me, I didn't say nothing about what I was giving him in the duffel bag. On account of I felt shame to be giving dresses to a boy. It was like all the other children at our school was standing there by the riverside, and if I said anything about the dresses, they'd laugh at me.

I opened the duffel bag, took out my leather billfolder and gived it to Malice. While he was putting his own money and the money that Sam gived him in the billfolder, I put the pillow case Sam done brought in the duffel bag.

Then we headed for the highway walking along the edge of the river down the riverbank so nobody wouldn't see us. Back in them days if any grown person seed children walking on the road when they supposed to be in school, some backsides would burn. That was right after Huey P. Long done gived poor folks free books. Didn't nobody take no excuse for no child not being in school.

The most dangerous part of our journey was when we

cut across Little River Lane and went through the thicket between Little River Lane Plantation and The Fairlane Place. On account of grown folks all the time be in that thicket picking up pecans, looking for muscadines or taking a short-cut to somewhere. But that day The Lord was with us. We made it to the highway, and in a little while the bus comed along going toward Shreveport.

Sam flagged it down because he was the biggest. And he told the bus driver a big lie about how Malice was his little brother on his way to Shreveport to see their poor sick grandmama.

"Look after him for us, please, sir," he begged.

The bus driver promised.

Wasn't nothing left for me and Sam to do but go back home. We knowed that Booger and Noon and Rena and Malice's little sisters done already told the teacher that we supposed to be bringing Malice to school. So if we showed up there without him, what we gonna say? Tell the truth, and the teacher'd get in touch with Old Man Dufour. Then he'd call the bus station in Shreveport and get them to take Malice offa the bus and bring him back home. The old man owned the plantation, so folks in high places took his word to be law when it comed to his hired hands like us.

On the other hand, we knowed that if we didn't tell the teacher the truth, just as soon as the grown folks found out that Malice done runned away from home, we'd get a whippin' for lying.

Soon as I got home and put my dinner bucket and book-sack down, I went out to the plum tree and broke off about five switches. On account of I knowed I had a big whipping coming for what I done done. I hadn't had no whipping for nigh onto two years. On account of Mama told me I done got big enough to make up my own mind if I want to be something in this world. She said all she can do now is talk to me and try to get me to see that when I do bad things I hurt my ownself more than I hurt anybody else. But not one time in my life before had I done something as bad as giving away the only duffel bag we had to pack our clothes in when we go visit kinfolks, and giving away so many of my clothes and alla my money. So I figured I'd get a whipping to match the crime.

After I pulled the switches, I picked the leaves off them and laid them on the porch. Then I sot on the edge of the porch and cried about what done happened to Malice and about the awful whipping I knowed I had coming.

First thing Mama did when she walked into the yard and seed me was ask me if I comed home from school because I was sick.

I felt the quicker I got this over with and got the whipping I had coming behind me, the better off I'd be. So I told her what happened from the time that we comed upon Malice's little sisters crying by the side of the road. I didn't try to talk myself outta nothing. And I didn't try to make it sound like what I did was right. I just told what happened like it happened.

When I got to the part about giving away my dresses, I hushed a while to let Mama have her say.

She just looked at me straight through my eyes and out the back of my head and all the way through Prudhomme Woods that lay behind the plantation, all the way through that to the other side of the world. It looked to me like all o' the strength in her body done got up into her eyes so that she ain't got enough left over to open her mouth and say nothing.

I went on and told the rest of the tale up to Malice getting on the bus. Then I seed again how frail he looked, and I knowed that if anything comed up against the boy, he wasn't gonna make it.

And didn't nobody care.

Mama, she still didn't say one word. She didn't even grunt. All she did was turn herself around and walk off outta the yard and down the lane.

I figured what I done made her so mad at me that she had to take a walk and cool her temper down before she whipped me. Old folks always said ain't nobody supposed to whip no child if they mad.

So I sot on the edge of the porch and waited.

It was a long, long time before Mama comed back. When she did, she sot down on the edge of the porch next to me. She looked at me, and this time her eyes stopped on my face.

I seed from the red in her eyes that she'd been crying. On account of she had feelings for Malice.

"You pray for that poor boy, you hear me," was all she told me.

I didn't get no whipping that day and never again.

Years and years after that, after I got grown and married and had children of my own, me and my family went to visit our kinfolks in California.

Sam done moved to Oakland and got married. Him and his wife took me and my husband out to this nightclub where they had this absolutely beautiful blues singer named Mae Alice.

Lord have mercy! Spitting image of Malice!

Sam told me no, he done already checked. She born and raised in Chicago.

Sometimes I think maybe Malice done got to be a big-time blues singer, too, because he had a good singing voice. Every once in a while I see a black woman singer who look exactly like him, and I be happy he doing so good.

Then again, sometimes I think maybe he didn't even make it to wherever he had it in his mind to go that day he runned away from home. Somebody like him born different from most other folks, need a whole lot of love to make it in this world.

Seem funny to me that folks who claim God created the world and the folks in it most times be the same folks who ain't got a speck of love in their hearts for folks like Malice. Look to me like if God made man, he musta made us so some could be born morphadites. Reckon he trying to show us something?

You Can Hold Back Dinner,
But You Can't Sundown

The first Sunday in May was the day that life began. The very first time. Before the world was created. The movement that God put upon the face of the waters before he said, "Let there be light" was the first Sunday in May. A man could feel it in the early morning sunlight pressing cool, damp fingers against his skin with the gentleness of a delicious woman. He could hear it in the soft breeze that whispered praises without words and aroused desires for what he had never had before and could not name. The first Sunday in May wrapped up everything that had ever been and everything that was to come in a teaspoon full of time that a man could sniff a taste of just once, grab for but never touch. A snatch of time that could break a man's heart or give him a glimpse of Glory. Both at the same time.

All this Alphonse Cox felt as he stepped out of his front door onto his porch. The morning was so fair. So bright. And as far as he could see all of Little River Lane Plantation was covered with fresh, fragrant life blooming in all the colors of the rainbow.

"You musta overslept yourself."

The voice of the day that brought life to the world floated to his ears up from the beginning of time. And it tinkled with everything good and sweet that had ever happened. He turned toward the sound and was delighted to see what the years had done to Spizetta, the little girl who was born half a mile up the lane from his house not too long ago. She was sitting in the swing at the far end of his porch dressed in a sky-blue sharkskin dress that hugged her two-handsful of waistline like any hot-blooded man would yearn to do. The collar of her dress was low enough to give a man hopes of sneaking a peep to see if she had flesh and blood titties in her bosom or nothing but the sweet, ripe muskmelons that seemed to be there. Her head of long, curly black hair was topped with a straw hat, and the brim of it was covered with blue flowers.

She's all dressed up for church much too early in the morning, he told himself. Something's up.

To Spizetta he said, "No, I didn't oversleep. I had a bite to eat before coming outside to shave myself."

He could almost see angels pinning down the four corners of the world so that no wind could blow. His eyes got stuck on her beautiful face, and he held back his thoughts. He held his breath. Time stopped. Forever.

Then she floated out of the swing with the ease of the lightest butterfly, held her arms out from her sides, circled around and asked, "How do I look?"

Do Jesus! Why would she ask me a question like that? was the first thought that came to his mind. Then he batted his eyes a couple of times, took a deep breath and told her, "You look nice," knowing that she was looking for more praises than he felt free to give.

"Alphonse Cox, do you think I'm blind? I done seed the way you been looking at me ever since Miz Frozene died."

The soft music of her voice turned her words into a song, still what she said hit him like a hard fist against his chin. For he thought himself a decent man much too respectable to run behind young women.

Then he saw himself on that same porch a little over seven years ago when his son, A.B., was only seventeen. Alphonse heard again the tone of the boy's voice when he told Spizetta that she was too young to be his girlfriend. The boy said something about the diaper that Spizetta was wearing, and Alphonse knew that these words were especially painful to the girl because at that time she was eleven, much too old for diapers.

Remembering this now, Alphonse realized that he could not make the same mistake and use the young woman's age as a reason for rejecting her. So he searched his mind trying to find kind words to wrap around and hide the truth.

That he knew he wasn't strong enough to cover the years between her eighteen and his fifty-two.

"Pecan been in the pen almost two years," Spizetta told him. "I can get my divorce from him any day I want to. You free. I'm free."

Her lips eased into a smile that seemed to be begging for a kiss. At the same time both of her gray-green eyes shot out one beam of light that latched onto his eyes and spelled him so that his mind went blank.

"That's nice," slipped out of his mouth. And for a few moments he lost himself in the beam from her eyes.

Then all of the decency that he had mustered in fifty-two years of living turned into a silent shout. That girl is too young even for your son! Don't make yourself her fool!

This jerked him out of the spell, and he cleared his throat, getting rid of words he wanted to say to begin plans for their future together.

"That's nice, Spizetta. Any man in his right mind would be tickled to death to have a fine-looking wife like you."

That's no way to put off a hot-blooded young woman, his decency shouted from deep within him.

So he quickly added, "Like Moeese. He'll be glad to marry you. He's been sweet on you ever since he found out the difference between boys and girls. And he's free, too. Never been married. Much younger than me. Much better looking, too."

"Don't you tell me nothing about Moeese!" she snapped. "He don't care nothing about me! He ain't got no respect for me! He all the time be asking me to do it with him. I ain't speaking to him. Never no more!"

Her words shot through Alphonse's ears and balled themselves up in his throat, cutting his breath off. And while he struggled to swallow this ball, he remembered the many times he had stumbled into the blazing anger of a woman who got upset when he asked her to "do it." Does she want to marry an old man like me because she thinks I won't ask her to "do it"? he wondered.

"Anyhow, Moeese can't marry me because he ain't nothing but sixteen!" Spizetta snapped. "And his mama been going around all over the place telling everybody that she ain't never gonna let her son marry no second-hand woman like me."

On Little River Lane Plantation one of the few forms of entertainment was talking about the comings and goings of neighbors. So Alphonse had already heard about Moeese's mother's opposition to her son's interest in Spizetta. But living around the young man had shown him that Moeese was head-strong. So he told the young woman, "I bet you when Moeese comes of age he'll marry you in spite of what his mama says."

"But I told you, all he wants me for is to do it!" she snapped. "That's all Pecan married me for. I ain't never no more gonna marry no man to misuse me like Pecan did." Alphonse remembered how unhappy Spizetta looked during the short time she was married to Pecan before he was put in prison for stealing. His mind got stuck on her word "misuse," and he wondered exactly what did she mean by it. But he dared not ask.

"I know you'll respect me, Alphonse," she said in a voice that suddenly switched from vinegar to honey. "You just as good-looking as any man half your age. And you got a good head on you, too. Better than any other man I know. And I never will forget how tender you treated Miz Frozene when she got on her death bed. Every last woman on this here plantation done said they wish their husbands be good to them like you was to your wife."

Alphonse remembered his wife's final illness most vividly as a struggle that he lost. The year that had passed since that awful time of his life only slightly dulled the pain of his disappointment that all of his efforts to save his wife failed. His eyes went looking for the beauty in the day to comfort himself with the feeling that had delighted him when he first set foot on his porch. But he saw that the moment had passed. Time had flattened the first Sunday in May into just another spring morning. Then Spizetta's words pulled him out of his own sorrow.

"...married mens and all. They be all the time begging me to do it with them. And don't none of them mean me no good. All they want is to use my body to pleasure theirselves. Then they'll chunk me aside like I'm nothing but a wore out whore."

Alphonse looked at Spizetta standing before him, and it seemed to him now that he had never seen her before. For it hit him that for too many years his eyes had stopped at her gorgeous face. Now he saw what pain was doing to her beauty. Not distorting it, but chiseling her nose so that it stood out like a sharp line cleaving her face in two. And chiseling her lips, too, changing them from a soft, rosey heart into two tight lines of stone spread across her face. And even chiseling her eyes into pinpoints of dying light fading into tears that would not come free. Because her tears, too, had turned to stone. The sight of her pain stabbed him like an ice pick all over his body. He had to struggle to breathe.

"I don't never want to be no loose woman in this world," she went on. "If you marry me, Alphonse, all them mens will stop running after me all the time. I'll have a husband to stand up for me."

Time and sorrow had taught Alphonse that words don't work in all situations. So he went to Spizetta, lifted his arms and hugged her. Even as he did so he realized that might not be the best thing for him to do. But it would get both of them past these moments that were too painful for either of them to bear while standing alone.

She had about her the fragrance of a cape jasmine flower blooming in the sun far away, so that the sweetness of her body was delicate enough to give him some ease. He felt her body shaking as if she had come down with a chill, so he drew her closer to him and tried to will the heat of his own life to flow into hers. After a while he noticed the short and quick jerky way that she was breathing, and he realized that she was crying. He tried to comfort her by gently patting and caressing her back. But this did no good. After a while it seemed to him that all of Little River was flowing from her eyes and through his chest and into his heart.

How is it that I've been knowing this poor girl all her life, but I didn't see how miserable she is? he wondered.

The river of tears flowed on and on until Alphonse began feeling it trickle down his own cheeks.

Dear Lord, God Almighty, please have mercy on this miserable child, he moaned silently.

After she cried Little River dry, Spizetta stepped back from Alphonse, pulled a dainty white handkerchief from the pocket of her dress and gently wiped the tears from his eyes. Then she asked, "Is you gonna marry me, Alphonse?"

When she spoke he saw hope beaming like a light from her face. How can I reject her? he asked himself.

But how can a respectable man marry a girl who is too young even for his son? his decency wanted to know.

Then his heart replied, "You deserve much better than me, Spizetta."

"Ain't no better man than you for me nowhere else in this world, Alphonse," she told him in a sad, serious voice. "I done spent the happiest days of my life here at your house. When you bought that gramaphone for A.B., it was like you done it for all us young folks on this place. Where else can we go to listen to records and dance and have decent fun but here at your house?"

"Spizetta, I'm not going to have that gramaphone much longer. The only reason A.B. left it here when he moved to California is because he couldn't take it with him on the train. But last week he wrote and told me he's married now, and him and his wife are coming home to get that gramaphone."

"You think that's all I want you for, Alphonse? Just a old dead wood music box?" She shook her head from side to side a full minute, then added, "I want you for the kindness in your heart. For the love you show to everybody you meet.

I want you for the tender way you hugged me just now. I want you because you didn't try to kiss me. And you didn't even think about asking me to do it. I need you, Alphonse. Because I need somebody to care about me. And I see caring in your eyes."

He felt her words wrapping around him like sweet ointment easing over his naked flesh, easing through his mind. And it eased his mind into knowing that nothing else in the world mattered but her sweet, wrapping words.

He took both her hands in his, brought them up to his lips and kissed first one, then the other.

"Even if you ain't aiming to marry me, Alphonse, make pretend. Just for today. Treat me the way you used to treat Miz Frozene. Just for today. Please."

When these words came to his ears it was not her voice he heard. Instead it was the voice of the day speaking in warm sunshine and a cool breeze and all the brilliant colors of May.

But this day is slipping away. And it's never coming back. This thought sent a shiver through his body as if he had already lost the sweetest, most precious possession of his entire lifetime. The grip of his hands on Spizetta's suddenly tightened, and this gave him the feeling that he was trying to hold onto something that he never had, never could have. Still he brought her hands up to his lips and kissed them again. For this was the only reply that he could bring himself to give her.

He turned away from her and walked to the hand-made wash stand on the porch where he kept his shaving tools. He began setting up his razor strap, straight razor, shaving mug and brush to cut the stubble off his face.

"I'll stay here and ride to the baptizing with you," Spizetta told him from the swing, to which she had returned.

Every year since he first moved to Little River Lane Plantation as a young groom, Alphonse had attended the Evening Star Baptist Church baptizing in Willow River in the town of Morgan on the first Sunday in May. It was one of the biggest events of the year, and most folks in that part of the country went to watch the baptizing. As he lathered up his face to shave today, he felt that all of those other excursions to the baptizings had filled up only one cup of joy for him. But this day alone would fill up another entire cup of joy.

After Alphonse finished shaving and dressed himself, he cranked up his Model T Ford, and he and Spizetta took to the road. On the way to the town of Morgan he picked up five other neighbors, Little Jessie and Clenord Burns, their girlfriends, Simmerlou and Ollie Bee, and Spizetta's youngest sister, Violene.

When Alphonse parked his car under a broad limbed gum tree along the side of the road where the baptizing was to take place, he saw a large gathering of folks, both black and white, standing on both banks of Willow River.

"Look to me like everybody in this part of the country comed to the baptizing today," Little Jessie said.

"All the folks know the Holy Ghost be stronger here than it be anywhere else in the world," Simmerlou, his girlfriend, replied.

"That's sure enough the truth," Ollie Bee agreed. "I done seed the Holy Ghost moving so swift at baptizings here that mens be shouting like womens. And y'all know that's something mens don't hardly never do."

Alphonse was pleased to hear his passengers talking as they got out of the back seat of his car. This gave him a chance to tread time and fiddle around with the shift of his car and his steering wheel until one of the young men opened the front door and let Spizetta and Violene out of the car. But doing this made him feel deceitful. For although he hadn't promised Spizetta that he would make pretend he was going to marry her, he hadn't said he wouldn't, either. So he got out of the car, walked around to where Spizetta was standing, smiled at her and crooked his arm as a signal for her to take it and walk with him.

Although the crowd that had gathered to watch the baptizing was large, Alphonse heard a Sunday-morning quietness in the talking of the folks. Any other time in a large gathering like this, there would be loud laughter and all kinds of racket. But these folks were talking low the way that decent folks always do in sacred places. This brought to his mind the tale that folks told about the river.

Willow River ain't nothing but a lake made outta a piece of sky that fell to earth and went to sleep, the tale went. By the time the first folks found it, a thousand of the most beautiful shade trees in creation was standing around enjoying this miracle from Heaven. For it was one of the prettiest sights on earth. So pretty anything that laid eyes on it can't hardly never leave it.

And that's how come the town of Morgan comed to be built along the banks of Willow River, the tale went on. Because them first folks who found that miracle from Heaven stayed with it for the balance of their days.

"Hey, Alphonse! How much do I owe you for giving my woman a ride to the baptizing?"

Alphonse turned his head and saw Moeese Wilkins running toward him. He stopped and looked at how big and hard the young man's muscles were and how thick and bushy the dark-brown hair grew upon his head. And he saw how smooth, like a baby's skin, the young man's face was. Yet it was as square around the jaws and chin as the face of the strongest of men. And he had to admit to himself that even in his young days he did not look as handsome as this young man who had just called Spizetta "my woman."

Moeese could make Spizetta the kind of husband she deserves, he told himself. He'll be here strong enough to take care of her and protect her long after I'm dead of old age.

"I ain't none of your woman!" Spizetta was telling Moeese in a sharp voice. "Your mama done runned around all up and down Little River Lane telling folks I'm too old for you!" She tugged at Alphonse's arm and told him in her softest voice, "Come on, honey. Let's find us a good place to stand."

Alphonse tried to think of something to say to Moeese to ease away the questions that he saw on the young man's face.

But all that came to his mind was the memory of Spizetta's voice when she cried out earlier.

All he wants me for is to do it!

I ain't never no more gonna marry no man to misuse me!

Alphonse wanted to walk over to Moeese, take the young man's hand and teach him how to treat a woman. But the acute pain that he saw on Spizetta's face when she talked about Moeese earlier seemed to be trying to tell him something important, but he couldn't understand what.

Spizetta pulled him so hard that he had to follow her.

"Woman, don't you see how folks be shouting with the Holy Ghost every time I be singing with the Gospel Spirits?" Moeese called out behind them. "The Lord, he fixing to call me to preach! When I get to be a big-shot preacher, you gonna be sorry you didn't marry me!"

Although the young man's words were boastful, the tone of them was like a plea for help from a hurting child.

Spizetta led Alphonse to a knoll along the riverbank where they could stand and watch the baptizing looking over the heads of the other folks.

The voice of an old woman began singing.

"Gimme dat ole time religion,
Gimme dat ole time religion,
Gimme dat ole time religion,
Lord, it's good enough for me...."

The soft buzz of conversation along the riverbank slowly faded into the song as the folks stopped talking and added their voices to the giant open choir. Slowly swelling as more folks joined in, the singing floated out over the waters of the river and was met by the singing from the folks on the opposite riverbank.

In the middle of the river where the voices met, at the touching spot of the singing, there God himself set up a choir of his best angels to help the folks sing in order to let them know that he was pleased with the way they were worshiping him.

It seemed to Alphonse that the wind and the trees and

the water itself joined in the singing. He felt his heart swell with the ringing voices.

After the first song, one of the deacons read from The Scriptures and offered up a prayer.

Then two deacons and the pastor of the church waded out to the two wooden stakes that had been set down in the bed of the river to mark the spot where the candidates for baptism would be buried in the water and snatched up born-again Christians. As they waded the waters, the folks along the riverbank sang.

"Tis that ole ship of Zion,
Tis that ole ship of Zion,
Tis that ole ship of Zion,
Get on board, all God's children,
Get on board, get on board…."

When the preacher and deacons were set, two more deacons walked to the line of white-robed candidates for baptism who were standing on the riverbank. They took the hand of a tall, thin young man whom Alphonse recognized as Slow Kid, one of his neighbors.

"Slow Kid stayed a mourner for two or three years," Spizetta said in a low voice. A person who was praying to "get religion" was called a mourner. "I'm glad he finally got religion. He ain't bright enough to walk and chew gum at the same time, but Heaven wouldn't be Heaven without him."

As she spoke Alphonse heard Slow Kid's voice going against all the other voices and singing as loud as a ringing church bell.

"I'm so glad, I got good religion!
I'm so glad, I got good religion!
I'm so glad, I got good religion!
I done found myself a resting place!"

Alphonse saw that the young man had waded the waters out to the wooden stakes. He was clapping his hands and jumping up and down as he sang.

A man's voice shouted, "Lord, I know for myself you done converted my child's soul, 'cause I done seed a change in him."

"Amen!" someone else shouted. "I done seed a change in him, too!"

Other voices shouted, "Amen!"

At the same time still other voices shouted, "Thang God!"

And here and there scattered among the crowd other voices shouted, "Hallelujah!"

All of these voices came together in perfect harmony like notes from musical instruments playing together in a symphony. It sounded like they had practiced together for weeks on end to get the rhythm of the sounds exactly right. But Alphonse knew that this special music burst forth from the hearts of the folks, not because they had practiced together, but because the Holy Ghost had touched them. They could no longer control this force of joy, so it exploded from them in bouncing words like overheated popcorn.

Alphonse not only heard these voices, he also felt them with his chest and his head and his feet. And his lips smiled. And his hands began clapping. And his eyes saw more than sunshine in the sky. For the tongues of fire of the Holy Ghost that lit upon the folks on the day of Pentacost were more clear in his mind than sunshine. And he not only saw, but he felt. And the fresh fragrance of the breath of God rode the breeze all along the riverbank. He knew that this was why so many folks came to the baptizings in Willow River – to feel the presence of God.

After the baptizing, Alphonse drove his passengers to Evening Star Baptist Church for the right-hand-of-fellowship service that would welcome the new Christians into the family of God. The entire host of folks who had lined both banks of the river to watch the baptizing were now making their way to the church, some walking, some riding on horses, some riding in horse-drawn wagons, and a few in automobiles.

The newly baptized Christians had to pull off their wet baptizing gowns and dress up all in white for the fellowship service. While they got ready, the folks gathered in the yard around the church and talked to one another.

As Alphonse moved around the churchyard socializing with the folks, Spizetta walked beside him holding his arm. Every time that she laughed or even smiled, he felt warmth flowing from her hand through the spot where she touched his arm, and this warmth flowed directly to his heart. After a while, even the sight of her became warmth flowing into him.

Look to me like Spizetta is so happy being with me, he told himself. Maybe she needs me to marry her. And maybe I need her, too.

"Plenty folks done started going inside the church," Spizetta told him. "Me and you better go find us a seat before they all be gone."

Walking up the three steps into the belfry of the church, Alphonse kept his eyes on Spizetta. So he didn't notice Moeese standing off to the side. Anyway, the young man had his back turned. This Alphonse discovered only when Moeese whirled around and thrust his foot into Alphonse's path. It was in the final second before his head hit the floor of the belfry that Alphonse realized what had happened.

The first sensation that hit Alphonse after his fall was a scream from Spizetta. Then he became aware of strong hands lifting him off the floor and holding him as if he were totally helpless. He recognized his helpers as Little Jessie and Clenord Burns.

"Moeese, I'm gonna kill you!" Spizetta screamed.

"Hold on, Spizetta!" Little Jessie spoke up. "Moeese is my own flesh and blood cousin! My first cousin! I'll handle him! I'm gonna give him a good ass whipping that'll make him wish he was dead!"

"Little Jessie, I didn't mean no harm!" Moeese said in a voice that sounded like he didn't want to risk a fight with Little Jessie. "I swear to God! Alphonse tripped over my foot because he wasn't watching where he was going! I raise my right hand to God!"

Alphonse had stood on his feet and found out that nothing was hurting him. So he spoke up. "You two men don't forget where you are. Respect God's house. I don't have any animosity in my heart against Moeese. So the rest of y'all leave him alone."

"I gotta lam him just one time!" Little Jessie insisted, advancing toward Moeese, who backed away.

Alphonse caught Little Jessie's hand and led him back out into the churchyard, intending to talk him down.

Elder Butler, one of Alphonse's neighbors, ran up to him and said in an excited voice, "Alphonse! They told me you just now fell with a stroke! Is you on your way to the doctor?"

"He ain't got no stroke," Little Jessie explained. "Moeese tripped him up. That's how come he fell."

"Lord, have mercy!" Elder moaned, "When I seed Alphonse walking around here with Spizetta, I knowed there was gonna be trouble. Spizetta done got to be a loose woman. She ain't gonna do nothing but have mens fighting over her all over the place."

"Elder! You lay off Spizetta!" Alphonse snapped.

"See, I told you," Elder said in an humble voice. "Forty some odd years me and you been knowing one another. Never had a cross word. Now, do you see how you looking at me? See what I mean? Loose womens cause trouble like that! The man turned and walked away.

Alphonse saw several more of his neighbors making their way through the crowd toward him. And he suspected that all of them would blame Spizetta for what happened because folks always laid the blame on women for almost everything bad that happened.

"Come on and drive me home," he told Little Jessie. "Then you can come back and drive my passengers home after church."

"If you're hurting, I'll take Simmerlou along to stay home with you and see after you," Little Jessie offered.

"No, I'm not hurt. I just know if I stay around here and listen to folks bad-mouth Spizetta, I might punch out a few eyeballs."

Later as Alphonse was getting out of his car in front of his house, he heard a voice singing out from Little River.

"Oh, my bucket got a hole in it!
Wasted alla my beer...."

After Little Jessie drove off, Alphonse walked across the lane to the edge of the riverbank and saw Old Man Beauford, one of his neighbors, sitting in his fishing boat in the middle of the river. He knew that this old man usually spent his Sundays rowing his boat up and down the river and drinking moonshine.

I reckon drinking moonshine is the only thing he gets pleasure out of these days, Alphonse thought as he watched the old man.

For a few seconds he wanted to run all the way back to Evening Star Baptist Church and go back to pretending that he was going to marry Spizetta. All of his flesh seemed to be crying out for a few more minutes of the warmth that came to him from the sight of her and the sound of her voice.

Then Old Man Beauford's singing made him feel the strangle hold of time around his own neck, and it hit him that he was trapped by that which never fails to destroy. Hit him like a sledge hammer blow to his belly. Knocked the wind out of him. And he didn't even try to go back to breathing again.

That's me out there in that boat, he told himself. About a dozen years from now.

Spizetta told me that I look as good as any man half my age. This thought came to him like an angel bent on snatching him back from the brink of misery. And he held tight to memory of the sound of her voice saying this, trying to stave off all other thoughts. But after a while his grip slipped and his mind wandered.

Half my age. That's a little over twenty-five years back down the road from now. But Old Man Beauford is only about a dozen years up the road from where I am today.

You can hold back dinner, but you can't sundown.

All of the voices who had ever spoke this saying throughout all the years of his life came together in his mind as one voice powered with the strength of all. It was to him as if he heard the voice of God himself telling him that this saying of the plantation folks was holy and true.

The saying likened life to a day on the plantation. While working in the fields it's hard for folks to tell when dinner time comes in the middle of the day, but it's easy to see when supper time comes at sundown. In the same way, it's hard to tell how old a person is in mid-life, but it's easy to see when the vim goes out of life and the shine wears off in old age.

Alphonse felt a misery gathering first in his knees, then in his shoulders. He felt as if he had been picking cotton and dragging a sack heavy with wet cotton up and down the fields all day. His body seemed too tired to move. The sound of Old Man Beauford's singing began to scratch on his nerves. He slowly made his way to his house and changed out of his Sunday-go-to-meeting clothes into a pair of overalls. Then he sat in his swing and tried to comfort himself by remembering the sweetest moments of the morning that he wanted to keep alive in his mind forever.

But memory of Spizetta brought back the pain that he saw on her face, and the pain he felt flowing from her body into his.

Such a precious, sweet, beautiful woman, he told himself. Look to me like a man would do everything in his power to make her happy.

Ain't no better man than you for me nowhere else in this world.

Her voice floated up from the morning as clear to him as sunshine. And he told himself, Maybe I will marry Spizetta. I'll make her happy, even if I have to give my life to do so.

Then Old Man Beauford's singing came up from the river and whirled around him like a go-devil, showing him how close he was to sundown.

Maybe I won't have a whole lot of years to enjoy Spizetta, he decided. But one day with her is worth more to me than a thousand years without her. He settled himself in the sweet comfort of this decision.

Late in the afternoon Alphonse saw Little Jessie driving his car home. Behind was another car, the Model T of Hillary Melancon, the plantation overseer. Alphonse saw that L'il Hill, the overseer's son, was driving his daddy's car. As soon as these cars stopped, several young folks hopped out, most of them carrying bundles.

Spizetta was the first to come into his yard, walking fast and swinging her hips. "I done baked you a pineapple coconut cake, Alphonse!" she called out.

"Me, I baked you a pound cake!" Simmerlou called out.

"Old Man Dufour sent you a whole case of soda pops from the commissary!" L'il Hill called out, walking toward the gate toting a wooden case of cold drinks.

Alphonse walked out to meet his future bride. As he reached out his hands to accept the cake that she had brought to him, the desire to hug her rose up like a wild bobcat inside of him so that he had to struggle to control himself.

"Moeese done promised me he ain't never gonna try to hurt you never no more, Alphonse," Spizetta told him. "And me, I done swore to God I'll kill him if he ever try."

"My mama done fried up this great big old dishpan full of meat pies for you, Alphonse. She be begging you to please don't put bad mouth on her first-born son."

It was only when Moeese spoke that Alphonse recognized that the young man was among the many folks coming into his yard. This was because his eyes had been fixed on Spizetta.

Hearing the word "bad mouth" put a lump in his throat so that he was unable to say thanks for the gift that the young man was bringing. He felt that he had already been convicted of a wrong that he didn't do. Plantation folks claimed that an old person who was insulted by a young person could say all kinds of bad things were going to happen to that young person. And these bad things were bound to come to pass. Whenever a youngster died, some-body went searching through the history of his life and dug up at least one incident where "bad mouth" had been put on the poor child. Although Alphonse didn't believe in the "bad mouth" curse, he felt that if something tragic happened to Moeese, the plantation folks would say that he, Alphonse, put "bad mouth" on the young man.

"Moeese done cried his eyes out over what he done to you," Spizetta was saying. "And all day he been just as good as gold to me. So me, I'm gonna give him another chance."

"I'm gonna get me a job working on the WPA," Moeese said. "Then me and Spizetta gonna get married."

Alphonse realized that he was still holding out his hands to accept the cake from Spizetta. He felt himself looking old and stupid standing before her trying to grab. What? Ask her to do it?

You should have known she'd go back to that young man. An old goat like you ought to run down to the river and jump into that boat with Old Man Beauford. Shame shouted from inside of him louder than all the audible sounds around him. Even the loud talk and laughter of the young folks coming into his yard were drowned out by this silent shout from his own shame.

Spizetta will be better off married to a man her own age. He tried to rub this thought like a balm to ease the raw pain that was throbbing through his body. Then he noticed that the late afternoon shadows of his house and the trees around it had almost covered the world. Only scattered scraps of sunshine still touched the ground through the leaves of the trees and the spaces between the trees and the house.

Sundown is so close.

This thought made him feel as if he was standing there looking down on himself on the ground, helpless with old age.

His next sensation was of the cake that Spizetta placed in his outstretched hands. It seemed to him that he had suffered through an entire lifetime since he walked off his porch coming out to meet what he thought was his future bride. The weight of the cake in his hands pulled him up to face the responsibility of bringing Spizetta's gift safely to his dinner table. It also gave him an excuse to turn away from the young folks and return to the safety of his house.

All of the young folks followed him and set the food that they brought on the dinner table along with the cake. Someone had cranked up the gramaphone and put a record on it. When Alphonse heard the sad, sweet sound of Bessie Smith's voice singing, his heart crumbled. Not because of the words of the song nor the tone of it, but because he felt all the sadness of his own life and the sadness of Spizetta's life were somehow all wrapped up with the sadness that Bessie was singing about and all the other sadness in the world. Even the sadness of the passing of the day that brought life to the world was in that worldwide wrapping.

And there will be more sorrows tomorrow, Alphonse told himself. Because sorrows come of their own accord, and there's no stopping them.

He felt himself as helpless as the dying day trapped in the unmerciful grip of time, and he wished that he could die before the shine wore off his life.

"Hey! Hey! Mama, shake that thing!"

This sound came to Alphonse along with the tapping of feet on the floor of his front room, and it told him that the young folks had begun dancing. With the boundless vigor of youth – the way that he used to dance but could never dance again.

Alphonse felt the final minutes of this most beautiful day of his life slipping away as fast as dry sand through the bottom of a sifter. And he knew that he had to do something fast. Not enough time left for planning. Not even for thinking. Do something fast. Anything.

He popped the fingers of his left hand, and with his right hand he grabbed Spizetta and swung her around, then began two-stepping.

She followed his lead, laughing.

All of the man left in Alphonse shouted silently, Come on, sundown! I might not be as good as I used to be, but when you find me, I'll still be dancing!

Black Cat

This chick lumbered her two hundred pound butt
up the steps of #22 lugging
this great big old box with holes
cut all around the side with a dull knife,
raggedy holes cut catty-corner,
all kinds of ways like somebody was in a hurry
to get them done, like somebody else
was shouting from the front porch,
"Ain't you got them holes done yet?"
and the cutting hand got more and more nervous
and botched the job something awful.
And now here she come parading them old raggedy holes
before all them folks what ride the #22
like she ain't got no shame about herself.
Bus Driver, he ask, "What you got in that box?"
Fat Chick, she look at him with question marks
shooting outta her blue eyes
like she don't understand English.
Now she the color of skim milk
with raging fire red hair
and freckles all over her, face, arms, legs, everywhere,
and she trying to make pretend she Mexican
or Vietnamese or something what don't know English.
Bus Driver, he must think she deaf, so he shout
"What you got in that box!"
"Meow! Meow! Meow!" real loud and fast
like a dog barking, like,
Yeah, I'm here and you can't kick me out!
Bus Driver, he move hisself back real quick and ask,
"How big is that cat?"
"Just a little kitty," Fat Chick whisper,
flash her day pass, and stumble to the first empty seat.

179 | Pearl Garrett Crayton

"You let that cat outta that box one second,
 and I'll stop this bus
 right in the middle of the street,
 and out you go!" Bus Driver shouted.
 Fat Chick sort of shriveled herself up,
 pressed her arms closer to her sides,
 crossed her fat legs and drew her fat thighs in,
 folded herself into as small a package
 as she could manage,
 and kept trying to shrivel herself some more.
 And she glued her eyes to the box
 like if she didn't look at us
 we wouldn't notice that she was there.
 Then this old Japanese woman
 peeped into one of the raggedy holes,
 and the cat barked at her, like,
 If you want them eyeballs,
 you better get 'em outta my face!
"He's black!" Old Japanese Woman shouted,
 And her face shouted silently,
 Oh, no! Not another one of those people!
 We don't need another one of those people around here!
 Fat Chick, she shriveled herself up some more.
 Her freckles receded and became pock marks,
 her limp hair hugged itself closer to her scalp,
 and one of her hands caressed one of the raggedy holes,
 longing to touch this thing
 that she had been forbidden to show in public,
 this thing too loud, too animal, too black,
 too exciting for them
 that they did not want to deal with,
 did not want her to be seen with,
 did not want to see.

Three Ain't No Big Number

Cool it.
You gotta be cool!
Just stand here
under the lamppost with everybody else
and cool it.
Ain't your business to go lynching nobody
over what done happened.
The cops are handling it.
Don't look that way.
Three ain't no big number
when you think of all the children in San Jose.
Last census the population here
was something like over seven hundred thousand,
and maybe a fourth of that was children.
Think of all that many children
gathered here under this lamppost,
and you know that
if three of them walked away
you wouldn't even miss them
unless you had seen their faces
every single day for the past five years,
so just pretend that you had never seen their faces,
and you will understand that three ain't no big number.
And you be thankful
that the drunk guy driving that black Trans Am
didn't molest none of them.
He didn't even beat none of them.
He didn't even cuss none of them.
Nothing like that.
The man over there working on Elvin's house
said they didn't even see his car coming at them.
They were having fun playing in their yard,

so it wasn't all that bad.
A Trans Am is a big car with good shocks.
It roll over little bodies easy like,
and it was all over quick like lightning.
Everybody who saw it happen said so.
So don't freak out!
DON'T FREAK OUT!
Stay still and quiet like everybody else,
and stay here so the parents can look over here
and see the neighbors giving moral support.
Stay here until they see you.
Eventually they will see you.
They still have one child left,
so eventually they will stop screaming,
and they will need to see you standing here.

Nen-Nen

In 1946 Nen-Nen walked into the meat market
on Eighteenth and Capp,
ordered slab bacon, smoked sausages,
ham hocks, pork chops, ox tails, stew meat,
ground chuck, and turkey wings, then she died.
Safeway, Lucky, and other companies
built stores and markets all over San Francisco
and offered lower prices.
Black Muslims walked up and down
the steep hills of The City
preaching about the evils of eating pork,
her nieces and nephews turned vegetarian
and preached about the evils of eating meat,
doctors, nurses and other nutrition experts
preached from TV, radio, newspapers, and magazines
about the evils of diets high in cholesterol,
and finally Nen-Nen's heart and blood pressure
tried to get the message across to her,
but she hung dead in there
in that same meat market with that same order
that she made in 1946,
not moving one muscle of her brain
in any other direction.
When the family finally got around
to writing her obituary, we had to list
the date of death as 1995 because we didn't want
outsiders to know how long ago rigor mortis had set in.

Driving

I be trapped in the wrong lane on 280,
needing to hit the next Exit,
and this dude, he smile and wave at me
like, O.K., no sweat, go ahead,
pull in front of me, be my guest,
and right away I know goodness well
he got hisself a hum dinger of a job,
and not only that, he got his pockets all
stuffed to the bursting point with his paycheck,
and not only that, he be a hot-popping papa,
he laid back,
he been tantalized and satisfied,
and he ain't sowing his seeds in no ants' bed, neither,
no, alla his seeds be jumping,
playing hop-scotch, pitching balls,
so he wave at me like, go ahead mama,
I ain't in no hurry to go out and get me none,
I done already had it all.
But anytime I be trapped in the wrong lane
and this here other dude, he act like
he gonna fracture my back end
if I so much as move one inch toward in front of him,
I know right off what he ain't been getting lately,
and I know everything he ain't been able
to get up and get tight right.

God

Look to me every time I get on
the #22 County Transit uptown,
God, he got to get on, too,
decked out in them old faded clothes
he always be wearing,
like he don't know they got
almost new pants and shirts
at the Thrift Store on First Street
two dollars apiece,
and they give discounts to old people like him,
and I know he got that much money
on account of anybody skinny like him
sure ain't wasting their pension check on food,
so he must have a few dollars
stashed away somewhere,
maybe in that old greasy backpack
he always be lugging around,
and God only knows what he got in it,
like it be smelling,
and me, I be praying every time I see him
get on the bus
that he don't come plop down
in no seat next to me
with them old, yellow, rotten teeth of his
what don't smell no better than that backpack.
And I be knowing alla the time
the minute I make it across that Chilly Jordan
and walk through them Pearly Gates,
the first sight I see gonna be him
decked out in them same old faded clothes
lugging that same old greasy backpack,
and he gonna be telling me

that bit from Matthew 25
about how he done been
all the least of the little ones back on Earth.
And me, I'm gonna be asking him
how come he didn't bathe.

Afterword

I grew up an only child on a cotton plantation in Natchitoches Parish in Louisiana where I was born on September 26, 1932. The plantation was a large plot of land that included many small farms, all belonging to one white man. If you were a sharecropper, you made a deal with the owner to let you use his mules and ploughs and hoes, and you gave half of everything back to him. If you were a renter and had a big spread, you had to buy your own mules, your own plough, your own hoes, you had to finance your own operation – you didn't get anything from the man. But you worked when you wanted to, the overseer didn't come by your house; it was like your family farm. At the end of the year you gave one-fourth of whatever you cleared to the landowner.

My grandfather always rented. My father was a sharecropper, a very poor one. He loved farming, I think, he had a garden, raised his vegetables, but he just wasn't good at cotton. He didn't stay on the plantation for very long. In 1939, when the government started building army camps here in Alexandria, my Daddy came and got a job. I was "farmed out" for about three years to my grandparents; they were nice people, not as religious as my parents – I was taken out of the briar patch and put into heaven. I finally came to live with my parents in Alexandria in 1942.

The Garden God created when he created heaven and earth must have been like the place where I was born – rivers and bayous and lakes, alligators and snakes. We had everything. We hunted, fished, grew our own food, made our own clothing. We were self-sufficient – we only went to town to buy shoes, coffee, sugar.

Edited from a taped interview.

187 | Pearl Garrett Crayton

I knew only a little bit about segregation while I was
growing up on the plantation. If you don't have the money
to go to the picture show, you don't know that you have to
sit upstairs while white folks sit downstairs. If you don't have
any money to go to the restaurant, you don't know there are
certain restaurants you can't go to. When you go to town,
you don't look for a water fountain, you take your own water.
There were so many poor whites and poor Blacks, that I
didn't equate whiteness with prosperity. I knew about slavery,
but I didn't know about the segregation situation until I
came to Alexandria when I was eleven.

My entire world was right there. I didn't know anything
about the federal government until FDR got polio. I knew
about Huey B. Long, because I had seen him with my
own eyes, but I wasn't terribly concerned about the world
"out there." It was a good life for us. Decent people worked
on the plantation where I grew up. The owner wanted to
know who you were before he let you become a sharecropper. He didn't accept just anybody – he checked you
out. If you had what they called "bad blood," if somebody in
your family stole, or you had been in trouble, he didn't
want you working for him. You could not be the kind of person who went to prison and live on that plantation. Of
course, we had a few people who were sinners, who didn't go
to church; we had a one-eyed Cajun who made moonshine –
everybody made moonshine in those days.

We didn't have a whole lot of money but I didn't miss it.
We were very close, the community was very close, we had
extended families. It was a wonderful world – now it's different. The church was extremely important in the life of
plantation people. You had three sets of parents: your mama
and your daddy, your grandma and grandpa and God and
Jesus Christ. You communicated with God who was your
invisible parent through the church and through the
preacher. God was the one who saw you, everything you did,
the one you couldn't hide from, the one you couldn't lie
to. The church told you that all the time. It was the moral

leader of our community. Some of us children didn't really believe it until we got caught doing something.

I should have turned out a holy person. My Daddy was superintendent of the Sunday school, president of the Star Benevolent Society. The pastor of the church was my Daddy's first cousin, Joe Nash. He was always telling me he wanted me to be "a good girl." The church was also a part of our social life. When the Benevolent Society had a turnout, we would march down the road about a mile, with somebody playing the "juice harp" or a guitar, everybody dressed in black and white, singing and clapping. People would set up stands to sell ice cream, hamburgers, hot tamales – homemade.

All my stories are about the cotton plantation where I grew up. That's my world. In literature today, you read mostly about contemporary Blacks and the contemporary problems of Blacks. But I feel a contemporary Black person has a history, ancestors, bloodlines, culture, socialization that go back, back, back. I feel that it is important for America to understand what shaped contemporary Black people. We were slaves, but when we were set free we had no place to go. A lot of us went to work for the same people who had been our masters, or if we didn't like that master, we went and worked for some other master. This is the life I am trying to preserve in literature. I want people to know what my childhood was like.

* * *

I started writing in 1945 when Joe Nash's son, L.T., came home from the War. He was president of the choir at our church, Mount Zion. Once, when a convention of churches was meeting at Mount Zion, he wanted me to deliver the welcome address. I said, "I can't do that." He said, "Yes you can." I said, "Are you going to write it?" He said, "No, you're going to write it." He was my Sunday School teacher; he said, "When you talk on a lesson, you have such good ideas, Pearlie Bee." They always told me I was smart; everybody in my family said I was smart. When I told my Daddy, he said, "Why don't you try." I didn't try – I cried.

My Daddy called L.T. and said if he wrote it, my Daddy would make sure that I memorized it. I went by his house to pick it up, but when I read it, I knew that was not what I wanted to say. I didn't tell anyone but that night I sat down and wrote my own welcome address. I knew it had to be really, really good so I put in a lot of Bible references, worked myself to death. When I gave the welcome address on the day of the meeting, my Daddy went to L.T. and said, "That's the best thing you have ever written. That's really good." And L.T. said, "That's not what I wrote." Daddy said, "Pearlie Bee, where did you get that from." And L.T. said, "I told you she could write it."

That started me writing. I would read papers at meetings, I did welcome addresses, I did a little talent show, people asked me to speak on their funerals. For a time, whenever somebody died in Mount Zion, I would be asked to write a poem for that person. I got into writing through the church. But some writing I was doing for myself. When my Daddy's aunt, Aunt Minnie, got ready to go to California in 1935, she gave me some of her books, including poetry books. When I read those books, I started writing my own poems, but I didn't let anyone know.

I started writing on a regular basis when I was about fourteen. My English teacher, Mariah Louise Beaty Lawson West, liked my essays. When I finally got up enough courage to tell her I wrote poetry too, she asked me to give her some of my poems. She sent them away to the *National Anthology of High School Poetry*; I had my first poem published there when I was in the 11th or 12th grade. She encouraged me to write; after I got out of high school, after I got married, every time I saw her, she would say, "Pearlie Bee, are you still writing?"

After I graduated from high school, I went to nursing school in Kansas City, Missouri. I found I could do jet airline piloting better than I could do nursing. It felt like people were all the time dying and it was always somebody who shouldn't be dying – not one time did I run across anyone who should have died. And there was nothing you could do. I like people, but I don't like death. I don't like sickness either and I got to a point that I didn't like the smell of the hospital. I wasn't cut out for nursing.

I came home and got married. I married the kind of husband that God allows to teach wives the saving power of prayer. He did at least a thousand things that drove me to seek help and comfort from God. While I was married, I wrote for the confession market. When you're married to a man who is terrible, you can always write good confession stories. I sent something off to *Negro Digest* that they published. I kept writing – it was just a part of me. If I breathe, I write.

In 1965, just before my Mom died, I had another story, *The Day the World Almost Came to an End*, published in *Negro Digest* in Chicago. (Both of those stories have been reprinted in anthologies. My first story has been reprinted four or five times.) I told three people: my Mom, my Dad and Miss Emanuel (my teacher's married name) – she was so happy. After my Mom died, I got a letter from Langston Hughes saying he wanted to include my short story in *Best Short Stories by Negro Writers*, the last anthology he did. I couldn't believe it – I hurried up and signed the paper he sent me. I thought there was something flaky because I never heard another word; it was a whole year before I got the book and a check. Miss Emanuel was elated; she showed the book to the pastor of her church and I was asked to be the Mother's Day speaker that year. It was her being proud of the little things that I did that made me continue. My parents had always encouraged me too.

* * *

My first job when I got divorced was with a weekly newspaper; after that, I worked for an insurance company. Then I decided that I needed to get some office skills, so I went to stenography school. In 1969, I started to work for Sears, and worked there forever and ever and ever. I was in the credit department. When I found out you could transfer to Sears in other cities, I told the manager I was thinking of moving to California. After my Mom died, her sisters wanted me to go to California where they lived, but I said no, I don't want to go to California. But the people who had always been the closest to me were all in California; for twelve years, they tried to get me to go. One by one they got my kids to come and finally they convinced me.The manager called a colleague in Hayward which is close to Oakland and got me an interview there. I went, was very impressed, and, when four months later someone quit, I got that job. I left Alexandria in 1977 when I was grown, divorced, with five grown children.

After I worked for Sears for awhile and decided I wasn't making enough money, I passed the test to become an insurance agent. Then I decided I could make a lot more money if I had an education. I found out you could go to San Joaquin Delta Community College for five dollars, so one day I went in, laid down my five dollars and said, "Now what do I have to pay?" The woman said, "That's it." I went to evening classes for a semester.

English 1A was one of the prerequisites for the AA degree. Since I had been out of high school for 900 years, I wondered how in the world I was going to be doing all the required essays. So when someone from the developmental education department came to class and said people who were having problems with their writing could get help, I whipped on over right after class with an essay I had scribbled together. I gave it to the tutor, Beverly York, who looked at it. When she didn't put any red marks on it, I knew something had to be wrong. I had seen her put red marks on other people's papers.

She asked me, "Are you a writer?" I said, "I do a little writing." "Your use of imagery," she said, "is wonderful. This is so good." I said, "Thank you. I want it corrected." "But there's nothing wrong." "What about my punctuation?" She said, "Your punctuation's fine." "My spelling?" She said, "How would you like to work here?" I said, "Doing what?" She said, "Being a tutor." I said, "I don't have any experience at that." She said, "But you know how to write. You must have been writing." I said "Well, I worked for a newspaper. I have a few stories published." She told me to go over and talk to Mr. Pikes and take him my essay. He said, "When can you start to work?" I held on to the insurance job for a while, but when they wanted me to work full shift in the writing lab, I quit the insurance job.

While I was working in developmental education I had a whole lot more time to do my writing. I wrote a lot of short stories, I did poetry, entered poetry contests. I started getting a lot of journal and small magazine publications. During my last year at Delta, when I was looking for jobs, I got a call that I had won a scholarship because of my grades. I went to the University of the Pacific and got my B.A.

* * *

After I graduated, I moved to San Jose and worked as staff support in San Jose State University's English department. Naomi Clark, a very talented poet and executive director of the Center for Poetry and Literature there, liked my work and included me in programs at high schools, nursing homes, museums – wherever she had a poetry reading. When Alan Soldofsky took over the job, he asked for my resume and samples of my poetry because he was applying for a grant from NEA. He said, "I need a Black person, because I don't have one." I said, "Great. I've become a token." Several months later, I met him in the hall and he said, "Hey, Pearl, you know that grant I applied for? I got it." I said, "Great, man, that's great." "And we start teaching in March," he said. I said, "Wait a minute, Alan, my degree's not in teaching. I don't know anything about teaching." I went into the bathroom and I cried.

A poet friend, Gabrielle Rico, rescued me. She took me through her class at the university, so when I went out to teach at the high school, I would know what to do. But I still had to design my own program. After she introduced me to my class, quoting from my very respectable resume, I said, "The important thing you need to know is I don't know beans about teaching." And when I said that, they clapped their hands; they were sick of teachers. I told them we would work together and that's what we did – it was absolutely marvelous. I have a book of wonderful poems that first class prepared for me at the end of the semester. For example, next to a drawing of a truck a student wrote:

> "This truck reminds me of
> Pearl, because I think I know
> Pearl, because when Pearl picks
> up a car, I know that she is
> going to pick up a good car.
> Like a GMC truck. I just
> know that Pearl is not going
> to take a trash car and drive
> it around...."
>
> (José Figueroa)

Eventually, I applied for a grant from the California Arts Council and got approval to do poetry and fiction writing workshops on my own. Working with those kids, 3rd grade on through 12th, helped me more than anything else in the world. I found out a lot about myself, I learned a lot about writing and the kids learned something, too. For many of them, English was their second language. Mr. Riley, at the developmental education center at San Joaquin Delta, used to tell me, "Whatever you do, Pearl, don't mess up their pretty way of saying things. Just make sure it's grammatically correct." I learned not to say things like a regular English teacher would. I learned to speak like a Vietnamese, like a Cambodian, Iranian, Chinese, Japanese. After that residence, my writing got much better – it really did.

* * *

But after a while, I got too old to stay in California – the pace of life was too much for me. What really brought me home was the fact that I was getting to retirement age and was living in a place where I would never be able to buy a house. I was not even going to have enough money to pay the rent because after I had got the grant, I quit my job, gave up all my benefits, all the perks of working for the state of California at a state university. I knew that here in Louisiana I could buy a house for nothing – a nice quiet place. This is it. I came back here in 1991.

Back here, I'm close to the language that I'm using in my work; there are people here talking the same way that they talk in my stories. And being here, I can go and look at the places that I'm talking about. That has helped me a lot. I think if you're around famous writers, as I was in California, you begin to depend on them, they give you leads, they recommend you to this, to that. I wouldn't have known that California Arts Council grant existed if it weren't for being around those people. They opened doors for me. I met Adrienne Rich, Carolyn Kizer, Gwendolyn Brooks, Lucille Clifton, Toni Morrison, Sharon Olds. Sometimes I think you might get caught up in that.

Around the time I moved back to Alexandria, I won the Frances Shaw Fellowship for women who have made a serious commitment to writing later in life. The "prize" was two months at Ragdale Foundation, an artists colony in Lake Forest, Illinois. The award came at a time that I was discouraged. I feared that my work would never be accepted by the literary world because my writings are so different from what is being published today. Winning the Frances Shaw Fellowship was an affirmation of my worth as a creative writer and gave me hope that my work is significant. The time that I spent at Ragdale gave me an opportunity to look at myself as an individual away from my family and friends. In a strange place, among strangers, my writings were the only familiars that I had to cling to. The setting at Ragdale, the meadow and the woods, reminded me of the setting of my childhood, the places that I was writing about. A log cabin on the property was perfect for me. I "visioned" out the electricity and modern conveniences and walked back into yesterday every time that I visited that cabin. I feel that my time at Ragdale helped me become a better writer.

*   *   *

Wherever I am, I can write. When I was working at Sears, if I got an idea for a story or poem, and my break time had passed, I would get a piece of paper and pencil and go to the ladies room and write. If I sit at the typewriter, there's something that comes between my mind and the paper. If I hold the paper in my own hand, then my mind will communicate with the paper – there can be no third party. I write best when I'm sitting in my rocking chair in my back room looking out the window. Or in that swing out there. Or I can walk the trail down the street and write in my head.

There was a time in my life when no-one saw a story of mine if it was not published. Now there is one person I can show it to, before it is published. He has an analytical mind, an iron point of view; he dissects it, sees all the little errors. But I do not share my unfinished work with anybody. I want to write what I'm going to write. Once a friend said, "Pearl, when are you going to stop writing this didactic poetry? Make up your mind, are you a preacher or a poet?" I told him all poets are prophets. But it's really my background – because I started writing for the church, church occasions, funerals.

There is in me this very well developed sense of right and wrong. Sometimes I choose according to taste, instead of morality, but the older I get the more I go toward trying to do what is decent, what is honest. As a writer, I feel I am supposed to bring some light into a person's life through my writing. I don't think there are any grants out there for that.

Take the story, *How Deep the Feeling Go*, for example. There are people who are born both male and female – androgens or pseudohermaphrodites. We act as if a person has to be either male or female, but God has made it possible for people to be both. When I was a child, my father told me that when he was a child, one of his playmates who was supposed to be a girl turned out to be a boy. "She" went to California, became a preacher, got married, but she never had kids. He didn't know what she was, but he really liked her. That's a seed for the story. And in my family one of my grandsons was born a true hermaphrodite – surgery corrected the condition. After he was born, I wrote the story. I think we need to be aware of the fact that this does happen to some people. Then we will be a little more understanding of people who are out and out homosexual. We need to have another, kinder way of looking at homosexuality; we need to look at it through the eyes of love like this little girl in the story did.

Florence Weinberger

For my daughters, Amy and Jessie
and my grandchildren, Sadie, Jason, Zane and Zachary

Mame Loshen, the Mother Tongue

Yiddish, my first language, you were
given to me whole, with your wild colors
intact, your bent humor, your centuries
of bottled-up rage and richly-imagined revenge.
How else could my father have heaped curses on
my mother with such violent originality, called
my dates names vicious enough to make me ashamed
I walked down the street with them.
And still I believed in him, believed
the wisdom he borrowed from ancient proverbs was his,
believed in his dazzling litany of dirty jokes,
believed in his gossip, believed in his criticism,
believed in the shop details of his paranoia,
believed in his poker-player's paranoia,
because out of this avalanche of language,
punctuated by deep painful rasps of breath
as he battled bronchitis and then emphysema,
still smoking those pungent Turkish cigarettes,
came the rhythm of my poems, like hard slaps
with an open palm, panic he would run out
of breath and die at the door of our third-
floor apartment, die in the middle
of a shout or a story, but
where in his mouth were the milk and the honey,
and where was his boyhood, and David's, and where was the
sheepherder's whistle calling down the steep slopes of Hebron
and where in his mouth were the biblical mothers
Sarah, Rebecca, Rachel and Leah and where
in his mouth was his own mother Rachel
who taught him the one song he sang to me
when I was a child?

From Where the Feet Grow

Curious how Yiddish won't translate easily
into American idiom so I can share with you
the graze of my father's judgment, but I knew
exactly what he meant when he said
She wants to know from where the feet grow.
I was someone who needed to find the hidden
wellspring of things; no answer would end it
once and for all, none would be perfect,
even come close: feet grow from inches,
from dresses, from socks and buttocks,
feet grow straight out of the flesh, they descend
from hems, they fall from ankles thick with sorrow,
slim with grace, they stick out naked in horses.
My father thought I wanted illumination.
I only wanted to hear him name me in Yiddish,
his voice modulated so I understood
how bemused he was by my brightness,
how charmed by my lust.

Mouth

My mother is smitten by silence.
A woman kisses me on my mouth
a moment before departure.
Stingy giver, who sends me these
truncated dreams, like treasures
buried at the bottom of dumpsters.
Maybe they're about revenge.
My mother grunts a few guttural
sounds, so I know she's had a stroke.
I pick her up and carry her, an
uncommon tenderness in my arms.
I never knew whether she loved me;
she never said. During the Great
Depression of the thirties, when even
words were spent judiciously, it was
necessary to understand the smallest
gesture. Now my daughter
works with the deaf. Holding her love
inside her body, she teaches her
eloquent hands to speak, while
her eyes add nuance. Her big soft
brown eyes. Those were the words
I heard as the dream vanished.
Now my granddaughter carries
my mother's name, her mother's
eyes. But there's that shadow woman
who kissed me on the mouth
and asked me to miss my boat.
Go home a different way, she said,
go home by way of Hong Kong.
She offered distraction, a chance
to shop, but I've been to

Hong Kong, I've eaten duck
roasted in clay, breathed the hot air.
I bought a notebook there, white
pages with red lines. I've kept my
dreams in it for years. I'm through
shopping for other gods. When I sit
cross-legged, fingers touching,
breathing in a deep yoga breath,
I exhale a Jewish sigh. When I go
to a gentile medium, he conjures
an Eastern European shtetl, he
produces an accent, he brings me
my immigrant mother. It seems
she has changed, she's regained
her speech, adopted American ways.
She says she approves of oyster white
for my daughter's living room. The fan
in the bathroom, she says, needs to be
oiled. She says she can see
into my heart. She says
she has come this far to assure me
she loves me, and God is a woman.

The Power in My Mother's Arms

My mother stretched dough thin,
thinner, to its splitting edge.
All that certainty gripped her
wrist, while she sieved
bread crumbs through her fingers,
nuts, sugar, apples, lemon rind,
laying down family legends
like seams in a rock; then
she rolled it all up
the sweet length of the dining room table.
Beaten egg glazed the top, and still
aroma to come, cooling and slicing.
I didn't mind her watching me
eat; I'd give back the heat of my
need gladly, fuel to keep the cycle
elemental, if you've watched birds feed
their young.

To every celebration, she matched a flavor,
giving us memory,
giving exile the bite of bitter herbs.
God's word drifted in fragrant soups,
vigor in the wine she made
herself, clear and original.

      My mother's death
changed the alchemy of food.
            Holidays run together now
like ungrooved rivers. I forget
what they are for. I buy bakery goods.
They look dead
under the blue lights.

I don't do anything the way she taught me
but I get fat.
I don't look like her and I don't sound
like her, but I stand like her.

There must be rituals
that sever what harms
our connection to the past and lets us
keep the rest.
If not, let me invent one
from old scents and ceremonies.
Let me fashion prayer from a
piece of dough, roll it out,
cut in the shape of my mother,
plump, soft, flour-dusted,
the way I once played cook with clay.
Let me keep the cold healing properties
of female images,
their power
to hold fire.
Let me bake her likeness in vessels
made of earth and water.
Let me bless the flames
that turn her skin gold,
her eyes dark as raisins.
Let me bless the long wait at the oven door.
Let me bless the first warm dangerous taste of love.
Let me eat.

It's the Bronx Again

turning up in my
dreams   women hung from
walls of windows   they
cleaned them then looked out
for hours   watched their kids
come home from school   their
men   laid off   clutching
their tool kits under
their arms   everyone
knew Lensky was a
bookie   called us to
the phone   for a five
cent tip   you won a
contest   a voice said
your essay   *why I*
am proud to be an
American   did you
write it yourself   or
did someone help you
my parents don't speak
English   who helped you
no one   where did you
type it   at a friend's
house   what's her name and
so forth   like being
touched by a stranger
at the Ward Theatre
Saturday after
noon   if you don't have
a date Saturday
night   roll your hair in
pin curls anyway

they'll think you have a
date on Sunday   once
my father caught me
meeting Jake at the
subway station   he
promised not to tell
my mother   but he
did   did you know Carl
Reiner's from the Bronx
so's Peter Levitt
so's Hank Greenberg but
who remembers him

Bury Me in front of Urban Turbulence

Bury me at Isla Negra
in front of the sea I know, in front of every wrinkled place
of rocks and waves that my lost eyes
will never see again. – Pablo Neruda

For him, the choice was simple. He owned the place,
every wave that came ashore, and the salt view.
When my parents moved from New York to California
and had to leave behind the site they chose,
we bought a row of burial plots, my sister and I,
to calm them, to show them there would always be
six of us lined up: us, them, our husbands. In 1978,
our parents claimed their spaces. Then one husband
left; he will be buried elsewhere with another wife, ·
the third, or maybe the fourth.
                    Last week, my sister and I visited
the graves. We laid a towel I found in the trunk of my car
across the vacancies beside them, and sat together
on a green sloping hill looking down at our view, a
freeway busier each year, an airport just over the
horizon. While we talked, we brushed away the thick
straying grass and felt the two bronze plaques warm
under our hands. Miriam buried her husband
on the other side of the entry road in 1966, a son
twenty years later, her second husband in 1993.
Ruthie's parents, once my parents' neighbors in the Bronx,
have become neighbors here again.
            We chose six plots sight unseen from a dour
salesman in a three-piece suit. We were young and
nervous then, and we needled him with smart-alecky jokes:
Were Jewish gangsters like Bugsy Siegel buried in his Jewish
cemetery? My husband asked if we could picnic there.
The salesman never smiled. Everyone was still alive.

I had no thought of my own eternal vision.
Of course I'd have wanted an ocean at my feet,
but for now, I'm not going anywhere, I'm unprepared
to range the world's beaches for better spots;
it would take time, and I'm busy with the grandkids
and the poems and the friends I have left.
I still have questions for my parents,
and sometimes I have a need to sit and rest, watch
the cars struggle to move like fleas stuck in wet sand.
I like to feel the ground shudder, wave after wave of
747's flying out of Burbank airport, right over my head.

Uncle Sandor

Uncle Sandor was growing old
and he hated it. He'd phone
and complain about his losses
from his body's heat to his long-time friends.
You listened and later told me
what he said. At the end
Uncle Sandor stopped complaining
or even remembering who was gone
and where the pain was landing.
You're seventy.
All your uncles lived long lives.
I see the signs. Everyone sees the signs.
Not just you. Our friends, too.
The way the afternoon wears out.
You don't complain. In 1945, a soldier in
the American army told you you're free.
You walked for months, until you got home.
Since then, you have been home free.
I watch you age. No soldier comes to liberate me.

Spring, Passover, Anniversary, in That Order

You haven't changed, you weigh the same,
look the same. Yes, age, gray, the usual
way bones lose their heft and shrink
a little. Otherwise, hard and soft still.
Two exceptions: you didn't have a
moustache then; you didn't have a
scar from the hollow in your neck
to the bottom of your rib cage.

But I've changed, haven't I? A new
shape every ten years or so, I've been
thin with smoke and deprivation,
bland and round as a jar, hair short,
clothes sleek, I've followed every fad,
sat at the feet of gurus, pursued mystics,
fallen in love with analysts, soul
hungry. I begin to know me,

but who are we? Maypole and
dancer, north star and seeker? Once
my poems were so obscure, I
wrote them on graph paper. Those who
understood them didn't, and those
who didn't, did. I hid desire like an
afikomen on Passover, the *seder* incomplete
until a child found the missing piece.

I dream a young girl comes to me and tells me
who she is. She always knew. I chose you
thirty-two years ago, myself hidden from self
like the sons in the story too insufficient
to ask the question, too simple to call it
love, too wicked to admit it.

The wise child hides behind the door,
listens to the voices, plots her life.

Survivor

He knows the depths of smokestacks,
from their bleak rims down
their spattered walls, from their ash cones
to the bone-bottom ground.
Once he could see under skin,
inside the body, where deprivation
thins the blood of all desire
except hunger.
For years he wanted to forget
everything. He knows it is possible
to live only at the surface,
it is possible to work,
to marry and have daughters.
But his daughters
look like people he once knew,
and he dreams them.
He dreams them opening doors,
sending letters. When he wakes,
he knows he has been dreaming.
This year he will show his daughters
where he was born. He will show them
the chimney, the iron gate,
the deep oven where his mother baked bread.

He Wears Old Socks

He wears old socks,
pajamas full of holes,
saves shoes, saves
everything, stuffs
large amounts of food
in his cheeks, chews
slowly. So much is
his. This is how
he once survived.
Now he has means
to buy new socks,
eat in restaurants.
It isn't that old
habits die hard,
or even memories.
It's the way he
represents the dead,
with his own bones,
not knowing
where the others lie.

Speak without Faltering, If You Can Bear To

You meet them wherever you go.
On a cruise ship of 1000 people,
the one other survivor
sits down at your table.
You start comparing notes, camps,
liberation dates. Nearby,
a survivor's granddaughter eavesdrops,
then joins your conversation – soon
everyone around you is in tears.

Survivors' children find you.
You look like their uncle, they want to hear
your story. You seldom tell. Meanwhile,
the survivors dwindle. They're down to a handful.
Tell, I urge you, tell it
on paper, on tape, but you'd rather
speak to the children, speak to the children
without faltering, if you can bear to,
you'd rather look into their eyes,
where they carry, carelessly revealed,
everything they own.

Suspects

In the small Hungarian town of Szentendre,
    where artists and writers live,
my husband buys thirty-two pieces of strudel
    for his wife and his daughters.
He has come back after forty years.
He wants us to taste the substance of his return,
    he wants us gorged with freedom
and more sweets than anyone needs.
    We eat them all on the train to Belgrade;
butter glazes our lips and fingers.
    We become European, a family
eating on a train while the train
clatters through the countryside.
    At the Yugoslav border,
the train stops. The conductor slides open
    the compartment door, enters,
holds out his hand. He seems
    both old and young, careless, yet
expedient. Stacking our passports
on top of one another, he shuffles them
    like a deck of cards, opens each one,
stares at our pictures. He matches the
    faces, his head bobbing up and down,
his eyes looking straight into ours.
    Hours seem to pass, perhaps even days
before he smiles, hands them back,
bows, and leaves. It takes us a long time
    to become a family again,
    to tell our jokes and hum the latest tunes.

Yes, Apple Pie

When the vigilant guards on the gun mounts,
the oven architects and virtuosos of the *verboten*
doled out your simplest tasks, told you
where to walk, what to eat,
when to sleep, speak, defecate,
even xxxed out your name, you escaped
to the menu of your mind, landscaped
the splintered barracks and the greenless yard
with your mother's meals, easily slapping away
your burly brothers' grabbing hands, a family
slide into the love and jab of uncompleted sentences
where you ate your fill of foods
slippery with butter, glistening with chicken fat.
All day you moved rocks, dreamt of eating
as much as you could hold
until you came to America where
your uncle took you to the Carnegie Deli
and let you scan the lush prolific mounds of food
the way Moses scanned plains of infinite harvests;
you got to choose.

Fifty years have passed.
I feed you now.
Though there's plenty, I think about your arteries
while doling out the red meat, the egg yolks.
But today's your birthday, and I'm baking
an apple pie, your favorite, I'm piling on lots of
sugar, I'm using real butter, I'm licking my fingers,
letting the scent permeate the rooms in which you feel
rescued. Let this be the birthday of desire
in the safe house of excess, where globs of fork-mashed
crust and softly melting apples find their way down
into the protected crevices of your body

to which nothing should ever be denied.
Let this be the open house of goodness, the table piled,
dishes always brimming.
Let this be the uninhibited country
in which you get to choose apple pie over pumpkin
and the road you walk on.

Driving California

for Judy

Driving down 101
with your uncle, I thought of you alone
in your car, collecting towns, connecting yourself
to the state's gold-and-wine itinerary.
You would have stopped
in Crescent City, stepped right up to its
abstract monument of timbers stacked
to look like tepees or cathedral spires, to read the
plaque and learn exactly what its symbology means.
You would have had a ball
in Jacksonville, sifting through thirties stuff
my mother threw out long before it got so
bent and caked with rust; lured to rustic
roadside stands, you would have bought
tickets to the mysteries of caves and trees,
snubbed the redwood bears to sample local fare.
In and out of old
towns, legendary tasting is your way. We passed
them all, found a hotel next to a lake, breakfast
included, luxurious sheets that matched the walls
and shades. I drifted down to the log cabins rented
to citizens who cook outdoors.
I found today's America. You
find restored Victorian inns, visit all the wineries,
learn which grapes were brought from Hungary,
a straight peaceful road, not the bloody way
your parents came from the death camps
and landed you here too.

Meditation on the Hebrew Letter *Zayin* after a Santa Barbara Retreat

I'm salting the tail of a dream
I'm trying to find my way back to Santa Barbara
to get on a train and follow the coast north
     without danger of rain or conversation
to watch from the safety and charity of poetry and dream
to smell the wet leaves
to focus and float through days of rest and beseeching
to see that lonely chair I stumbled on as if a film director
     put it there and said, look, you come upon
     a metal rusted folding chair at the end of a
     slippery path, and it says someone else
     walked this far, for the walk, for the height,
     for the sight of the sea and the little town
     of Santa Barbara, on a day like this, after rain, then
to go back to the black mystery of the letters
to merge into a circle of seekers
to know I am chanting a word over and over
     and the greatest joy is not to hear it
     to hear it fall out like a loose thread
     to hear it inside my head, after silence
to write the 22 letters as if I were nine years old
to begin a new language old in me
to reassert the first metaphor
to become *aleph,* the breath and *bet,* the house
     with no back door
     as becomes a language that speaks about soul,
     sin, satire, diplomacy, war, prayer, mystery, division
        and return
to return to its mystery
to shuffle the letters and ask for an answer
to pull the letter near the end of the twentieth century
     that is the sign of the end of the first week

221 | Florence Weinberger

that is God's first day off
that is the confluence of male and female
that is the very answer to my very question
to find my way back to the question
to understand the question
to wonder who asked the first question
to remember my first question
to offer thanks for the answer
to question the answer.

What Counts, What Doubts

        The Torah scholars say they know God's way, it lies in numbers added, subtracted, multiplied and divided; they say the gorgeous sly combinations are cosmic prescriptions, holy games that predict the future. They say God hid signs inside computers. To search for them is to follow God's mind, to find them is to know God's heart. The truth is so simple.

        I say I know some numbers too, six million is one, one is one, and how many survived the flood in pairs; I say yes, six million is proof infinity exists: isn't it incomprehensible, difficult to teach, impossible to picture, divisible and repetitious as a number should be, yet easy to remember, as in: "Let us remember the six million"?

        And even if each one of my aunts and uncles and cousins died alone as trees, aren't they also a part of "the six million," one of God's own numbers to which there is neither an end nor a reality? And when the scholars uncovered the sequence of numbers that spelled *hitler* and *holocaust*, was it also revealed what God is thinking, what God wants them to tell me

        about God, when God is a lover, when God is the trickster, and what is the end of these means? And what is the meaning of one, which is the number I know best, because it is of myself, I am the onest of one God, we are one by one by one, we are the one son my friend lost yesterday in the vastness of God's numbers, and where was this death foretold,

        and what is the number of God's consolation?

Varieties of Prayer

I dream of prayer
on the way to the house of a famous novelist,
her language rife with color, excessive,
as if the overrun can be used as sacrifice.
But sacrifice means giving up
that which is most loved, a tithing.
Addicted to fixing
daughters without money, depressed friends,
desperate charities, I consecrate myself
to a life of writing American poetry,
an inadvertent witness thrown into communal fires
in the image of the tortured mystic
who, in his death agony, flung the letters of the Hebrew
      alphabet
into the air, crying out *Make of yourselves*
the necessary words.

A Dead Los Angeles Poet

Do you know the dead poets of Los Angeles? a friend asks me.
Those who never got widely read but kept on writing
just the same? He's putting together a book. I name a poet
who put herself in a book before she died, though I, so much
younger then, sniffed at her sensual flights, ellipses that felt
    like failed endings. My friend says *I trust your judgment,*
    pick five or six you like best, let me have a look at them.

And suddenly she's back, with her impolite juxtapositions,
her labial flowers and her Buber aphorisms and the tragic
death of her son and a thwarted life and the losses of age
and the dying of passions. As I did once before, I judge like a
Nazi: You should have killed that crippled line, weeded out the
lame metaphors, the sentimental gaze, but at the same time,
    I'm writing down page numbers of poems that somehow
    claim a hold, with their unspoken reasons for inclusion.

As I descend into her language, some lines begin to tremble
like Old Testament leavening; I grasp the sharp wire of her
mind and follow it down so much deeper than I once fathomed,
to her rocking sorrow, the way she knew herself and gave up
her self-knowledge to the poem, pitiless, without irony,
letting me see her plain once-lovely face fade into age
    with finesse, with some measure of resignation,
    with a prescience she could not have anticipated.

She could not know I'd reread her poems years after her death,
savoring at last the tender facets of their bravery as I
reach the end of a trying year, her age and her cancer now hot
in my hands as I age with my friends who grow wild things
in their unsuspecting bodies, as I learn to love the late hour
with its liquid lucid moments, as I shake with the questions
    she wouldn't contain, her unquiet acceptance,
    and how she forgave the Hebrew God.

225 | Florence Weinberger

The Light Gatherers

In their passion for completion, the devoted – dry-lidded,
holy and haunted – poke among the blasted pieces
for traces of what newspapers call "human remains"
but something, of course, will always be missing.

Impossible to get it all. All that once had a semblance
reassembled to be buried close to wholeness. As if they
can ever resemble themselves again. Leg by cell by
eyelash, they will be gleaned by the *hesed shel emet*

faithful who are hoisted aloft to lift human flesh
off the trembling leaves. Before the last light, the first star,
they will sift the shards of colossal explosives,
combing through tangles of rubber, singed wire,

glass, shoes, the body shells, every crumb of skin,
ash of hair, finger nail, the clotted blood, the cracked skull,
the broken armature of bones; they will climb the sides
of buildings carrying plastic bags filled with cotton balls

to blot the stunned bricks, the smoking windows.
While dazed mourners try to find a *minyan*, they will pick
at the bark of trees, scour flag poles, every house and
lamp post they pass to bundle up what once were children –

there are always children – busy women who shopped early
for produce still livid with soil, readers and smokers and men
who sold diamonds. Even if these burial crews come home
to their wives washed clean,

who wants a job like this, without pay, restless, sleepless,
their fingernails cut to the quick, their pockets emptied.
It is not written *You shall bury him intact,*
only *You shall bury him on the day he dies.* To do it right,

they would have to save the very air around the deed,
even the man who strapped explosives to his chest.
His severed head. His squandered heart.
Everything that belongs to each dead. The last blood

that leaves the body contains the soul, it is written.
The last breath contains the awe, the last sight an after-
image that cannot be imagined. Once bound to the task,
they must gather with charity all that is commingled: the killer

and the killed, when one left home to board the bus,
the bomb hidden, the infant held, the terrible misconception
of the teaching, the non-believer settled in beside the devout,
the words they were about to utter to each other, the sweet

subtext of country. This is not a country easily divided
from the body. Because every Jew carries it, it scatters;
Jews have been found in cellars, their scrolls in caves,
their rituals in Mexico. An exploded bus is a Torah destroyed.

The gatherers, meticulous to the point of madness, are like
crows in the field. Avid and silent at their work, they bring back
to their young their stories which are passed
from mouth to mouth with loud cries or an unbelieving stare.

Joseph and Potiphar's Wife

a painting by Marc Chagall

In the Bible he is blameless, he came to work.
She lurked around him. When he saw the marred light
in her eyes and heard what she wanted, he said no and fled,
leaving behind the garment she had torn from his shoulders.
Adapting the loose fabric of story, the rabbis
and scholars mounded their sharp little stones
and threw them at Potiphar's wife, wounding her
fatally. Choosing the bright stain of the words, Chagall
painted the surface of story, mostly in whites and blues.
Potiphar's wife is completely nude.
She's what you see first, she's in your face. Joseph lies
on the bed
behind her, a blanket pulled up to his chin. His jacket's blue
and it's off to the side, as if it's hanging on a coat rack, as if
he took it off carefully, hung it there himself. Got into bed,
waited,
like a man waiting.
Or asleep, and dreaming, of Potiphar's wife,
naked. A dream that does not seem, at first, as augural as
Joseph's big dreams, with their far-reaching political
implications. The naked woman is lovely,
surely Chagall
made this story up
out of the nature of seduction, out of his desire
to keep what he created, to canonize what he knew of lust,
what he knew of the crucified Jesus, surely he was a man
caught
between the hell of concealment and a passion for
confession, a friend's perhaps, some poet he'd known
in Paris
who'd once turned toward adultery but took time to consider
what it means to hide out in cheap motels,

meet at odd hours, freeze when the phone rings
during dinner.
             The blue jacket's hanging next to a chair,
it's not in her hands, and where are his pants? around his
ankles? in case Potiphar's meeting is cancelled
and he arrives home too soon?
                      And is the cat
under the bed Egyptian, or Chagall's Freudian nightmare
of hairy vaginas with teeth.
             And what do I wait for in front of this painting,
in a room full of portraits and studies.
A stranger joins me. We talk together.
        The stranger moves on. I don't mind.
            He's not the one I am dreaming about.

Hiding

In the Garden of Eden, there are no mirrors,
no locked doors. There is trust.
We call it ignorance.
The snake said I will show you
the other's back, the other's dirty mind.
Soon you will understand
how desire makes you devious,
how hunger makes you suspect.

It became necessary to hide;
this is the origin of engorgement,
of cabinets with locks the size of vaginas,
phallic keys, and all the accouterments
of concealment, like blankets, clouds,
newspapers, and the smoke
of the everlasting pipe in my husband's hand.

In the Garden of Eden, I saw a man.
He was very beautiful. I was curious,
and curiosity turned to trouble,
and trouble turned to interesting times.

I saw his back only when he turned from me.

It is I from whom Adam was hiding, I,
who knew the meaning
of inside before I was born,
when I still lay curled and waiting
under his anxious heart.

Distracted by Horses

Softened by smoke and wine, I can glance at
miles of film my friend took on a recent trip, pigeons over
the plazas, the overwrought churches, the narrowness
of Anne Frank's house, the cold scraped ovens of Auschwitz.
By the time I reach roll nine, I'm numb, so what it takes
to shake me up is a short sequence of photographs, six or
   eight
men on their horses, and I know, out of my family's past,
they are the cowboys who roam the *hortobagy*, the great flat
Hungarian plain; they are the iron Catholic essence of gentile
Hungary, as remote to Jews as their monarchies. I note that
in passing; actually, I'm oblivious to social and historical
   context,
fixed as I am on the flanks of their horses, their blue flowing
outfits, black hats, stiff leather boots, the cinnamon mud
they've stirred up, their stunts and sticks and whips
as they straddle the gorgeous animals, ride them
reined and unsaddled, make them rear and kneel
and lie down at their knees. I've been taken; I don't know
the name of the need, but I get the pictures copied
to keep for myself. The next time I see them,
I'm stuck with the lust they evoked
when my mind was messy and raw as wild cactus
and my blood raced with their flagrant stride. Not once
had I given a thought to the history of Hungary's Jews,
how full it is of whips and pillaging, and how I forgot the
   shrugs
of those who say it was not they who hated blindly and passed
the arbitrary laws, it was their fathers, and their kings.
And don't I love the possibility of detachment,
the luster of good wine and well-composed photographs,
brooding landscapes that are only themselves, blue-eyed

men sweeping in from another century. And wouldn't I
relish the oneness of the universe,
in which the daughter of Hungarian Jews moves to the
American West and falls in love with its drunk, unruly
　　　　　cowboys
and its thundering horses.

Angles

A Palestinian Arab is shooting my daughter.
Circling her for advantage, he works his way around
      obstacles,
keeps her locked in the cross-hairs of his sight. Now he is
      able to
see her head-on and in the round,
he can pick his moment.
Indulging his trained maneuvers, she smiles and smiles for
      him.
It is her wedding day. He assures us
he has photographed Jewish weddings
many times, he understands our rituals, when to film, when
      to look away.
I watch my daughter in his hands.
He twists the lens, zooms her closer, he's got her
mugging, relaxed, nothing but marriage on her mind.

Apple

The man my daughter married is in love with his wife,
his son, his car, his state-of-the-art computer;
I don't have to know the exact order of things.
Playing like all the citizen gods lodged in front of their screens
he conjures up a copy of his wedding portrait,
imposes over it the enlarged startled face of his infant son
and prints out a clear and ghostly double image.
I see my grandson afloat in the ozone
like one of Wordsworth's babies cradled in aboriginal wisdom.
Spread across the black and white print his great toothless grin
widens further when he first spots his parents taking their vows
under the ample branches of the mulberry tree in my backyard
and later when he decides it's time to be born he remembers
the happy guests who came from New York and New Jersey
to dance the hora and drink up liters of chardonnay.
He remembers me standing behind my daughter during the
ceremony grinning like a fool and don't doubt this for an instant,
he sees exactly what passes between the pair when
the Hebrew prayers are read though they both would have said
they didn't understand a word and he sees that they understand
the deepest meaning of crushing a glass underfoot
and he hears the glass breaking and the burst of joy
that comes from the guests and he sees the goodness of the day
lifting its way into the universe and he knows
then and there he will enter their life when he is ready
and the man he'll call father
will fool around with his computer until he burns
onto a sheet of Sublimation Printing Paper the image he created.

Sheltered

On the first day of Rosh Hashanah,
the old new age rabbi explains the Aliyah
this way: *all those who will spend the coming year*
as caretakers, for your giving, for your replenishment,
rise and come forward. In the Diaspora,
the synagogue may be a rented auditorium,
you may not be ready for the early onset of an autumn
reckoning, your children may live elsewhere,
so it happens it is my sister's son who sits beside me,
rises with me and draws us into the press of worshipers.
As the rabbi begins to chant from the Torah portion,
my nephew bends to tell me *This was grandpa's talles.*
Nearly twenty years have passed. I had forgotten
which grandchild was heir to my mother's wedding gift.
I look down at the discolored cloth,
the tiny holes close to the fringes.
Is a damaged *talles* kosher? Who whispers
into my nephew's ear and causes him to drape
around my shoulders a corner of the worn *talles?*
We stand touching and swaying. This year to come
I will see my husband through his cancer
treatments. My father's cancer did not kill him.
The rabbi chants over the heads of the supplicants,
sending out a web of healing sound.
Sound and sorrow cover me. Still, still, I am consoled.

Jews Don't Eat Green Jell-O

When Lenny Bruce said Jews don't eat green Jell-O, they eat
      red, I knew what he meant. A gentile salad is
cottage cheese on a bed of lettuce, topped by a slice of canned
      pineapple, a maraschino cherry;
gentile men become pilots, deep sea divers, race car drivers.
      Deft and irreverent, he drew the dark lines, the familiar
and the foreign, what was allowed, what was indiscreet.
The Bronx street where I grew up was a safety zone with four
      sides; everyone had a face I recognized.
When my daughters meet a new friend, they can't tell.
      They don't even think they have to,
all the world's benign and color blind. That's a sweet belief,
      no need to fear the drunken *goy* on a Sunday rampage
      who terrorized my mother's Carpathian village.
Though their father's a survivor of similar distinctions,
they've lost their paranoia, their edge, their clothes of thick
      skin and humor, the torn decision to stay or run.
They have ignorance and bliss, which they pass on
      to their American children. My granddaughter owns
a Native American Barbie. They rejoice in the markets
      around them. They can buy hush puppies, sushi, sopa,
pasta, falafel, pad thai, chow mein and kim chee in minutes.
I hope I can get comfortable. I hope I can get used to this.

American Beauty

I was staring out the window across my lawn
when my daughter told me on the phone
her newborn son's face is asymmetrical.
I said everyone's face is asymmetrical,
to protect me from fear that the two sides
were more than misarranged.
The fruitless mulberry is lopsided
from this distance, every bush is bare
somewhere as leaves fall and are replaced;
there's always shade in the wrong places
stunting the oranges, making us want
to fix things up with fertilizer
or prayer.

Claribel Alegría
said her asymmetrical face made her a poet;
one side could fly, one held the earth.
Even at birth, we enter unruly
hearing the ragged scream when we are torn.
Since that call my grandson and I have met.
He sings a loud exultation to me in infant tongues.
His fists beat out his first rhythms.
When he laughs, one cheek
is round and smooth with mirth

but it is the other that draws me,
a flawed reflection of family lore, faulty histories
from Eastern ghettos to the middle-East,
rabbis and bureaucrats, gamblers and shleppers,
or maybe we were truly blessed, meshed by some
wayward wind with *wabi-sabi,*
the Japanese aesthetic
that looks close at the commonplace and loves what is

bruised by chance or misshapen by use. Maybe
it is from this distance
my grandson's face blossoms into perfect beauty.

Afterword

When I hesitated about being interviewed for this After-word, you told me that one of the reasons you include the personal voice of the author in your books is that you want to demystify the writing of poetry. But there's a part of me that likes the mystery of writing poetry – and romanticizes it. When I was growing up, I cloaked myself in that mystique. Both my parents' highest aspiration for me was to be a bookkeeper. So I led a separate inner life. I read a great deal and that made me feel separate – there were no books in my house at all. Anything I ever did in connection with my writing was totally on my own. I wanted to hold on to the myth that they didn't understand me and never would.

In fourth grade I wrote a Halloween play; in sixth grade, in a special class for gifted children, I wrote a book of short stories. I was published in the school magazine and then the high school newspaper. When I was in eighth or ninth grade, I was accused of plagiarism and again in high school for a short story I wrote. But I also had very good teachers who supported me. Still, when I left high school I don't think I had a sense of a career as a writer. My parents didn't particularly want me to go to college, so I went at night, on my own. I worked at Metropolitan Life Insurance Company for five years as an actuarial clerk, sitting and doodling my little poems and sticking them in the drawer. I never got very far there; I didn't quite know where I belonged.

I remember meeting a young man at my sister's wedding – I was turning 21 – and saying something about wanting to leave home. And he said, *why don't you implement your attitude*. I absolutely didn't understand what he was talking about – put your money where your mouth is. There were women

Edited from a taped interview.

who left home but not many, not in my circle. You didn't move out of your parents' home until you got married. That's what I did, stayed home until I got married.

But I continued writing in college. I had a wonderful teacher, Judy Brayer, who permitted us to pour our hearts out. In an assignment she gave us to "write me a letter," I bemoaned the fact that I had to read Shakespeare on the subway on the way to work in the morning, because I worked full time and went to school at night. I even complained about my dumb boyfriend from Brooklyn and whatever popped into my head. I still have her response which was lengthy, detailed and very encouraging.

I went to Hunter College evening school for five years and then switched to day session for a year so I could do my student teaching. I taught third grade for one hideous year, one of the worst years of my life. I probably became pregnant sooner than I should have so I could leave. That last year in college I had another English course in which I wrote something the professor liked a lot. She said to me: *Whatever happens to my women poets? They graduate and they get married and I never hear anything about them again.* And she was right. After I got married I did not write for nine years. Everything else seemed to take precedence.

And then I started in a frenzy – it was all backed up. I wrote short stories for awhile and got a few published – in *Nimrod* and Harry Smith's *The Smith*. I wrote two novels, neither of which has been published, though I've had mentors who tried their best. One of them, a distinguished novelist, said she would publish my novel herself if she could. And I got deeply into poetry. There is something very seductive about writing poetry; it's a quick fix in one sense – I get lost in it. But I fight getting into it. I used to call it writer's block, but I don't think it is, because I'm always thinking about something. I'm not really sure what it is.

I'm not prolific. For someone who started as young as I did and who's been writing as long as I have, I don't have a large body of work. I get bogged down. I've had years of depression on and off, a lethargy that overcomes me periodically. It is only very recently that I've personified this lethargy as a female who weighs four hundred pounds and blocks me, just drags me down. Before that I'd been very glibly saying I'm a lazy person. In fact I used to think if I worked hard, I would get so successful that I would have to leave home and travel and break up my marriage and things would change so drastically that I just couldn't bear it. What an excuse for not doing anything! My husband said, *I really don't mind if you make more money than I do. It's okay.* Well, there is something else going on and I don't know what it is.

When I turned sixty in the same month that I found out both of my daughters were pregnant, something happened in my psyche. My joy was boundless, but at the same time, it was a period of stark re-evaluation: here I am, I'm sixty, I don't even have one book out, I was voted the most promising *blah blah blah* when I graduated from high school, nothing has happened. That's how I perceived it. I went into a funk that lasted three or four years. I'm just coming out of it. Therapy helped, but when my husband had melanoma and I focused all my energies on him and helping him, I was present finally. I was able both to deal with him and to start writing again. Very strange.

One of my big jobs for myself is getting to know myself. Out of the skillions and trillions of things that I'm confronted with all the time, certain things demand attention. That becomes a way of knowing who I am – why this, not that. Then I need to go more deeply into it, just as I have to go deeply into a dream, just move in. I try to get as close to the bottom emotionally as I can.

In my poems, I make an effort to extrapolate from who I am, what arouses emotion in me, to the general human experience. It's my life, but it's the lives of a lot of people. In a conference on spirituality that I went to, somebody said that spirituality is really a way of dealing with reality. That was fascinating to me, and yet I was already aware of that – as in the way I write about my mother making strudel and soup and her own wine in *The Power in My Mother's Arms*. Basically we have to make the daily holy. I have an awareness of the extraordinary that's in the ordinary. That to me is the greatest gift, to be able to express that, to be able to touch that in other people. Of course when I sit down to write, none of this is in my mind. I just need to get the best way of saying something out there on the page and it's much, much later that I ask myself these questions.

* * *

I've been studying Jewish spirituality for a good many years. I had an excellent teacher, a rabbi named Ted Falcon, one of the first in Los Angeles to integrate meditation with Jewish spiritual practice. It was a breakthrough for me, studying kabbalah, very expansive and, at the same time, it gave me a structure within which I could operate. When I took a four-session course from Rabbi Jonathan Omerman on Jewish meditation, though I came out with what Oscar Wilde talks about as "a smattering of ignorance," that didn't stop me from writing a three-page poem about Jewish meditation – a whole series of impressions and self-examinations. Out of that writing came the impetus for going ahead and exploring more deeply other Jewish topics. Coincidentally this happened close to the high holy days last year, when I had the experience of my nephew putting the prayer shawl around my shoulders, which I write about in the poem *Sheltered*. I loved that. One thing after another that happened seemed to have a thread – which I followed. It became a conscious act not only to look at what demanded my attention, but to look at it from the point of view of a Jewish woman – what about my own sensibility is responding to this.   Before I found myself concentrating on writing poems with a Judaic thrust to them, I had done such poems sporadically over the years. But when they were sandwiched between all the other work, it didn't seem like any kind of trend. I had always allowed myself to range all over the place – subject matter, size, shape, my poems were all different. I always fought being labeled anything. Getting caught up in these Jewish poems gave me a focus that I have never had before, other than in writing a novel. And I found that within that category I could still have a lot of freedom.

I don't think that Jewish women's voices have been heard enough. I don't want to say I am *the* voice, that my voice, just because I am Jewish, is like everyone else's Jewish voice. I'm not observant, I don't practice ritual. But I have been stamped from birth. Both my parents were immigrants, I grew up in New York City, in a Jewish neighborhood. The extent to which that influenced me and what I brought to it subsequently has to be expressed. I think I've barely scratched the surface.

I haven't mentioned that my husband is a holocaust survivor, how that has affected my life. My first novel dealt with that – or tried to. I remember naively asking Elie Wiesel, when he had just published his first book, *I don't know what to do about my husband.* I baffled him by the question. What I meant was, how do I write about this without damaging him personally, how do I treat the whole subject with reverence and not glibly. That's been an ongoing struggle for me. I haven't done it a lot because of that concern, that it's not mine. I took it on, when I was very young, in the shape of a man who was hurt and wounded. I took on a healing function that I was not totally equipped for and ignored my own need for healing at the same time, because his wound was worse than my wound. That's the way I saw it. In some respects this work that I have done was healing for both of us.

* * *

When I first started writing poetry, my poems were cryptic. I don't know when I shifted from not being accessible to being accessible – it was not a conscious change. Now I am hearing from people who are reading my book, *The Invisible Telling Its Shape,* because I'm their friend or their mother-in-law or I gave them a copy, that though they don't read poetry or don't like poetry, they like my work, I am very accessible. I have a very mixed reaction to that still. Part of me says maybe I'm too accessible, maybe I should just try to scramble things up a little more. I look at poets like Ann Lauterbach or John Ashbery – I don't know what they're saying, but they get published. Many years ago Ann Stanford, a wonderful poet I worked with, gave us an assignment to write nonsense poems. I really let loose. I have never sent those poems out but I love them. Periodically I look at them and say to myself, take a chance. But I have not been able to do that because, basically, they don't make sense to me. It seems unfair, like a trick; I feel poetry should say something. Maybe it's not always evident to the reader what I'm trying to say, but I am trying to say *something*, to connect. It's scary, and the older I get and the more I do it, the more I realize the danger in it. You get very vulnerable. On the other hand, it seems to matter less and less to be vulnerable.

I had a wonderful experience about a year ago. The daughter of a woman I know wanted me to read my poetry to a group of 75-year-old women in her backyard for her mother-in-law's birthday party. It would have been very easy for me to put this whole thing down – oh they're just a bunch of old ladies, Jewish mostly, liberal East Coast women (this was California, but they all had that sensibility). I think it was a turning point for me in gaining a respect for my audience. Some of them came up to me afterward and thanked me and I thought, I'm really reaching these people, why am I being so pejorative about my own work. Was it Groucho Marx who said *I wouldn't join any club that would have me.* This is the way I used to feel: if they understand my work something is wrong with them, I'm too accessible, not even accessible – I'm ordinary.

I'm very competitive. I was never as clear about what I wanted before one of my latest forays into therapy when I put that into words. I was seeing other people "getting ahead," getting books published, getting read, getting readings. I really was envious. It didn't feel good to me at all.

And then I'd read work and I'd say, my stuff is just as good, it's even better. I was becoming bitter. I'd never said that about myself before. I'd always believed that the work would find its level, it would speak for itself, but it seemed like that wasn't happening. I was very angry for quite some time that I wasn't being heard. Except that I *was* being heard. I wasn't being grateful enough for those people who were supporting me and did understand my work. I've had to make a shift, to remember that I really love doing the work, that I'm blessed by the ability to do it, the desire to do it. I'm working on that. I'm not all the way there.

But I'm still alive and I'm still working and I'm working on me. One of my favorite things I remember is my niece, when she was fifteen, asking my sister, do you like the way I turned out, and my sister saying, *why, are you finished?* I'm not finished. I don't want to be finished. I'll be finished and I'll be dead the next day.

One of the things Brugh Joy, one of my "gurus," said when we did a conference on "the dark side," was, *You are totally in touch with your dark side, it's your innocent child that's in the closet.* For years I have been really struggling with that. My father tended to put down simplicity, being "out there." He used to criticize my sister because she smiled too much! He himself had a sister who was a warm, giving person and he regarded her as not terribly bright. He had a very dark side obviously – I've written about that; and I've modeled myself in many ways after him. I put a great deal of importance on intelligence and achievement; the simpler more spontaneous ways of doing things I make judgments about. This is why I have this struggle with being accessible; it is right on the edge of being not too bright, not too cautious.

In another workshop with Brugh Joy, where we worked from images evoked by highly amplified music or highly charged films, I had an image of myself as an eagle and also as a sparrow. He felt that I did not honor the sparrow enough, I wanted to be the eagle, I wanted to soar, be big. Recently my therapist told me about what the sparrow represents – which I promptly forgot – but it was something really nice. And my Yiddish name is *Feigele,* little bird – that was what my father called me. I have not honored that aspect of me. It's very difficult even now to acknowledge my voice and at the same time be humble, to honor my own uniqueness without overinflating it. I guess I'm talking about balance, about equilibrium.

Eileen Tobin

To Phyllis, Sarah, Kateri and, especially, Ray, whose gifts of friendship triumph over age, space, time and even death. May I be worthy.

Bog Oak

My memories of my father begin in 1918 from before I was three years old. I hoard these jewels in a Pirate Chest on the floor of a narrow river, a river that is both gentle and wild.

I do not know why the Pirate Chest is in the river and not in the sea. I do not know what pirate put it there. I only know that it is mine, and that I found it when I was seven or eight years old and needed a place to keep things, things that were really mine. Things I remember.

> *I am under the big brass bed where since my father died I sleep with my mother. The bedspread reaches to the floor on three sides. The fourth side is the wall against which I lean. My cove smells of recently disturbed dust and lemon oil, but it is mine. I try my new trick. I put my head in my hands, close my eyes and repeat Me Me until I am inside myself. I find the river, plunge deep, go even deeper, and there is the Pirate Chest, that place of my own, where I store the treasure my mother will not let me talk about, my life until I was five-and-a-half years old.*

For too long I have merely gazed at the jewels, possessed them in secret, so that they remained still, never changing. Although I did not hear the sound, these internal jewels began at some time to explode like birthing stars to seek a fuller life in other parts of my being. Like all jewels they have survived time, fire and water. They wait for me to notice them. To see that they are alive. They need to come home, to move and to grow as I move and grow.

Some time ago I was encouraged to expand my written memoirs. I begin by a raid on the Pirate Chest and remove two of the jewels. One is the color of mud, rich and dark, with lights embedded in the stone. The other jewel is dark too, purple, like a bottle of port wine held up to the light. Both are memories from the birth of my brother.

I close my eyes to own the darkness. I see the image of my father. He is bending over my mother as she lies on the floor. Her legs, spread wide apart, stretch into the dining room. The crown of her head is toward me as I watch from my crib in the bedroom. I see my father's warm bathrobe, the color of port wine. His head is lost. He is reaching into my mother. Her fingers grip the ovaled threshold that separates the two rooms.

I tighten my grip on the jewels until my hands sting. I want to see more. I want my father to lift his head. After a while, a long while, my throat tightens as though a blunt instrument were being forced inside. My eyes burn. The pain is a good-bye pain. I release my hold on the jewels and return them to the chest. I fasten the rust crusted latch. Then clinging to nothing I submit myself to the cool wash of the river.

What else is there to see? And how do I see it?

I swim in water, river water, that tosses me in many currents. I struggle between frozen and authentic memory and the freedom of imagination, as though truth were a separate entity.

"You're a storyteller!" my mother tells me. Her voice is at an anger level just below fury. I see the anger. I see the fear that levels it. I have seen them before.

> *"Do you remember the cherry tree we had in the yard of our house in New Jersey? Remember daddy holding down a branch so I could pick some?" She does not answer. "Do you?"*
> *"Go change from your school clothes."*
> *Unshared memories widen the space between us. Our voices fade, or are projected onto pretend personalities, like ventriloquists in a puppet show. My brother had no memory of that world. He was too young. He is safe. With him, she can try to find her way in the new world.*

We are late returning from school. We are asked where we have been. *Norway,* I say. Frank, still excited, adds, "She took me there, but we weren't really lost."

We had taken another route, passing by an excavation with sand and rock mounted high on two sides of a narrow street with empty lots on either side. Water had been pumped in to clear the debris. We climbed to the top of one of the mounds, then holding on to each other we watched the wild water as it shoved sand and rock in the direction of the Bay. I saw us on a fjord. *Norway,* I told him.

Norway, I tell my mother. Storyteller! She slaps me, but not hard. It is my brother who cries, and as my mother comforts him, he looks pleadingly at me. *Take me to those places.* But I decide it is better to travel alone.

I continue to swim. The water turns dark and grimy. I come to an iron door. I tell myself that it is familiar, that I will come again and again. The door is the entrance to my Story.

The iron door opens and a cascade of white foam hurls and then drops me into deeper and even more raging water. My fingers find a sharp boulder protruding from a cliff, invisible in the dark. I claw at it. Lose hold. Claw again. Lose hold. Exhausted, I surrender to the roaring but sensuous current. It undresses layers and layers of tight skin before plummeting me into a whirlpool of laughing water. Although stripped and lanced by rocks chiseled by time into unsheathed swords, I leap like a salmon and find a hanging branch. My fingers clench and unclench. I feel the hard wood of the branch.

It is May 4, 1918 at one-thirty in the morning. From the far corner of my crib, I stir. Whimper. Burrow deeper. Stir again. It is a nonsound, the restlessness of a new day trying to push back the night. But I am awake, and I am clutching and unclutching two of the wooden bars of my crib.

My first instinct is to demand attention, but I am stopped by a tangible break and scent in the air. My father is passing the crib. His hand touches the top bar. But the touch is not for me. The touch is to guide him in the dark. He is warm from his bed and strong in his step. Scent and step say *daddy*.

"Frank!" My mother in a new voice, both demanding and dependent. It crashes through my last link with infant sleep. I lift myself to my knees and stick my nose through the narrow ribs of the crib as I struggle to feel and sniff what my blinking eyes do not see in the dark.

Dark is an early version of the great iron door, but I am innocent and do not know or accept jammed barriers. I let out a rippled roar like a weaned cub.

A light goes on in the dining room, the room just off the bedroom in this railroad, first floor flat of a two-story brownstone at 352-72nd Street in the Bay Ridge section of Brooklyn.

I let out a second roar. It is drowned out by my mother's second call, "Frank! Help me to the bathroom!"

Now I see my mother's movements. They are even more astonishing than her voice. She struggles to sit up, bends over, then squeezing the edge of the mattress and breathing heavily, she puts one foot on the floor. Now moaning, she twists her body and throws herself back on the bed. Frantically, she grips the blankets and buries her head between her closed fists. There in the big brass bed into which I had been born two and a half years ago, she lies quiet.

My father is back. I pull myself up again and press hard against the crib's edge. I lift my arms expectantly, but he goes directly to my mother. I lose my balance and fall sideways against the long side of the crib, hitting my head lightly on the bars.

My outcry is lost in the sound of my mother's voice, her normal voice, the caretaker's voice. "You'll get cold, Frank, close the windows."

Then my father's low laugh. Tender. Words are not needed. I have heard that laugh before. It is his evening sound, the sound he makes when he comes home from work with a package hidden behind his back.

This time the sound is not for me.

Shocked, but too curious to cry out, I watch this totally new scene.

Holding on to each other, they pass by the foot of the crib, while I stumble, fall, then creep over my crumpled bedding until I am at the foot of the crib.

I can almost touch them.

"Put me down, Frank! Put me down *here.*"

I do not know what is happening. I am afraid.

I see my mother begin to slide down the length of my father's body, pulling them both to the floor, his arms still cradling her. "Agnes," he says. His voice is strange. I think he is crying. I begin to whimper, low and rhythmic. My mother is sprawled across the threshold, gasping at first, then taking long deep breaths. He lifts himself to a squatting position. I change my sound and begin to mimic her. I gasp and breathe with her. They hear me.

"The baby!" I do not know that I will never be that to my mother again. "Cold," she adds. Her concern is for him and for me, but he springs up and heads toward the big bed, stopping by my crib to cup my face in his hands and kiss the top of my head. From the bed he seizes a sheet, blankets and pillow. Returning to my mother he throws the blanket over her body. More gently, he crouches, lifts her head and pushes the pillow beneath it. Awkwardly, he rolls the sheet around his arm, then puts it under her between the rough wood of the threshold and her spine.

He is up again. *Windows.* This time as he passes, he stops to lift me up and place me at the head of the crib. Firmly, he tucks me in. "Sleep," he says. I hear him pad across the parlor to the windows. Obediently, I close my eyes, but I do not sleep.

I hear the thud of the windows as he closes them. The throaty sounds of the foghorns quiet. The damp breeze ceases. Open windows, day or night, are part of my early memories. Tuberculosis is fought with air.

He returns, more quickly now, his eyes accustomed to the dark, ignoring me as he passes the crib. He ignores my mother, too. I hear him crossing the dining room, entering the kitchen, turning the lock and going into the hall.

Upstairs, our landlord has a telephone.

My mother screams. *Frank.* She says something about water. He is back in an instant.

I loosen my tucked in covers, twist around so that I face the foot of the crib, then worm my way under the blankets till I reach the foot. There I claw at the firmly tucked barrier. My head pokes free. I get to my knees, grab the bars and push my nose through. Now I see my mother's face and hear her breathing. I see my father lift my mother's nightgown, lift her legs and spread them wide apart. He drags the sheets and pulls them further down so that they are under her buttocks.

My father's thick brown hair is in a wild mass over his intense face, but through the strands I see the long horizontal line of his undisciplined black brows. He is flushed more than usual, moving his arms with even firmness. But with something else. It is the way he lights the candles on the dining room table at night, his sense of life and the sacred.

The heavy blanket, high on my mother's chest, is now hiding the action. I pull myself up as high as I can get. Everything becomes quiet except for my father's heavy breathing and my mother's synchronized guttural gasps. At last she whispers a sigh. He gives a raucous yelp, and I see him pull from my mother something that in the faint light looks like a wad of rags. The wad is the color of mud. Gently, with one hand, he pulls the sheet from beneath my mother. He is laughing and crying as he winds the sheet all around and around the mound of wet mud.

I shake the bars in fury. I do not know this game, and I want to be down there. I want to be on the floor with them. I see him smile, that familiar smile, so intimate that not a second lapses between it and your own. God pushes the same button.

Once again, the intimacy is not for me. I stop shaking the

bars to watch as he takes the swaddled lump and places it across my mother's breast. His chin rests on the strange bundle. He bends to kiss my mother. She has her arms off the floor and around my father and the bundle of mud hiding in the white sheet. "Agnes," he says, "we have a son."

I do not know what he means. I do not know what the whole mysterious event means. I only know that beyond my crib there is a world I have never seen. A world I am not supposed to see, but in it is everything that is mine. And I cannot climb across.

I am on my father's lap. We are in the mahogany rocking chair with the green velvet seat. I look over his shoulder and across the length of the parlor to the bedroom. The light from the brass Tiffany lamp on the dining room table is still on. The flickering beam worms its way into the bedroom and sways against the brass bed giving enough light so that I see the outline of my mother holding my brother. Brother. It is a new word.

The windows are open again, but only slightly from the top, enough for the tangy smell of the salt air to wrap us in all that is familiar. It is almost four o'clock in the morning, that time when night cannot make up its mind whether to hold tight to the freedom of the darkness, or reach for the brash warmth of a new day.

My father's robe feels solid, rough and wonderful under my chin. Like most families in the years immediately following the First World War, we own several surplus khaki army blankets. One is now wrapped around both of us. Coarse of texture, its association is with trenches, wounds, fear and exploding shells. But this night it is a tent of velvet.

My father fingers his rosary beads, but is too excited to concentrate. He kisses the cross and puts the beads into the top left pocket of the robe that is the color of port wine, but now, in the fog, is the color of the night. My cheek is against that pocket and I feel the beads hard against my flesh. I lift my left hand from beneath the blanket and place it between the pocket and my cheek, so that the beads now join his heart and my hand.

From a few blocks away a mournful buoy rocks a lone seagull in the early salt-laden fog. I settle in to the muffled beat of my father's heart, joining us like an umbilical cord to the slight creak of the rocker. He hums my name song, *Eileen alanna, Eileen asthore.*

Hardly more than an infant, I could not have understood the power released on the night of my brother's birth. Fog and the coming of dawn invaded my father with forces that transcended his frail body.

How do I remember it at all? And how do I seem to recall that in some way I knew that that brief time was filled with mystery? The silent energy of the night was being fused into me from my father. I was being conceived again. I was in a new world, a world that would destroy my childhood, but break the hard ground to my womanhood. In early childhood, following my father's death, I clung to the clear immediacy of early memories. If I did not let them move, perhaps they would not go away, and they must not go away. In so doing, did I block, or freeze, the tremendous force of that night?

As a child I had discovered an alternative world when I sought solitude under the parental brass bed. In ancient Irish culture, the ability to enter easily into the "otherworld" was a natural thing. My maternal grandparents came from Dublin at the time of the American Civil War. My grandfather was a Fenian and a hedge teacher. In secret he taught "the faith," Gaelic, and the legends from the old culture. When discovered, he had escaped with my grandmother, leaving an infant behind, and was smuggled onto a ship headed for New York. Both died before my mother married. On my father's side of the family, it was my great-grandparents who emigrated in the dreadful days just beyond the acute years of the famine. My father's people were among those descendants of Irish immigrants who tried to hide their Irishness, victims of the low self-esteem common to a persecuted and conquered people.

So, how do I come by my ancient Celtic psyche?

In these final decades of my life, my spiritual journey has led me into the great adventures of inner myths and dreams. The journey has also led me into the struggle to write again. I see both of these developments as one.

Most Irish citizens, as well as we exiles from Ireland (no matter how many generations have passed), have been deprived of their language. Loss of one's own tongue starves the spirit. Instincts and vague longings that were expressed in the words and experiences of a people, now swim around in the inner being, finding their outlet in dreams, myths and art. Timid as I have appeared to others, I have always had a raging storm within, a desire to plunder the high sea of the other world, the alternative world, the world which our enemies have labeled superstitions, calling its inhabitants *little people, faeries, gnomes*, in search of my own self. I believe my father had this same drive, as did his uncle for whom he was named, another Francis Tobin. And certainly my maternal grandfather, David Kidney (even his name was taken from him) knew the hungry call of his own lost tongue.

Something of that force lived that night. It was all around us, whispering in the mist, groaning in the fog horn, scratching in the thick blanket, passing into my deepest being.

That night, what does it feel like now? Currents of a sacred energy burn through my throat, chest, mouth, shoulders and groin. I am the seed.

I am having my hair cut. The hairdresser is from Galway. I ask about her family.

"One of my brothers is an artist," she tells me. "I remember that when I was little, he used to take me very early in the morning, just before dawn, into the bogs to look for buried oak. At that time the mist is so thick it hugs the ground. He would hold my hand as we felt our way through the weird light of the mist. It is really no light at all because we could

*not even see each other. You have to keep going, feeling your
way, and hoping, until you see a spot where the mist has
not settled, there you see a piece of the bog. That is where you
dig because buried under there you might find an ancient
oak that has survived the ice age and water. From that wonderful wood, Conor carves his statues."*

She speaks these words casually, seemingly unaware of
their beauty. I gasp and grip the chair. She wants to know if I
am all right. I am still in that scene, knowing that mist, feeling that need to hunt, hoping for that treasure.

Embarrassed by my emotion, I tell her that she has just
given me the title for a book I want to write, *Bog Oak.*

The product's name is "B&P Standard Loose Leaf Record
Book." It is a heavy gray canvas volume, reinforced with steel,
filled with yellowed and brittle 8 1/2 by 11 unlined, blue-
margined, fine quality legal paper. The borders, tabs and
spine are of maroon-colored leather embossed with gold leaf
letters. Its once elegant label is rent diagonally like the veil
of the Temple or the garment of a mourner. The maroon
color of the label is faded, but subtly rich, a compromise
between a dimly remembered smoking jacket worn by my
grandfather and a well-remembered robe.

The book came into my possession in 1988 following the
death of my brother Frank. The label reads:

RECORD BOOK
The minutes of the M. J. Tobin Co., Inc.

On page 61, dated June 20, 1920, the entry reads:

RESOLVED, that a leave of absence be granted to
Francis C. Tobin for one month with pay.

My father's signature, F. C. Tobin, Secretary, concludes
the page. It was this abbreviated signature that struck me
when I read it for the first time, some 68 years after he made
it. Frances C. Tobin loved the flourish of his full name. His
capital letters were calligraphically shaded. His signature

cascaded and rolled across a page like an incoming tide. He must have known when he signed this entry that he would not return. The F, though, seems defiant, its thick black descender stroke heavier than usual, so that for me life jumps right off the page, defying the entry on page 81 of the same volume, made almost ten months later.

> Whereas it is with sincere regret that the Board has learned of the death of their fellow member and Secretary of the Company, Francis C. Tobin, who died on the second day of April, 1921, and
> Whereas this company has suffered an irreparable loss....

Little Frank was almost a year old and I three-and-a-half when, in April of 1919, we moved from Bay Ridge to our new house in East Orange, New Jersey. The drier air of the Oranges, it was believed, would help my father.

The wood frame house had a porch where we sat at night, the air slowly filling with the sharp smell of citronella as my father with his long fingers, still strong, massaged the oily liquid over my arms and legs. At the curb, cracking the sidewalk that separated it from the lawn, a maple tree bent protectively toward the house. In the evening it whispered, lulling even the menacing hum of the fierce Jersey mosquitoes.

In the back yard a cherry tree, fat, red, and bursting like a merry cook, made my father laugh. He would lower a branch so that I could reach a cherry. Sometimes it was sweet, often sour, and I would spit it out to be grasped by a grateful squirrel.

I try but cannot remember the merry cook in the lacy pink of her spring innocence, perhaps because it would be in the third spring that I would be taken away.

But, as time went on, and I was approaching five, the center of my world was the attic, a great sunny space that stretched the length and depth of the house. Its sounds and colors were another world, and like most otherworlds, it was reached by uneven narrow steps. The back of the attic narrowed off to make a wall for the great climb. Storage boxes and a large black trunk were stacked in the corner beneath a tightly closed high and narrow window. By climbing up the trunk and standing tiptoed, I could see the cherry tree.

Filled with intimate creaks, soft echoes and silence, the great room was almost empty, save for a couch that extended into the room from the long wall at right angles from the wide, curtainless French doors. To that couch my father came every afternoon from June till late August of 1920, when he became bedridden.

Downstairs, my mother and brother napped.

Several feet from the steep steps that led to this magic place I played with my father, he across the long room by the French doors, I on the opposite end near the stairs. Leaning in my direction, propped up by pillows, he would tell me stories or call instructions on how to form the letters of my name. When tired, he would suggest I draw the cherry tree, and the echo of his voice would rise to the beams of the high ceiling and rest with him.

My companion on my side of the attic was my favorite toy, my blackboard. Dark as night it was, my blackboard, waiting for my sticks of colored chalk. Propped against the wall and held firm by two bricks, it was large, much larger than a child's slate.

Each afternoon my mother placed a bowl next to the blackboard. In the bowl was a clean wet rag. Before being called back downstairs at the end of our time together, I had to clean the blackboard and put all of the pieces of chalk back into the sturdy cigar box. "But," and she would hold my shoulders firmly when she said this, "if daddy coughs, you are to clean the board immediately and come right downstairs. You must come backwards on your hands and knees so that you don't fall."

The afternoon sun played with the maple tree whose happy leaves cast shadows across the vast empty floor. The floor was a wide and beautiful river, but it was filled with whirlpools. River and whirlpools marked the division between me and my father, a division I was forbidden to cross. Above and all around this river was light and air.

But didn't we both know that it was all one place?

Toward the end of March in 1921, I was taken in my sleep from our house in East Orange to the home of my aunt, my father's younger sister. This sprawling and comfortable house was a few blocks away from where my brother and I had been born.

Awakened by a blinding light, I defensively turned over and buried my head in the blanket. Something was wrong. I was someplace else. This was not my crib. Or my blanket. I turned over again, covered my eyes with my fists, and peered through the fingers. They were like the bars of my crib. I was looking at the splintered glare of the morning sun. Where was I?

I lowered my fists. Fear mingled with wonder as I slowly entered the scene. I was on a glass enclosed upper porch that stretched the entire width of the back of the house. The porch, just outside the room of my seven-year-old cousin Kathryn, was a combination playroom and schoolroom for Kathryn, a victim of the 1917 polio epidemic. Her legs were useless. Her grieving parents had compensated by becoming her subject.

On that morning, Kathryn was at the far end of the porch holding on to an executive size mahogany glass-topped desk. The desk was surrounded on two sides by windows, and on the third side by the gray shingles of the house. She was encased, waist to toes, in great ugly steel and leather braces.

"When you get dressed," she proclaimed, "you are going to play with me."

I did not answer. Stared. Who was she?

Where was my daddy? My mother? My little brother? This must be the wicked fairy. What would she turn me into?

On a hook between the north wall of windows, a few inches from the ceiling, hung a teddy bear dressed in short red pants and a red knitted sweater. Was that my brother? Daddy had told me in one of those lulling moments in the attic that a handsome prince, or Jesus, always came and turned everybody back to what they were supposed to be. It was done with a kiss. My father was both the handsome prince and Jesus. Until he came, I would keep away from this wicked fairy whose legs of leather and steel could make the floor shudder like the earth beneath Jack the Giant Killer.

"Do you have any toys?" Kathryn moved one hand over the other and tried to push herself toward the back of the desk chair in order to get closer. She couldn't.

I slumped back on the couch and looked down at my pajamas. They had blue stripes. I remembered that a strange lady, dressed in white, had helped me with the buttons the night before when I was in my own house in East Orange. She had kissed me even though I did not know her, and had smiled as I climbed up and into the crib. There were two cribs in my house, the other belonged to my brother. The room next to ours was empty. Some day it would be mine my mother had told me, but now it was used for visitors, like my grandmother, or Lizzie Manning, my mother's devoted friend from school days or, like last night, by the lady in white who came to help my mother take care of my father. A small bed that was supposed to be mine was in the room with my parents. My mother slept on it near the window, close enough to hear my father, but far enough so that she would not get sick too. "When he gets better, things will change."

"Well," Kathryn screeched, "do you? Do you have any toys?" Her voice was a slung arrow.

I was surprised to hear my voice, surprised too that I recognized it. My shouting was part of this new world. "Yes. I have toys. They are in a box in my room. My brother has some too. They are in another box."

"But you haven't got them with you."

I began to cry. "Where am I? Where is this?"

"Shut up!"

Terrified, but now the fear was that I would lose what was mine. I threw my feet over the side of the couch and stood up. "My favorite toy is not in the box."

"Where is it?"

Caught between pleading and defending, I opened my arms in her direction, but my fists were clenched. "It's in my attic where I live, where I play with my daddy. It's a blackboard. I have lots of chalk, all colors of chalk." I fell back to the couch and began to sob.

"A blackboard! That's for school. I have a big ball. But I need you to throw it to me. I need you to get it when I throw it too far."

My aunt was at the door. She sat on the couch and held me, but only for a moment. She reached across and touched her daughter gently. She turned my face toward her. "Don't you remember me?"

I did, but only as someone who came to see my father for brief visits, standing at the door, afraid to get close.

"She's a crybaby," Kathryn said. "And she likes to play with a blackboard. She even thinks it's a toy."

In the afternoons, Kathryn, after rubdowns and exercises, during which she screamed and scratched, would be dressed in Lord and Taylor children's clothes and brought downstairs to her wheelchair. She was pretty with shining light brown hair and blue eyes. Her shoulders were strong and broad. They defied her legs much as the fierce blue of her eyes defied a world that tried to cripple her.

She was not the good fairy. And the teddy bear remained on the hook. I wondered if my kiss would work, but I was too little to reach. I climbed on the desk and tried when no one was looking. I stretched and stretched but could not reach my brother. He did not look back. He did not know me any more.

During the last days of March, in the afternoons when the sun was on the enclosed downstairs front porch, Kathryn and I played there. Her favorite toy was the challenge of a blue and white beach ball. From behind her wheelchair, I stretched as high as I could to pull back the handles of her chair as she leaned forward as far as she could to bounce the ball with a skill I envied. Once she came so close to toppling over that I screamed. Aunt Lily came rushing out to see me struggling to hold the chair back while Kathryn's strong hands gripped the wheels so she could propel herself in my direction.

"Why did you let her do that?" Aunt Lily pushed Kathryn back and grabbed the chair from me.

"I didn't," I whispered. "Kathryn wanted to bounce the ball all by herself."

"Eileen wanted to see if I could do as many bounces as she could," my cousin lied.

"Play with something else," Aunt Lily ordered.

When she left, Kathryn thrust her hand down my back and drew her nails deep and hard into my flesh. Simultaneously, her other hand covered my mouth. "Tell and I'll do it again."

After my bath that evening, Aunt Lily applied a stinging liquid to my back. She told me that Kathryn had been very sick and in the hospital for a long time, but she asked me no questions about the long scratch on my back.

The next afternoon Kathryn taught me how to play Parcheesi. The day was cloudy. We were at the dining room table which had been stripped of its engraved silver bowl, matching candlesticks and elaborately embroidered runner. Now the wide grained and earthy colored wood held neat stacks of drawing paper, coloring books, crayons, and the open Parcheesi board. I liked the table better when it was not set for the evening meal. At night it made me sad. I remembered a table so like it with my own mother and father. So long ago. "Is my daddy better?" I asked once. No one said anything, not even Kathryn. At last my uncle said, "We hope so," and I did not ask again.

Suddenly Kathryn swept the chips to the center of the table and closed the board.

"Do you know how to dance?" she asked.

I shook my head.

"Then I'll show you." She pushed her chair closer to the table and placed both arms on the table. "Move over." I got up and moved my chair to the left and sat down again, glad of the space.

Kathryn flexed her powerful fingers. She held up her right hand and stuck out her index and middle fingers. "This is the boy," she explained. She did the same thing with her left hand, extending the corresponding fingers. "And this is the girl."

I became fascinated. She sensed my interest and was pleased. "We should have music." She began to hum. Then with great dexterity, she wove the four fingers in and out, touching and withdrawing, twisting and swaying. I put my arms on the table and tried to imitate, then afraid, withdrew. "Go ahead," she said in an even voice. I was no match for her dexterity and strength. My fingers got tangled and my thumbs kept wanting to break in. We both laughed. It was the only time we had laughed together since my arrival a few days before to stare at the teddy bear who was my brother under a spell.

After a while she began to move her torso in rhythm with the dancing fingers. She removed her arm from the table and rolled herself away to the large open space that marked the division between the dining room and living room. There, with the wide and clear space of the vast front room in front of her, she worked the wheels of the chair in three quick circles, then she reversed and turned the chair the other way.

I watched in admiration as my cousin, beginning to breathe heavily, continued to shake her torso in rhythm with the revolving chair.

When she stopped, I thought the performance was over. "You can dance very good," I said, but she was not finished.

"Come on, put your feet next to mine."

I looked down at her useless, tiny, make-believe feet that had not grown with her. She had carefully placed those feet on the footrest by reaching down and lifting each leg with her two hands, manually moving the patent leather covered stumps far enough apart for me to stand. "I'm afraid I'll make you fall over, like yesterday."

"No you won't. I'll lean back. I am much bigger than you."

I held on to the arms of the wheelchair and placed my feet between hers. Her legs and feet were weightless. I was in the middle of nothing, only images.

Kathryn started to hum again and roll the chair. Our bodies began a ritual of pendulum like swaying, until flushed and gasping we stopped.

Aunt Lily was at the far side of the dining room. But she was smiling.

"Kathryn can dance with her fingers," I said.

She came over to us. Gently, she stroked our heads. "You are both getting too tired." She stretched her arms and drew us toward her. She looked happy. I smiled up at her. I was happy too.

Kathryn pulled her chair back, bent slightly forward and looked at my legs. Anger darkened her eyes. Her voice was thick, not like a child's voice at all. She turned her head and looked directly at her mother. "But Eileen has feet."

I stood still, and looked down. I did not know how to hide my feet.

A week later, on April 2, 1921, in the early afternoon, I was on the floor beneath the triple windows that opened onto the downstairs porch. Although the porch faced west and had the afternoon sun, today my cousin and I were not allowed to play out there. The shades of the porch had been lowered to the sill.

Inside, the dark green velvet drapes were drawn across the triple window above where I sat on a rug. I was protected from an attack by Kathryn's wheelchair by two upholstered chairs separated by a table with a fringed lamp. Aunt Lily had put on the lamp so that I could see my coloring book and drawing pad.

I was wearing my black everyday shoes that laced to above

my ankles. My dress was a deep blue with a smocked yoke beneath a white Bertha collar. My mother's friend from school days, Lizzie Manning, often came to visit during my father's illness. While she talked to my mother, or quietly talked near my father's bedside, she would work diligently with brightly colored yarns, smocking and embroidering the yokes of dresses she had made for me. The dresses were all the same, but the colors and themes between collar and yoke were different, crisscrosses, leaves, fruits, flowers and birds.

From the kitchen I heard Aunt Lily and Kathryn talking in low voices, but I knew Kathryn would come soon. I spread out my coloring book on the floor.

I was using a red crayon to draw cherries onto a stark black-and-white tree stenciled in the book. The trunk of the tree I had already colored with a brown crayon, but now, instead of leaves, I wanted to make cherries like the tree in my backyard at home. Gripping the crayon, I was in the picture, underneath the tree. Daddy was shaking a branch. I saw myself reaching, and laughing and stretching.

I heard the branch move and saw it quiver.

It wasn't the branch. Kathryn's wheelchair had bumped against the upholstered chair, that wall of my safe place. The motion had moved my arm.

"Your daddy is dead."

I looked down at my cherry tree. I saw the crayoned cherries, but I could not see daddy or the branch, only the partially colored outline of the stenciled tree.

The wheels backed up. Kathryn solemnly rolled her chair to the center of the room. I heard hurried steps across the dining room. "Kathryn!" My aunt stopped by her daughter's chair. Both were staring at me.

I was alone. Safe. *Dead.* I had never heard the word before. What was it? What did it have to do with my daddy?

I didn't know what I was supposed to do. I wanted to go home. I wanted my father. I wanted my mother. I needed my attic and my blackboard. And I wanted my brother. Dead must have something to do with the knowledge that that was not my brother hanging from the ceiling, turned into a teddy bear. But dead did have something to do with the kiss of a prince, or of Jesus.

The kiss of my father. Why was I here?

Aunt Lily lifted me from the floor and fell into the chair, crying as she held me to her. Kathryn reached across. She touched me. Dry-eyed, I repeated the word to myself.

"What is dead?"

"He is in heaven," Kathryn said.

"Yes," Aunt Lily's voice was very low. Then stronger, she said, "God loves your daddy so much he wants him to come for a visit."

"Oh," I said. Now I understood. "*I* am visiting. I don't live here. Daddy is visiting God."

I smiled. To myself I thought, *He knows he doesn't live there either. He will come home.*

Aunt Lily said she would make some cocoa. Kathryn went with her. Back in my safe place, I closed the coloring book and opened the drawing pad. I drew a big oblong frame, found a black crayon and filled it in. Alongside it, I made streaks of varied lengths using every color crayon in the box. Like my chalk, it lit up the pad, but I couldn't make the crayons show on the black the way my chalk showed on my blackboard. I tried to draw a couch, but it was just a thick blue line, so I colored a little square and put it next to the thick blue line. I used purple, the color of my father's bathrobe.

A few days later my mother came.

She stood on the winding carpeted staircase on a step just below the landing with the stained glass window. I was looking up at her. I do not remember her entrance, nor the earlier part of the day. Nothing, only her appearance on the staircase. She peered over the banister. Holding on. Very still. The mother I remembered was constantly in motion. Stairs were for climbing, for reaching the man in bed who was my father. Stairs were for mounting. Stairs were for finding an attic with a couch by French doors and a balcony. A couch I couldn't draw.

Stairs are magic. They connect. They get close to the sky. Stairs are filled with story.

But this woman on the stairs was like a slow moving cloud. She had only the suggestion of a face. And this stair-case led to Kathryn's room and the porch with the terrifying leather and steel pretend legs. This staircase led to a teddy bear hanging from the ceiling.

She did not speak as she stood there. My aunt's hands were on my shoulders caressing them with tense, even strokes. The woman had a long black veil. A full black skirt swept over black shoes and wafted over the steps. A ship was departing and a gangplank was being pulled up. Soon the whole staircase would float off with the veiled woman lean-ing there, not even waving.

Sometimes I wonder if that veil ever lifted for me.

Dead was a word I did not know then, but the sound of it, with its short guttural beginning and end, was what I was looking at then.

Dead was a woman veiled in black leaning on the railing of a receding ship, and when her daughter said timidly, "I want to go home," she had called faintly from the distance, "Soon, it will be soon."

Soon. It hummed a droning tune through my body and eventually was still, like the East Orange mosquitoes, but there was no pungent citronella, no loving rub. There was no sting either, and no itch. I stopped waiting and asked no questions. I did not want to hear any more words that had sounds I did not know.

Summer came. Aunt Elizabeth and Aunt Josie, two of my mother's sisters who lived in Bay Ridge, came to see me. Aunt Elizabeth was very tiny with beautiful brown hair piled high on her head. Her wide brown eyes looked deeply into mine. She held my gaze. What she saw made her weep. Taking my cheeks firmly in her hands, she spoke in a strong deep voice, "Your mother is getting everything ready for you and your brother. It takes time, but she will be coming. I want you to understand. You must understand. It will be soon."

I nodded. I wanted to please her, but *soon*, like *dead*, had no meaning.

Aunt Lily and Uncle Bill took me with Kathryn to Sea Gate. When I broke loose and ran into the waves, my uncle after me, I felt excited and happy. I belonged there. I thought I had been there before. Didn't I know the rush of the water? Didn't I remember a gentle rocking. It didn't matter where. It was mine.

In mid-July Aunt Lily sat me on her lap. "Tomorrow, *tomorrow*," she said, "Uncle Charlie is driving your mother and little Frank over here. They are coming to take you home."

We were on the front porch. The white wicker furniture was full of summer, its dark green pillows now covered in bright cretonne. We were waiting for my mother and my creeping, walking, climbing, squawking little brother, and, I secretly thought, maybe for my father, if he had finished his visit with God.

Kathryn's wheelchair was in front of the screen door between Aunt Lily and me.

"Is it almost time?" I asked.

"Any minute," my aunt said.

"When Uncle Charlie drives up, I'll let you go past me and down to see your mother first," Kathryn offered.

I heard an old sound, a sound that was part of a world before Kathryn, before a teddy bear dressed in red, even before the attic and blackboard, before a father who was in bed all the time. It was before *dead*.

And now here it was. A chug. A movement I could not see but knew it was there.

I pushed past Kathryn, taking her by surprise, shoved the door and was down the steps just in time to see the Ford with the big wheels and the black sides, black as my blackboard, the Ford my father once drove. It had turned the corner and was almost at the house. It stopped right in front of me. For a moment I almost hoped, but in an instant Uncle Charlie was out of the car.

He knelt. He kissed me. He held my face and drew his finger across my eyebrows and eyelids, just as my grandmother always did. I didn't know it then, but both were touching my father. Later, during lonely years of childhood, I would look into a mirror and sink into the reflection. My own eyes, loved because they belonged to somebody else, became another cut into the *me* in me, choking the struggling *I*. My own eyes were an annihilation and a revelation on the long journey to discovery.

Uncle Charlie removed his eyeglasses and wiped them on the collar of my dress. From the open doorway, Aunt Lily frowned and Kathryn laughed.

With a broad grin and great flourish, my uncle reached into the Ford and lifted my brother from my mother's lap. Frank held on to his uncle before turning shyly to me.

"Remember your sister?" our uncle asked.

My brother was now facing me. I tried to hug him. He reached for my big, dark blue hair ribbon, just the way he used to. With a touch of envy I stared at the white braid bordering the collar of his cotton sailor suit. While we were apart, he had had his third birthday.

He held up three fingers. "Me *free*," he said. We all laughed, even my mother still hidden in the car, her face still lost behind the black veil, but as I looked, she raised her hand and lifted back the heavy black lace. The darkness framing her blue eyes was deeper than ever. My mother's eyes took on many shades. All the shades, though, were blue, from sun on a lake to coming dusk in an October sky. On this day a pallor covered her face, except for the eyes, like a mask. First the veil, then the mask. Where was she?

I felt strong hands under my armpits as Uncle Charlie helped me up and into my mother's arms. Her arms grew tighter and tighter around me. She held my body without speaking. I held my fear without speaking. Where was he?

"Uncle Charlie, come up here." It was Kathryn. Our uncle left us and hurried up to her.

While Uncle Charlie talked to Kathryn, Aunt Lily came down to the car and gave me a package. My clothes were already piled on the back seat, along with a suitcase filled with Frank's clothes and new toys. "Don't open this until you are on your way," she said. I lifted my face to kiss her. Without Kathryn studying us, her embrace was different.

Most of the packages now got transferred to the front seat so that my mother could sit with her son and daughter in the back. After we turned the corner, I opened the paper bag. My mother helped me. Our hands were once again together at the same task. I remembered the trays we used to fix for daddy.

Frank gave a delighted gasp and tried to grab the teddy bear with the red pants and sweater. I held it to me. Frank screamed.

"It belongs to your sister, Frank," Uncle Charlie called from the front seat. "You have one, a bigger one, packed in with your other toys. Maybe we can find a sweater for him."

"You can hold it for a minute," I said, but as he took it, I held firmly on to his hand. "I used to think it was you."

Anxious for an opening to keep us talking, Uncle Charlie said, "You thought the teddy bear was Frank?"

My memory of that first morning was as dark as my mother's veil. "I thought Kathryn was the bad fairy who turned my brother into a teddy bear to hang from the ceiling. And I couldn't reach him."

Uncle Charlie laughed, a big real one this time, and even my mother smiled. Frank handed me a small metal replica of the Ford. He had been clutching it ever since they arrived. I didn't want the car, but I relaxed as Frank imitated me and hugged the teddy bear. Slowly, I moved the wheels of the toy as I let it roll up and down my legs, then up Frank's legs and on to the docile bear. Frank took the car and I took back my teddy.

My brother was here, a real little boy. The teddy was

here, now, at last, a warm stuffed little animal who soothed my memories. "I can't wait to see our cherry tree," I said.

No one spoke.

After a while, my mother said, "We are not going to East Orange. We are going to live someplace else now."

Frank moved his car across his mother's breast, then up her cheek. She smiled at him.

I curled up in the corner, clutching Teddy. "Where are we going?"

Uncle Charlie said nothing.

My mother spoke. In a more intimate voice this time. "You remember Aunt Maggie. You used to talk to her on the telephone."

In East Orange we had the telephone between the big bedroom where my father was and the door that opened to the attic stairs. Often I was asked to talk to her. She was funny and had a big voice. Aunt Maggie always asked me questions about what I did and what I played with. I liked her but could not remember ever having seen her.

"We are going to live in part of the upstairs of her house."

Dead, the unknown word was back. "Will daddy know where we are?"

Uncle Charlie's voice was low and husky. "Eileen, your father will always know where you are."

I twisted myself into a ball and hid my face in the corner of the seat sobbing into Teddy's bright red sweater. "Stop, Eileen. For God's sake, stop." Her voice had icicles, a new voice. Then softer, "We are going to be very happy there."

Lies. All lies.

The front of the second floor as well as the attic were sleeping quarters for Aunt Maggie's large family, two of whom were now married, making it possible to close off the back of the second floor to rent to us. The Canarsie section of Brooklyn was an older and less affluent community than Bay Ridge, but by moving back to Brooklyn, my exhausted mother was reasonably close to four of her six sisters.

The house had originally been built for two families, so there was a large kitchen and a bathroom in our quarters. In addition, there were two bedrooms, one barely large enough to hold Frank's crib, two trunks and a chest of drawers. The other bedroom held everything else.

Aunt Maggie took Frank and me upstairs, chatting all the way. Her voice always had laughter hiding in it. As she helped us mount the steps, I remembered our long ago conversations, and wished that I were back there, near the attic door, near my father, and telling her from a long distance what I had drawn on my blackboard.

When we went into the crowded room, the first thing I saw was our oval china closet. It was placed between the two windows. In it were our best dishes with the roses around the borders. The oversized platter formed a backdrop on the lower shelf. On the top shelf were the stemware and the cut glass ice cream dishes with their own matching platter. My father often held that platter up to the sunlight so that I could see the dancing colors. He told me they were happy angels who danced in their best robes because they liked to see families having meals together. So long ago it was when we sat around the oak table covered with the Irish linen cloth, the best dishes and candles in silver candlesticks. Even though I had to sit on a volume of the French Revolution and a dictionary, I remembered it as so much more filled with magic than my aunt's splendid dining room with the silver bowl of fresh flowers.

I looked around. "Where is our table?"

Frank had disappeared. Aunt Maggie went into the kitchen to get him. Holding him on her lap, she sat on the bed and drew me to her. Our big brass bed took up most of the room.

Nothing was where it was supposed to be. Across the room, crowded in the corner was a remnant of our former parlor, the mahogany set with the green velvet cushions. The rocking chair was not with it. Next to that was the tall chest that was supposed to be in the bedroom. But on top of the chest was the Tiffany lamp. That was supposed to be in the middle of the dining room table when it was not set for eating.

"Where's *my* table? My chairs!" *Our* had gone with the angels in their best robes. No one here knew their language. I was going to have to find everything myself. I was going to have to find a way to all my treasures, then find a place to hide them.

Aunt Maggie was speaking. "Your table and chairs are in our cellar, little one, all covered up for the time being. Some day you will move to a bigger place and there will be room for all that you do not see now."

Uncle Charlie and my mother came up with the packages from the car. I had already tucked Teddy underneath a pillow on the brass bed. Frank ran to his uncle who lifted him up and held him.

I watched as Uncle Charlie turned his back to us. His head bent over my brother as he kissed him again and again. He turned to my mother.

"Charlie." She spoke softly. "Charlie, I have just lost my husband. I am not going to part with my son."

My uncle put Frank down. He disentangled Frank's grip on his legs and left without speaking again. Frank tried to follow. Aunt Maggie was too quick for him. She lifted him up, kicking and crying, and handed him to my mother.

"Aggie," Aunt Maggie said, "you look exhausted. When you calm him down, put him in his crib for a while so that you can take a nap. I'll take Eileen downstairs and keep her for the rest of the day."

She took my hand. I looked again around the room where everything was in the wrong place. "Mother, where is my blackboard? Where is my chalk?" I broke free from Aunt Maggie. "Where?"

I buried my head in Aunt Maggie's skirt. She smelled real. She smelled safe and strong.

"It was too big, Eileen. We could not take it."

The familiar faces and furniture now froze, huge and threatening. I, too, froze into a formless iceberg till the wound became a stick of dynamite to scatter and tumble me downstairs to the front door in time to see Uncle Charlie drive away in my father's car. He turned his head, hesitated, then waved good-bye.

Last Christmas Frank had broken my favorite Christmas tree ornament, the round red ball with the gilded gold and green cords entwining white angels who danced around fir trees laden with snow. Uncle Charlie, married but childless, had come to East Orange carrying the tree and mysterious packages. My mother put all the packages in the hall closet, while Uncle Charlie set up the tree in a corner between the windows.

From his bed upstairs, my father, his voice amazingly strong, was calling instructions on where to put each familiar ornament. "I want to see it the way I smell the pine."

From one of the boxes, Frank took the precious ornament. He held it gently, but tried to trace the cords with his fingers.

Now I am back there watching the splendor of the glittering sphere tear apart. All around me are sparkling remnants of color. Each remnant glitters with splintered jewels. Each remnant is a well-aimed sword. Each remnant is as sharp as Excalibur.

Out of the Depths

Martha was eighteen. She and her name *Martha* were not best friends, and if asked – as if anyone would ask such a thing – but if asked, Martha would say that she didn't really dislike her name *Martha*, she just didn't know her. And one's name, Martha often pondered, ought to be alive deep inside you, breathing your breath and so intimately your other self that, like a loyal friend, it would rise to the surface whenever you needed to be strong. And Martha needed to be strong. Gumption, her mother called it. She needed more gumption to get along in this world.

And Martha is such a gray name, Martha's reverie con-cluded on this very gray and cold November day in 1934 as she removed the white woolen glove from her right hand so that she could check the contents of the deep flapped pocket of her heavy red coat. Martha loved red. Her mother had accompanied her to Kleins last Saturday to buy the coat.

Martha's cold fingers felt for the nickel subway fare. It was ready, huddled behind the lint collected in the lining. Almost unconsciously, she crunched her shoulders, letting her head sink deeper into the raised shawl collar of the coat like a turtle determined not to see the enemy. But that was there, too, away from the coin, lurking in the seam, so narrow that Martha did not feel it until she pricked her finger on the needle-fine point of the long black hatpin with the rhinestone tip. She put her wounded fingertip into her mouth, then withdrew it quickly as though sucking venom.

She was nearing Fourth Avenue in Bay Ridge, just a short block from the 77th Street Station of the Fourth Avenue Local. Once again, the whole unpleasant scene of last night rolled like a Pathe Newsreel through her mind and she was at the dining room table drinking tea with her mother and cousin Betty who had dropped by to see how she,

Martha, liked her new job, the first permanent job she had had since graduating from high school over a year ago.

"I hate it." Martha's voice, low and husky, fought its way up through a waterfall of anger, shame and depression to face a cousin, six years her senior, who was tall, confident and beautiful – all she could never be. She heard her voice shatter in unison with the teacup held between her trembling fingers.

There was a shocked silence. Betty understood her troubled young cousin, realizing too late that she should have talked to her alone. She looked across at her aunt who looked stunned, registering both concern and guilt.

At last, Betty said softly, "You need not be there forever, Martha."

"But it's not such a bad job," Martha's mother said placing both of her arms on the table defensively. "She doesn't have to work Saturdays, and she gets off every day at 4:30. Ahead of the rush hour."

"I don't beat the rush in the morning, though," Martha said. Her voice, still husky, had an edge to it.

Betty caught the wedge in the tight emotional curtain surrounding Martha. There was no way out now. She must pursue the subject. "What else is there about it, Martha?"

Martha's words were forks from a burning building. "It doesn't happen every morning, but it does happen a lot. You get squashed in so that you can't move and some man, most of the time you can't even see who…."

"I know," Betty said.

"Know what?" Martha's mother's eyes were large with fright.

Betty put a compassionate hand on Martha's arm. "A man takes advantage of the impossibility of moving and plays his hands all over the nearest girl's body, especially if the girl looks young and afraid and too embarrassed to scream."

Martha nodded as her mother stared at her. "This has been happening to *you*?" she asked her daughter.

"It's even worse in the summer," Martha said. "In winter

my coat helps and there are little tricks like holding your purse down low."

She drained her cup and was about to get up, when Betty said, "There is one more defense. I used it once, but it takes courage."

"What?"

"The hatpin." And Betty described its use.

"But the man might scream and everybody would know!" Martha cringed.

"That is just it!" Betty responded.

And that is when her mother said that she must have the gumption to protect herself and had gone into the bedroom and returned with the black hatpin with the rhinestone tip.

Martha's anger no longer flamed outward; it had become a dark cinder, swallowed alive, to sink deep, deep into the depths to challenge a gray name.

She had turned the corner and was approaching the subway steps where she could see the top lines of straphangers, five or six abreast, sinking inch by inch like a doomed army down into the first layer of the tunnel. As was her custom, Martha paused at the corner and turned her head west to feel and smell the New York Bay some four blocks away. She took a deep gulp. Its tangy familiarity was a caress.

Then, seeing her chance, she ran to the top of the steps and held the railing with her right hand, looking upward to demand one more look at the sky. She noticed other people doing the same thing. For the first few steps they were still people, Bay Ridgeites. After that, their eyes squinted, their elbows shot left and right, and the men folded their newspapers and snapped them smartly under their arms in order to free their hands.

Hands. Again, Martha envisioned the tiny weapon strutting its rhinestone as though it were Excalibur, intimidating the lowly nickel. Then she joined the silent and sullen strangers with the vaguely familiar faces, as one by one they dropped their coins into the turnstile and strove to stay upright for the final descent into the depths of the station, that place of constant roar and accepted civilized violence.

When the Fourth Avenue Local pulled into the 59th Street Station, Martha tightened her body and joined the mob molding itself at the doors. Grimly the unit sucked in a single breath and waited to be sprung like a poorly molted cannon ball into the savage mouth of the Sea Beach Express, which was already coming to a halt across the platform, belching with its overload of undigested workers.

As the momentum carried her off the local, Martha caught a glimpse of two of her former high school classmates making a grab for two of the vacated seats. She knew they were students at Brooklyn College and would not have to change to the Express. Their laps and arms were filled with textbooks and notebooks. An explosion of pain stung her eyes, but she did not have time for it to sink any further.

It began almost immediately. First the hand at the back of her coat. She wriggled slightly to the right. The woman next to her moved a little and for a moment she seemed to be free, but at Pacific Street, the doors cracked like the leak in the dike and another wave of uprooted human debris roared in. The woman who had cleared a little space was unwillingly carried toward the spot where the side seats meet the first row of aisle seats, and there she moored, knees forcefully buckling against the ungiving curve of the seat. Her arms flailed wildly with nothing but air to cling to.

Martha's tormentor, too, had moved, closer. She felt two hands kneading through her thick coat, feeling their way to the firmer barrier of her hip bones. The fingers were light but strong like an aroused jellyfish. Slowly, they were working toward her center.

She began to sweat. When she dared to look up he was almost directly beside her. He was stonefaced and middle-aged and had a lost, lonely look, so that for one awful moment she had a sense of identification. His coat was open. The train lurched giving him a little more room. He removed one hand from her and skillfully began to undo his trousers.

All she remembered of the next few seconds was that she was breathing in short rhythmic gasps with an energy she had never before experienced. The hatpin with the shining head was out of her pocket, while her heretofore helpless right arm was moving and aiming the hatpin directly at his left hand in the fleshy part below his thumb.

As she dreaded, he screamed. "Bitch!"

The woman with the buckled knees and flailing arms turned her head and screamed back, "You've had your hands all over that girl since we left Bay Ridge Avenue."

Martha was still holding the pin, both ends of which were now decorated, one with a rhinestone that had suddenly lost its glitter, and the other with a tiny drop of dark blood. Stunned, nauseous and strangely excited, Martha was St. George lifting the magnificent weapon from the flesh of the dragon.

The mob, who just minutes before had been sullen and bored loners, became united workers storming the Bastille. All of a sudden there was space for everybody to move. Two young men who had been hidden behind copies of *The Daily News* now held her tormentor in a tight grip.

"You filthy bastard," one of the long-lost heroes said.

"You're getting off this train," the other shouted, tightening his grip. The train was now in the open, crossing the Brooklyn Bridge, with its renewed hope of sun, sky and water. "Almost time for your exit," one of the young men shouted.

From an aisle seat, a woman's voice, "Make him close his fly first."

One of the men did it for him, then resumed his grip on the prisoner's arm.

Martha still held the hatpin. She wanted it to disappear, but to drop it on the floor would be an act of public shame. Agonizingly, she flexed her fingers and returned the weapon to her pocket, wondering if she would ever wear the red coat again.

Two people got up simultaneously and with tenderness and respect guided her to a seat. A seat was also given to the woman with the buckling knees. Martha met her gaze across the excited crowd. For the second time within a few minutes she felt an identity with another person. Her body was on fire. Embarrassment? Rage? Shame? All of these, but over them all there was an exultation. She looked around. Some people were laughing, all the way from a giggle to that dangerous tone that signifies unified action.

They were deep in the tunnel again and pulling into Canal Street. The prisoner was still pinned against the door.

When the doors opened at Canal Street, the captive was lifted by willing hands, swung for a moment to gain momentum, then tossed like an emptied trash can onto the narrow platform. Neither questioning nor shocked, the incoming crowd simply broke ranks.

The condemned man, silent and resigned, had a clear passage. As the train pulled out with its cheering prosecutors, Martha had a glimpse of the man pulling himself up and leaning against the wall. She closed her eyes, terrified that their eyes would meet and, once again, she would lose herself in his loneliness.

That evening, Martha told her mother she was going to the library. Except for a simple, "Are you all right?", she had not been questioned, neither about the hatpin nor further incidents.

The night air was bitter and a fine snow beat against Martha's face. She walked down Ridge Boulevard to 69th Street and west for the short walk to the Bay and the Ferry Slip. For a moment she thought she would take a ride across and back, but instead she walked behind the toll booth and down to the edge of the water. A ferry had just pulled out and its wash gurgled against the rocks. She listened and waited. It took a while, but at last it came, the calm she had always received from this body of water that was neither ocean nor river, but much of both. She held the sounds, the smell of salt and the peace. She held them like treasures she was about to lose.

There was just enough light to spot the rock she needed. It was a few feet from the shore, but its ledge was fairly smooth and slanted toward, rather than away from, the incoming tide. Its crevices were not deep. Anything placed in one of them would be washed away. She removed her loafers and put them on a rock well away from the water. Then she crouched to place her hands on the highest rock to balance herself. The shock of the icy water and the pain of the splintered stones cutting through her stockings made her cry out. She heard her voice roll and then return over the dark water.

Gasping, she knelt with one knee on the chosen rock. She reached into her pocket and took out her mother's hatpin with the rhinestone tip. She waited for the right moment, then placed the weapon in one of the crevices. Her feet were numbed beyond feeling, but Martha believed as she had never believed before that they would take her where she had to go.

Back on dry ground, she sat on the rock and rubbed her feet with her gloves. She watched until one vigorous wave of bubbling water covered the selected stone. She thought she saw the tip of the pin shine momentarily like a dying star. Then, as newly baptized, the mock sword and the stranger's blood were washed away and carried by the tide to a new existence.

Afterword

You ask me how I feel about myself, now, as an artist. I am uncomfortable when I hear myself so labeled. It's like voices coming out of the woodwork to challenge that label, *artist,* a kind of "Who do you think you are?" Your question, I suppose, touches on my sense of loss for what might have been. Yet I now believe that I am an artist. Stating that boldly is in itself great progress for me.

In high school years and in my early twenties I was told that I had promise as a writer, and I did write. But the absence of privacy haunted my early life. After my father's death, we made one move after the other. I never felt settled, always looking for the stable life I thought I had until I was five years old. I was in my mid-twenties before I even had my own bed. I slept with my mother. Any space that I could claim became an obsession – a drawer in a chest, a shelf in a bookcase, a hidden place behind boxes in a closet, even the top of a tree in a vacant lot.

After high school came years of responsibilities. And the responsibilities were not of the positive kind, such as raising a family or working on a career. The responsibility was for a parent who went from financial dependency to an illness without hope of recovery. But as I said, I did write, at least some, and when I did not, I longed for it. And it was in the actual writing, that stretching of imagination, memory and thrill of words that I was freeing myself, at least internally, from total stagnation, perhaps serious emotional illness.

I was forty-seven when my mother died. I think it was only then that I had the time to realize that most of my life had not been mine at all. Then I experienced anger and all its accompanying guilt, so that when I tried to write I had severe anxiety attacks. I feared it was too late. However, the power I had always experienced in words was still there. More than words, it was a deep spiritual and psychological need to create. I had, and knew I had always had, a dependency on images, images fed by memories, imagination, a need for adventure, a need for access to another world, but a world not separate from this one.

To be able to see my life as a whole has been a very long journey. What I once viewed as a fragmented life, filled with interruptions of what I was intended to be, I now see as the unveiling of layers of my own being so that I could become – I am still very much becoming – my true self, a self that is both writer and human being. Such energy, I believe, is divine. It is God. In Scripture, the noun *fragments* is frequently coupled with the verb *to gather.* Fragmented people gathered into a community, fragments of seed gathered by the needy, fragments of "loaves and fishes" gathered for unending distribution. My life's fragmentations made my life whole, made it one. Often it takes jolts terrible enough to make you scream for help to awaken the presence of that enormous gift. But that is ahead of my story.

* * *

My first five years of which I write in the memoir *Bog Oak* laid the foundation for my life. My father died when I was five. When his death was imminent, my brother and I were removed from our suburban home, separated, and sent to stay with different relatives. We never returned to that house. My mother sold it, got rid of much of the furniture, and moved back to Brooklyn so that she could be close to most of her sisters. We moved to the second floor of Aunt Maggie's house. We had a kitchen, bathroom and one other room into which almost everything was jammed. I do not know how a modern psychiatrist would describe what happened to me but, though I was less than six years old, I believe I was in emotional shock and denial.

That winter, less than a year after my father's death, my exhausted mother came close to death from pneumonia. Once again my brother and I were taken away from home, but this time not separated. I overheard two of my aunts speaking about what would become of the two of us. My brother, they said, would go to an uncle who was childless and wanted to adopt him. I would go to an aunt so that I could be a companion to my crippled cousin. Try as I may, I cannot recall any emotion when I heard this conversation. I'd come to expect nothing. My mother recovered, however, and our lives went on, not joyously, but I did develop. Imagination, though dangerous at times, was my avenue of escape and growth.

The September following my father's death and a few months before my mother's near fatal illness, I started school. It was a crowded, no-nonsense classroom. Our reader was about a boy called Dickie Dare. I was called upon to stand up and read. The text, which I could read perfectly, said "Dickie Dare went to school and on the way he met a cow. Moo, said the cow. Good morning, said Dickie Dare." I saw myself taking this amazing creature to the park and playing hide-and-go-seek with her among the trees. I read out loud what my imagination saw. I did not even see my classmates. I was in a much more interesting world. The teacher shrieked out a loud and shaking *zero*! In shock I saw where I was. The children were staring, held by the story, my first audience. Miss Strang, however, the first grade teacher, was frightened.

After the Dickie Dare incident I did not return to school. Aunt Maggie and her youngest daughter developed my reading skills with flash cards, encouragement and love. She told me that as soon as I could read everything with ease, I would be able to leap from one world to another like a happy rabbit. She did not read stories to me but told me many. I do not recall them, but I suspect they were tales she had heard from my grandfather who had been a "hedge teacher" in Ireland, one committed to keeping the legends, history and culture of his people alive in spite of brutal occupation.

Shortly after my mother's near fatal illness, we moved

again, to the Bay Ridge section where both my brother and I had been born and where my maternal grandparents had bought a home after "making it" in this country. Aunt Lizzie's family had just bought a house on a wide and spacious street one block away from the Bay. All the rooms were large and filled with the sounds and smells of the New York Bay that I remembered from my first three years. Aunt Lizzie was tiny with great dark eyes. Frail, but filled with an inner strength, she was something of a psychic. Family stories told of her waking her husband in the night to accompany her to a Mrs. So-and-so who had just fallen out of her window! Or Mrs. So-and-so who was alone and had just gone into labor. Always, she was right. Often, she would study the palms of my hands, then place my hands on her cheeks and kiss them.

When we were alone, Aunt Lizzie would talk to me about my father, a subject I could never discuss with my mother. It was she who sensed that I still watched for him to come home, that he had only gone to the mountains to get well and would surprise us. She told me how he would talk to her about food, its serving, table appointments, and that when she visited us, before I.was born, they would cook together and let my mother rest.

A Victrola and some fine recordings had survived our moves. But one simply awful record, of World War I vintage, was included in the collection. It was the monologue of a dying American soldier calling for his mother. To me it was my father calling. I would sob and hide in the closet. My brother, a terrible tease, would play the record just to see my performance. One day, I screamed for my mother to make him take it off. She said he was only teasing and that I didn't have to listen to it. It was a cold day, but I ran down the stairs and out of the house before anyone, even Aunt Lizzie, could catch me. Taking charge, she sent my tall, tender-hearted cousin after me. He carried me back to the house. In the interim, as I found out, Aunt Lizzie had sped upstairs, removed the recording and smashed it over her knee with her small furious fists. Next, she turned my brother over her knee and whacked him just as loudly. I returned to hear her say, "Can't you see what that record is doing to her?" Downstairs, Aunt Lizzie rocked me, wept with me, crooned, and wept again, but did not speak. I remember her as a source of courage and healing.

Not long after the record smashing, Aunt Lizzie was diagnosed with tuberculosis. My mother was terrified that once again my brother and I had been exposed to the disease. Our bright and sunny rooms were now needed for Aunt Lizzie's care and for some isolation from her family. Once again we moved.

Aunt Josie was two years younger than my mother and recently widowed. She occupied the parlor floor and basement of one of her in-laws' two houses. We rented the third floor. The house was ugly and shabby. There were rats in the walls and I could hear them at night. The two younger cousins were our age and delighted that we had come there to live. I resented the fact that they considered that all three floors belonged to all of us. Again, I had the sense of not belonging, of never coming home.

In spite of my yearning for a place to be by myself, a place to weep for my father and be with him in memory and imagination, the interaction with my cousins worked to my psychological advantage and growth. On the first day of summer vacations, the four of us would go to the library in search of a play we could work on for the summer. We assigned roles, made costumes, rehearsed and turned Aunt Josie's second floor into a theater. We explored the Shore Road and the park, pretending each section was a different country, then ran to the library to find out about the lands we discovered. My brothers and cousins would become exasperated when I distinctly saw what was not there so that our discoveries could conform to the books. My love of adventure was my answer to loneliness.

High school and adolescence brought many changes. Our economic situation worsened. Since my father's death, we had lived on the money from the sale of the house in New Jersey and from what money and stocks he had left. Amazing that a man who died at 35 could provide at all for a family for almost a decade! My mother did not look for a job, feeling strongly that a mother belonged with her children. As we became poorer, Aunt Josie's condition improved. She was placed in a job, then moved to a nicer place. Again, we moved, too.

By now, I was 15. This time we rented the first floor of a pleasant house. It was the first time we did not share a home with relatives. My mother was waiting for us to graduate from high school and find jobs. Meanwhile, dignity must prevail, so rent was always paid, but frequently we did not have enough food. My brother worked in a grocery store and caddied on a golf course, but with adolescence, my self-worth and isolation increased. My cousins, much more outgoing, did what was normal for teenagers, found other friends. My social life was worsened by the fact that I never had any spending money. After school, when other girls were going for ice cream, I would pretend that I had promised to come right home. After a while, I was ignored.

I came to life in our English classes. Shelley and Keats, the Arthurian legends and Shakespeare transcended my complexes. When called upon, I found it impossible not to express my thoughts. Although this was an ordinary public school, some students were offered the opportunity in the junior year to substitute a term of studying and writing short stories instead of the usual curriculum. Once a month, we were tested to make sure that the standard courses were being kept up. Thus began my writing life. One English teacher wept when she found that there was no hope of my going to college.

After high school in the early thirties, we were in the middle of the Depression. I had a series of dull jobs, all of which I hated. There was really no one to advise me on how to get further education. I was not aggressive or enterprising, and I was not very strong. While working at an insurance company on 23rd Street in Manhattan, I enrolled at New York University for a noncredit writing course. I wrote a story about the death of my father. Millen Brand, a young novelist whose first novel, *The Outward Room*, had been on the bestseller list and turned into a Broadway play, was a guest lecturer and reader. In front of a room with about fifty students, he quickly summarized the students' work he had read, then announced that he had found one story that he wished he had written – and that was something he never thought he would find. The story was mine.

He organized a small group of ten people, all older than I, and all formally educated. We met once a week for about two years. My whole world centered then around writing stories and the Thursday evenings when we met. The group had dinner in a little Village restaurant and talked writer's talk before meeting in whatever space we could get in the area. Clustered at small tables in the restaurant were many poets and writers who later became famous. Some years later, I would see so many of those faces on television during the nightmare years of the McCarthy hearings. At NYU I had stumbled into a world I felt was mine.

Millen Brand's work was being handled by the Leland Heyward Agency, then on Fifth Avenue near 42nd Street. His personal agent was a woman whose last name was Pindyck. Millen gave her several of my stories. She sent for me and told me to read all of the magazines and to direct my stories toward such popular publications as *Cosmopolitan, Colliers,* etc. Meanwhile, she did send out some of my stories to *Atlantic, Harper's Bazaar,* and *Delineator* (long since gone). They did not sell but she sent me the responses which were very encouraging. One story sold to a new publication called *Home and Food,* circulated for a brief time in the more exclusive food markets of the upper East Side.

I was now approaching my mid-twenties. About this time my mother looked for and found a larger apartment, the second floor of a two story brownstone. At last I would have a room of my own. With my brother and me now working, she felt we could handle it. It was now 1942 and most of the world was at war. My intensified reading, my association with Millen Brand and the sophisticated men and women in the writing group had deepened my interest in the struggles of ordinary human beings for justice. The Civil War in Spain, for instance, found me on the other side of the fence from most of the people in the conservative area in which I lived, from relatives – with the surprising exception of my mother and brother – and also from my church. Also, I had begun to wonder about limitations of my womanhood. Why, since I had an attraction to the mystical side of our lives with one another and with God, and found that to be at the heart of my Catholicism, why was it impossible for me, if I were free to do so, to be a priest? Fortunately, for that day, it was a very understanding priest to whom I spoke about this. He said that I could be a nun, that women in that role had throughout history done much to change society and even the church. That was not unappealing to me then, but since I had home responsibilities, neither was possible.

To get back to my story. A few weeks before we were to move to our next home, my brother announced that he had been quietly married for several months and that his wife was pregnant. My mother decided that, given our financial situation, we should move anyhow – all of us. I did have my own room, a small hall bedroom with a bed, desk, typewriter and shelves for my books. The thought of a baby coming thrilled me. Before she was even born, I loved my brother's child more than I had ever loved anyone since my father.

Home life was difficult, however. In less than a year and a half, there were two babies and four adults in what was now a crowded and disorderly environment. My first niece, my namesake, was born on December 14, 1941, one week after the bombing of Pearl Harbor. Our writing group broke up, since Millen was now writing for the government. When my second niece was six months old, my brother was drafted. Life became strained. Our lives were filled with worry for my brother, and terrible tension at home. I became something of a buffer between my lonely and restless sister-in-law and my distraught mother. Writing became impossible. I could not produce and lost my connection with the literary agent.

On the bright side, jobs opened up. I left the insurance company and went to work at the National Broadcasting Company. It was a very exciting place then and I loved passing the newsroom and hearing the ticker tape carrying the news. Toscanini would rehearse the symphony orchestra behind the locked doors of Studio 8H, a glamorous place, long since dismantled for television. I was able to do some publicity writing on a freelance basis. My eye was on the news-room, but without a degree in journalism, I could not get near it. Eventually I was transferred to the Voice of America which was then a part of NBC. I wrote letters, among other things, in which I was to imitate the radio rhyming style (like Gilbert and Sullivan ditties) of the director of the English language department. It was fun and helped offset the tensions at home and loss of the kind of writing I had so promisingly begun. Then the Voice of America was taken over by the government and moved to Washington. I was offered a job there but was not free to consider it. I stayed with NBC in the press information department, composing and setting up form replies for every conceivable kind of audience response.

My sister-in-law's mother died and she and the children moved into her mother's apartment. My mother and I then moved into a small apartment building. For the first time in her life, my mother took a job outside of the home. She became a waitress in the Charleston Gardens, a tea room in the B. Altman department store. At that time she told me that she hoped we could save enough money so that I could stay home for a year and write. It was a pipe dream of course, but I treasure that memory, since it was the only time that she made reference to my talent and gave herself a role, no matter how unreal, in nurturing it.

My brother returned from service. I was now thirty, my mother sixty-five. She now had all of 37 dollars a month in

Social Security. The few years she had worked at Altman's had helped my mother; she looked younger, fussed about herself, and had made friends beyond her close family circle. But by the middle 1950's my mother was obviously very ill. The word *Alzheimer* was unknown then. It was simply senility or dementia. She wandered the apartment at night, sometimes stopping by my bed to just stare. I had little sleep. Aunt Josie began to come daily to spend hours with my mother, relieved by Aunt Tessie who was now advanced in years. If there was too much time between their leave-taking and my return from work, my mother could be out looking for her father's house. I was exhausted and my job was threatened. When a nursing home was suggested, I looked at a few and was appalled at the conditions, and even my looking made my aunts and cousins very angry, not really seeing, or wanting to see, what was happening.

My brother and sister-in-law, now living in their own home on Staten Island, and the parents of four daughters, offered to take my mother. They had a room on their first floor that would be hers and there was always somebody at home. I knew it would not work. I sensed that eventually my brother was going to be torn between his mother and his family. By this time both my brother and his wife were deeply involved in extremist politics of the far right, a development that made communication between us already strained. But to everybody else this arrangement seemed like a most generous solution, so I agreed to the move.

Less than three years later, the situation was impossible and I had to find a nursing home. I placed my mother in a home near Central Park West in Manhattan. The emotional stress of such an act is overwhelming. Sometimes I wondered if I could live through this, but my sense of drama and my innermost conviction that life was a journey, though it had many stops – stations, if you will –, that it was a whole, and the connections or fragments had a destination, sustained me. My inner life and spiritual reading deepened. This was no mere pious or sentimental port in a storm. I still knew fierce anger, discouragement and helplessness. It was a reaching into what was already there. Writing was now story-telling to myself. When alone I would go in imagination to a vast and rocky desert, and there in front of a huge boulder, I would meet the Christ. I did not keep a day-by-day journal, but I did record much of what I experienced in this other world.

NBC went through one of its many transitional crises and I lost my job. From every practical point of view, this was the last straw, but I felt almost an exhilaration as if I were being told, *see*, something really wonderful is seeding. By this time, I had had to vacate my apartment, give away most of my belongings and move to a residence for business women who were either new to New York or struggling along on low paying jobs. The place was run by Sisters of Mercy. This was early in 1960. Manhattan was to become my home. This move was forced on me by most stressful conditions, but developments after that, painful and joyous, were to lead to a fulfilled old age that would never have occurred had I remained in lovely provincial Bay Ridge.

When my job at NBC was terminated, a friend in the news department took me to lunch to see what he could do to help. I told him that it was not possible for me to look for a "good" job. I was too exhausted and too shabby to even think of an interview. All of my money, except the $25 a month that I paid to the Devon Claire for room and two meals a day, went to the nursing home. In fact, I told him, I had just applied for welfare for my mother, an act which had my self-esteem at an all-time low. But in spite of my need for money, I needed even more a job that interested me and a place where I could make a contribution. He called Thurston Davis, a Jesuit priest and editor of the small, but esteemed, publication *America*. Father Davis not only made a job for me, but within the year had arranged to have my mother admitted to the Mary Manning Walsh home. It was then, and still is, a model for geriatric care. At last, she was really cared for, and I was in a publishing house.

Thurston Davis taught me everything about proofreading and editing. The pay was unbelievably low, but my name was on the masthead. And, the greatest thrill, I was there in the middle of the action when Pope John XXIII opened the Second Vatican Council. As the great historic documents were being released in Rome, they were rushed to our office, part of the staff got out the weekly magazine, but most of the Jesuits worked endless hours translating them into English. I typed. But to me this was not routine typing job. I was watching my early brash thoughts of what the church should be actually being talked about from the top. When I visited my mother, I found her smiling, with her hair braided with blue ribbons and bright chintz curtains on the windows. My mother died in 1963, the same year as Pope John, John F. Kennedy, John LaFarge and C. S. Lewis, all of whom I held as icons.

Somewhere in these years I took a correspondence course in writing for children. I did a number of stories but did not seriously try to publish them. With my mother gone and my life my own, I moved from the Devon Claire to a midget apartment in one of Columbia's buildings, but the building itself had an elegance that I hungered for. In my sixties, I was able to move to a middle-income co-op where I now live. Writing was now possible, but whenever I seriously attempted to work, I had anxiety attacks.

Back in the NBC years I had done some public speaking. The experience did much to increase my self-confidence and a realization of my need for human response, for an audience for who I am. I made a trip to Ireland with Bob and Kelly Wilhelm who had founded "Storyfest Journeys." On that trip to the land I feel is my own, I discovered my own ability to *tell* stories and to listen to stories. In recent years I have told stories on retreats and in groups. If you are a writer, you are a listener. If you are a writer, you release the power of the person within. It is a response to the Other and a plea for the Self. Published or unpublished, a writer is a creator and has a life worth living.

When the retirement age of 65 came along, I very much needed to add to my Social Security and to build some kind of savings. I was offered a job at Union Theological Seminary, about a three-minute walk from my home. Raymond E. Brown, who died suddenly on August 8, 1998, was not only the first priest, but the first Roman Catholic to teach at Union. He was the foremost New Testament Scripture scholar in this country. I first knew Ray as the distinguished, boyish looking scholar from Union who came every morning to preside at the 7 A.M. mass at the local parish church across the street from Union. As religious thought and churches became more open, Ray's fame grew, and so did offers of chairs and professorships from both secular and religious universities. Union did not want to lose him, so offered him personal secretarial help. He offered me the job. And so I began my last job, which I kept until I was just short of 75 years of age.

This last job, which on the surface was simply that of a secretary, was the most fulfilling job of my life, and the one for which I am most grateful. I handled Ray's affairs during his many world-wide speaking engagements, research projects and sabbaticals, but it was that spirit of the writer that really came into play here. He was a scholar, I was not. He was a *famous* writer, I was a writer. We shared, therefore, that spirit. It was in the transcribing that I realized why I was there. Not only to serve him, but to nourish my own spiritual appetite. With awe I began to realize that I was the first person to hear so many of his insights. The mystical side of this man and his own personal journey to God were vivid undercurrents on these tapes. And my writing soul was ready to hear. Sometimes, hours after a simple conversation with him, he would call me and say that he had caught something in *my* voice, and he would ask if he could help. He was attuned to mystery, whether in the ancient languages he loved, the darkness of history, the story behind the Scriptures, the mystery of God, or the troubles of a friend or colleague. And on that level we met, without either of us ever expressing it. I had had a childhood relationship like that with my father, both before and after his death. I am not so sure that I do not have it with Ray. The power of his life was certainly present at his grave.

*   *   *

In 1978 when Mary Gordon's *Final Payments* was published, a friend lent me his copy, saying "read this, it is a great novel and it is all about you." I read the book and all of her novels after, little knowing that in 1994, when I was 79 years old, I would meet her, study with her and have a rebirth of my writing career.

Morningside Gardens where I live is considered a NORC community, a sociological term meaning that it is a "Naturally Occurring Retirement Community." There are many programs here for older people. In 1994 Mary Gordon received a grant from the Lila Acheson Wallace Foundation. The grant included a public service condition. She offered to conduct a class in creative writing for interested seniors. I was the first to register. From the first thing I wrote, Mary was interested, not only because I wrote well, but because of the similarities in our lives – the influence of our fathers, both with mothers afflicted with dementia, and our Roman Catholic backgrounds. We talked frequently, often about religion. Mary is not only a gifted writer, she is a deeply human person.

In May of 1995, Mary invited Michael T. Kaufman, who then had a column in the *New York Times*, to sit in on one of our meetings. She had asked us to write about our names, and what they meant to us. I did a piece on how and why I was called "Eileen." When I finished, there was a long silence. Two social workers connected with our retirement center were weeping. Mary said to Kaufman, "So much for teaching." Kaufman's May 25, 1995 column opens: "The other day Eileen Tobin, who is 79, and Mary Harkins, who is 77, came down from their respective apartments...." I was thrilled. I had hardly known what it was to have my name in print.

Mary encouraged my memoirs. After her sessions with us were over, I kept in touch. At one point I gave her a section of the memoir that I thought could stand by itself. I didn't hear from her for a long time. Then she called and told me that she had read the story on her way back from a trip to Italy. "I love it," she said, "and want to publish it." I didn't realize that she was guest editor for the Fall 1997 issue of *Ploughshares*, the issue in which my story appeared. The first story I had published in some fifty years!

Where am I going now? I have begun writing poetry. It is a peace-filling genre for me. Perhaps because I can sit by the window and feel the pull of the inner self toward the pencil and onto the paper. So much more intimate than a word processor. I want to put my journals in order, and continue recording both dreams and thoughts. I want long periods of silence. I want more time to just *Be*. I am most grateful for my incredible friends, my home, for the trees under my window, full and moving as life is. I want to deepen my relationship with God.

I have a photograph of Raymond Brown at my retirement party. I was at the home of Phyllis Trible, scholar, feminist, and Ray's esteemed faculty colleague at Union. In the photo, Ray is holding up his glass of champagne in toast. I can still hear him call out, not in his pulpit voice, not in his lecture hall voice, but in the voice I heard for so many years on those tapes: "L'Chaim."

L'Chaim.

Carol Lee Sanchez

she) poems

she) remembered stilts
scraped knees and
summer afternoons
liberally sprinkled with
goathead patches and
lemonade stands where
5 cents bought a tumbler
of tart ice water

she) watched cutglass shimmer on
silk winds and startle crooked
cobblestones beyond repair

steamed acorns recall other days
whispered through soundtracks
and concrete returned to
abstract particles sized and
separated by tamarac
ivy and elm.

⊕

in the midnite of a lesser year
she) plaited braids in
her waist length hair
scratched food from his pockets
to feed her nestlings and
settled for more
another life away
she) breathed silent screams into
her nightly sleeps
planned instant flights –

daily disappearances from
diapers dishes and duty.

⊕

she) had to invent a new
hiding place and couldn't
remember why
her hobby was collecting
aquamarine time
packages of days or
even parts of days
that sang yet
remained translucent –
suspended in her mind
she) heard about others who
collected bits of violence
in paper bags –
cruel images of human
extracts rarefied for
continuous examination
   – oh
    how unrefined

she) noticed moths
springing full grown in
her carefully stored cornmeal
it was a lesson to
take note of

someone dear to her
mentioned that possibility
with specific emphasis and
she) wondered why he'd
conjured up this particular
pestilence –
this slow invasion of larvae
webs and furry wings.

⊕

she) dreamed of
other lives and places
covered over with
sacrificial moratoriums and
sacramental paraphernalia and
felt drowned each awakening

each choice was always adamant
no matter how
carefully considered and so
she) pulled the ballot from the rack
to make her thoughtful x's in each
appropriate box

she) pushed notable fragments
through her mind
assumed a different posture
momentarily
and resolved to note some
long forgotten medicinal recipes:

    boil pine needles
    to get tar
    or – place a stick
    in a pine tree
    no –
    that was too wasteful
    too cruel –
    sassafras tea!
    a general tonic!
    lots of sassafras is
    good for everything.

⊕

she) moved forward because
she) could no longer
hold the surfaces together
around her
they continually raised dust
would not glow anymore
no matter what
she) did or (sd.
and the yellow/gray
reflected everywhere
inside and out

she) pondered unyielding concepts
become daily presents to
unwrap quickly then
stow away on closet shelves
and reexamine on
another day.

she) wanted to remain a spy
undisturbed in her passivity
or a confirmed marxist with
no new creed to expound

the crisp edge of this
hallucination cut through his
tongue-thick-wobbly-words –
she) told herself the difference
was doing or not doing
the stuff they called
their life.

⊕

she) inhabited her universe tenaciously
holding onto the crevices and tiny
bits of obsidian singlemindedly –
her days froze in unison

and sometimes slid past each other
with no marks or scratches
for identification

occasionally
her memory coincided with a
particular day and
a forgotten friend
came to call

the visits began with gossip to share
out of date events to re-examine
and put away with several
cups of coffee and a
halfapack of cigarettes

she) reached conclusions that
heralded a new combination
of possibilities –

the friend always carried a
personal message for her
unaware most of the time
that s/he did so –   but
she) knew
and the messages
she) sent herself
moved her into other dreams.

⊕

she) wanted roses once a month
because she deserved them
she) believed that giving
was connected to loving
but she was wrong in
this case

she) wanted to tell him
that everytime he won
he lost more than he
could measure when the
tallies were counted

she) mourned those days of
intense drama
the words they flung
and emotional
roller coasters he and
she) had constantly created –

she) told herself
she) wanted peaceful quiet and
silent loving as replacement
high drama was too hard –
required huge frames of reference
meticulous accounting and
far too much energy to
track down the story plots
they hatched spontaneously –
at random.
she) dreamed simplicity
over and over while
detailed scenes from the
forties and fifties of
uniformed-g i-joes-
turned-cowboys
dancing rock & roll
floated about in her
consciousness –

she) added deep longing
for spice – focused her will
to strengthen the wish
and finally
her dream came true.

⊕

what clever veils
and marvelous gilding
she) had created to
scourge her memories of
moments not completed
and wishes left in storage
for some future empty day

she) cautioned herself to trust
her mirrors for they spoke the
truth at any moment of what
she) had to understand.
she) knew that
time and matter would always
comply when her visions
were concrete

someday – somewhere – somebody
echoed in her mind
beckoned her to notice all the
minutes these thoughts
filled her daily life

she) hadn't noticed these
packaged conclusions hanging
there til now
always tacked on –
trailing each risky action planned

she) told herself to
leave yesterday to ponder
its hold on tomorrow because
today is the key to anywhere
anytime you decide –

307 | Carol Lee Sanchez

she) knew
the dark side of anything
held mystery for those
filled with adventure
and fear for those
uninitiated into the
unknown

she) hated the notion of
love incorporating contracts
describing boundaries
of contracts designating
authority –
titles of ownership
vesting control over
such things as properties
and human destinies

love is: commitment (he sd.
not saying anything at all
even though the look of him
was filled with intense
concentration

commitment did not explain
her love for him nor how
she) came to know it
in this year of her
unfolding.

⊕

she) wanted to understand her
crumpled mood
to absolve herself for
feeling invaded – overcrowded
out of control

she) was unable to tell herself
she) had gone beyond
her body limits and
demanded more of herself than
she) could part with then

she) expected her muscles to respond
before they were ready and her
body to bend in unfamiliar ways
she) lost her cool and sent
waves of impatience and hostility
outside herself

she) noticed her need and
gave herself plenty of time to
shift paradoxes – tenses and
backyards stretching into woods
and fields

she) gave herself this new place
where time crawls instead of
rushing forward into
concrete and steel
this place
that doesn't dream progress
beyond bigger tractors
harvesters and mowers

she) watched crickets – spiders
mudders – beetles – barn swallows
and butterflies as they visited
her garden

she) noticed that her new
world contained expansive
horizons – magnificent sunsets
and intimate connections with
trees and creatures in
this place.

⊕

she) thought so many
thoughts these days –
sifted and sorted
examined – combined
to discover
she) liked her life –
so far.

she) thought a lot
about her babies now –
grown. gone.
building selves
beyond her reach
outside her daily concerns

she) felt the tug and pull
of their leaving
discovered she wanted to
hold on – keep them nearby.

she) looked forward (she'd sd.
to this time –
a time when her mind
no longer held her babies
day and night
always worried – wondering
if she'd done anything right

so inextricably bound
to all her choices
all her actions
they were her babies
for so many years

mother - mama - mom
she) would always be

to them
she) faced freedom now
without children at home
without mate to remember the
years of always being there

so many years of choices
husbands and lovers –
choices which were
hers alone
because she willed it so

mom - mother - mama
she) would always be
to her three babies grown
grown beyond her choices
grown beyond her dreams.

⊕

she) noted different days
and attitudes
surrounding her like
cream cheese and sunshine

she) tried to remember
other times and places
in accurate detail
found only blurred
images and fuzzy
emotions along with
apple cores and
sunflower seeds
tucked among faded
photographs

she) protested the wait for
new horizons to explore

while swapping recipes and
old stories of once was –
she) protested
so much time invested in
reliving past events
youth spent in glory days
of conquest and achievement

she) wanted to yell at herself
to stop the merry-go-round and
cacophony of raucous pretense
when so many untarnished days
held quiet reflections
simple satisfactions
easy content and
still more mountains
to climb.

⊕

she) sat in endless
meetings
organized moments
into being
discarded thoughts and
bits of herself
into days of no return

she) exchanged molecules
of matter for wishes and
dreams others held dear
while judgements rained
fierce all around her

she) remembered rain barrels
and cellar doors from
a childhood song –
thought about

all her playmates
across time and continents
revisited memory held days
embedded with laughter
and freedom
wished them back again

she reminded herself
tongue-in-cheek that
"life is serious business"
that every ladder to success
displayed that message and
expected her to believe it

she) pondered the success
of rainbows
cumulus clouds
spring blossoms and
winter storms
considered the seriousness
of sparrows and
lilies in the field then
discovered a kernel of joy
hidden in her coat pocket

she) noticed a familiar tune
playing over and over
in her thoughts
    "playmate – come out
      and play with me…"

                ⊕

she) remembered a far away
long ago daydream from
a san francisco
living room rap session
that created a citywide

poetry festival
and later
amidst howls of laughter
made up preposterous rules for
a new bardic tradition
they assumed none of them
could possibly achieve

now years later
she) noted that
without conscious intent
she) had mastered many
of the bardic levels – and –
she) wondered what the
spirits had in store for her
in this new home place

she) thought about trolley cars
and late nite fog horns
mixed with muffled drum beats
guiding dancer's feet
in a far off dusty village
and wondered how she'd
found the trails
to so many different
adventures –
just exactly how
she) had gotten here –
from then

⊕

twilight holds bouquets
scented with possibilities
for another day's adventure –
she) wanted to be
a life preserver –

some sort of savior
reaching out and
healing all wounds
everywhere

she) found her own impeccability
hiding in a corner of
her thoughts and
she) was unable to rise up and
proclaim her innate imperfection

   – all earth beings
rattle on earth   (she sd.
and knew
she) would be misunderstood
misquoted and therefore
hollow in the minds of many

in another world
a pool of misery beckoned
quietly asserting
she) ought to agree with
all the circumstances
posited there –
even the obvious
distortions

in that world
monologues continued to
disperse dictums and
sentiments at random
then impose facts and laws
on startled bystanders

she) reexamined all
common dramas once enacted
created internal
thought loops
to dovetail
back on themselves

go nowhere new
provide few answers to
any and every
what if?
imposed.

she) decided to disconnect
her feed back loops
disengage her thought forms
from
    repeat – repeat
    repeat – encounter

she) noted that reflection on
every perceivable outcome
of any event
consumed great volumes
of energy
to pinpoint
    which cause
    which effect
    which i sd. or
you sd. or he sd. or she sd.
to untangle
    all the i dids
    and didn't do's
remembered
she) saw star seeds of
peace, humanity, harmony
and hope filled futures
circle overhead within easy grasp
yet doomed to remain unplanted
in local present time

on the ground below –
tended with sporadic
voicings of limited endeavors
untilled fields lay waiting
while days were counted as

investments in
    just getting by.

        ⊕

in germany
she) thought about courage
and blood lines
her indian identity
entitlements and the
american dream
the vanishing indian
playing indian
taking dog & pony shows
around the world and
her nonindian identity

she) considered the frenzy
of documentation
in 'indian country'
exploration of detail
examination of culture
and family life
in 'nonindian country'
gave explanations
interpretations of all
symbolical references –
the meaning of this
the reason for that

are you real?
    (they ask
do you still make ceremonies
with dances and song?
    (they ask
or are you just acting without
knowing the meaning?
    (they want to know

she) heard their questions
outside her surprised thoughts of
    what are they saying? – oh
    they're hunting for indians –
    for *real* indians!

she) joined in on the projections
and explanations
dredged details from experience
to meet expectations
then lulled herself into compliance
with the scholarly tasks
at hand

she) remained transfixed by
this continued attention
toward every possibility of
indigenous aboriginal life
she) listened to monologues
listened to dialogues
heard all arguments
understood the necessity
for 're-inventing
the enemy's language'
and wondered when this wave
would crash into all the
other waves gone before.

in years past
she) had visited celtic
shrines and ludwig's castles
talked with shamans and
healers from various
parts of the world

she) had danced in
the dalai lama's space
moved parallel to

his movements in time –
coalesced energies within
nearby circles
in the mountains and
valleys among the
people who called her there.

⊕

she) posited new assumptions
outside biblical terms
    no trumpets blaring
    no archangels to
fix her position in time
and space like h.d. had –
    no european allegorical
    allusions or illusions to
    draw upon

maybe the wind brothers
guided her steps –
whisked her across
continent and ocean
to a cloud covered city
on the baltic sea

she) had come to speak
about the ancient ways
of the indigenous people of
her nation and noticed
her words touch oversouls
waiting to be connected again

she) wondered which faces
contained old friends
from other times –
wondered what future effects
these connections would seed

and if
she) would ever meet
these old friends
again

she) had arrived here
by 'accident and chance'
looked around and discovered
governments in reform
felt freedom seeking light
and was awed into silence
by this reality
she) was living.

⊕

back home
she) thought about her
european journeys
and decided that approbation
and acceptance were relative
she) watched blue jays scamper
among the bare twigs
and branches of her backyard
mulberry tree

this moment invaded her awareness
and she hugged herself –
draped herself
with a new gladness of
coming home
while a sense of belonging
permeated every cell
of her body

she) wanted to talk
about this new sensation

right away –
she) needed talking
required it to balance her being
she) could not imagine living mute
unable to impose sounds of
her own making into the universe
she) decided to immerse
herself in every aspect
of her home life
and thought about
the days tasks instead.

⊕

she) followed raindrops
to the bottom of her soul
and found lemondrops
in the back of her throat
she) leaned on hardwood floors
counted stars and flowers then
wished melodies outside her mind

sometimes –
longing visited her and
she) could not place its origin
could not locate the horizon
it beckoned toward and so
she) returned
to the daily ordinary –
pushed magic into view
to shift her focus
from barred windows
to open doorways because
she) wanted selfmade exhilaration
for her journeys through
ordinary days

images riding on the back
of an old song
filled her thoughts until
she) remembered they were
"only the echoes of her mind"

she) thought about crystal and topaz
mixed with opals and turquoise mountains
pondered her good fortune at length
and finally bathed herself in
the genuine acceptance
she felt in her new home

she) permitted herself to
experience this rare sensation
and watched lonesome fade
into silent background memories.

⊕

elements of surprise
filtered into her
daily routines
displaced her
doubtful moments and
she) wondered if her
time scattered projects would
ever meet her expectations –
relieve her anxiety
on moonless nights
and cloudy days when
pen or brush in hand
countless images
arose in her mind as
she) faced blank surfaces
unable to choose the
most unique among them

to place upon the page
she) watched january snowflakes
display themselves in
intermittent sunlight
noticed her correspondence
with the weather
wondered which it
would be –
dark skies and snowfall
or sunlight and snowmelt

she) moved into a new decade
in this year of her life
accepted her role as
grandmother
yet uncertain of her
role as   elder

she) remembered her
grandmother's stories
how the ancestors knew
this cycle well
understood the phases
of transformation
had ceremonies and
celebrations to mark
the transitions from
mother to grandmother
grandmother to elder
she) dreamed the songs
sung by those women
in the clans
the bands
the lodges
so long ago
so very long ago

in her dreams
she) heard the grandmothers
singing.

323 | Carol Lee Sanchez

⊕

she) pursued her versions
of reality
continued to separate
the caustic from
the sublime
reexamined anecdotal
testimonials – support
for her methodology

why on earth would anyone
want to discover nothingness?
   (she sd.

she) stumbled upon an argument
over enlightenment
almost entered the fray
with her usual
    – yes but
    what about
oh my
she) was guilty – oh yes – of
thought and deed contrary
to mainstream
whimsical fancies –
    – hear hear
liberation was now don't you know
it's a mainstream fashion
has been for decades
(they sd.
    – but you see
she) interposed
    – liberating
    saturated fat from
    human ingestion
(because it produces

bad cholesterol
clogs arteries
expands skeletal waifs
into overweight blimps
    – could be perceived
    as a vegetarian plot!
(a well organized
conspiracy to remove
animal fat, flesh, other
disgusting by products
from human consumption!

she) thought about visions
and versions of visions and
which version her intellect
measured compatible
with her daily life

she) posited priorities
(those choices acted on
and reviewed her versions
of terrorists
and terrorists acts
connected to causes
espousing liberation and
sometimes thinly cloaked
as virulent inquisitions.

      ⊕

she) considered tradition
as a concept
the importance of symbols
as conceptual referents
the significance of numbers
imposed on acts
of acts as events repeated

often enough to
become traditions
repetitious movements and
moments directed toward
some imagined goal

she) considered imagination
and human attempts to
embrace the unimaginable
(a thought/word that belies
its existence
she) named ritual tradition
a value system
a method for invoking
specific attitudes
ritual tradition as a
container for cultural dreams

she) understood how
'mom and apple pie'
        invoked
'family – hearth – home'
required deep attachment
to a cultural past
        imposed
reverence for traditions
        forbade
change of any kind

she) read somewhere that –
'a culture seeks to preserve itself'
        – yes but   (she sd.
it must factor in bizarre controls
brutal methodologies and
carefully organized religions
as perpetrators of
cultural survival

she) pondered current shifts

in consciousness
polarization of attitudes
ugliness in the streets in
cities around the world

cities – towns – countrysides
seemingly filled with
angry people unhappy people
desperate people hungry people
frightened people and
she) noted phrases like:
   world banking system
   global marketplace
   global economy
   global communications
were as commonplace as
'mom and apple pie'
were new ritual symbols
repetitiously invoked
calling alternative realities
into being
birthing a different set
of bizarre controls
renaming cultural survival
creating
techno-info theologies –
theoretical networks built to
catch cultural dreams
reaching for unified fields
   – all in a days work
she) told herself
musing over myriads
of circumstances

endless conversations
and favorite authors
jumped in and out of her
memory banks left her

exhilarated but drained
   – well
   i am not an accident
of molecular 'evolution'
she) told herself
   – i am a
participant in consciousness!!
an active co creator
evolving!

     ⊕

she) imagined mountains
across her path as
objects to climb
metaphors to move about
or objections to remove –
she) was always
testing her abilities
to survive and endure

she) forgot about cloud people
and rain birds
encircling the crests
another vision
she) could hold

she) wanted to:
state the problems
implement solutions
(the most effective
for any moment
in this place

she) wanted to
create a shiny image to:
invoke a startling metaphor
bursting with robin

wren and blue bird songs
with pen brush ink and paint
in sound filled colors and
muted black and white

she) reached for
enlightened forms
clarity of mind but:
pure essence evaded
her grasp
would not be caught
nor caged nor stilled
for lengthy observation
for indefinite consultation

she) dipped her soul
into spaces around her
her hands into substance –
(creative matter
found the whispers
between her thoughts
singing:
  i am light
  i am change
  i flow soft
  across a surface
  become a line
  then thicken
  expand into plane
  reborn: i am shape

  i am space holding shapes
  shape-shifter/trickster
  i shape-shift to volume
  disappear to other
  dimensions where:

  i am dark
  i am change

i reappear as you envision
i am raven
i am coyote
i am your vision

now spider is my name...

Afterword

Growing up in a small isolated country town, a person of mixed-blood, part of me felt I could never quite fit in any place. I was this or that or something else. And yet, I ended up in exciting places like San Francisco and Riga and Leipzig, doing incredible things that I only read about in books when I was a youngster. For example, I was director of Poets in the Schools for the state of California, I taught at San Francisco State, I was invited to Germany to participate in a healers' conference in '84 and as an author, lecturer in '94. The *she) poems* reflect the lucky, and at the same time, sad and confused young woman who was doing all these things.

I grew up in a land grant town in New Mexico that consisted of approximately twenty families. We lived right by the store, a general merchandise store my family owned, where people from both Navajo and Pueblo reservations came because it was a big trading company. We lived in a hundred-year-old adobe house – my grandparents lived right next door. That house in that small community was my reality for thirty years. No movies, no drugstores; our family and two other families in that whole community had the only homes with running water. For the first eight years of my life, we had no flush toilet.

My mother is a quarter Laguna and not quite half of French Canadian Indian. My grandmother divorced her first husband when my mother was barely months old – she wanted nothing to do with him and would give my mother almost no information about him whatsoever. As far as she was concerned that part of her life was done, over with. When my mother was four, Grandma remarried – a German Jew who was born in Germany, whom I knew as my grandfather.

Edited from a taped interview.

331 | Carol Lee Sanchez

In 1939, he brought his oldest brother and his brother's wife to this country and settled them in the little village where my folks lived. So I grew up hearing a lot of German.

My dad's Lebanese, first-generation American. His father was born in a little town outside Beirut. But my great grandfather had already come over alone in the late 1800's and peddled souvenirs from the Holy Land up and down Fifth Avenue in New York. He went to Woolworth's, bought rosaries and little lockets he filled with "true slivers of the cross." That's how he made a living initially. He wore his Arabic garb, the full burnoose, and was part of exotic New York. Later, he brought his wife and son to America and came West peddling and eventually opened a general merchandise store in New Mexico Territory. My dad was born in the small land grant town of Seboyeta, where his folks settled, and grew up speaking Spanish and Arabic. English was his third language.

My mother who was born on the reservation at Laguna went to school in Cubero, a Spanish-speaking community, after my grandparents moved there. Both my parents spoke Spanish when they wanted to talk about something they didn't want us to know. I picked up Spanish because I was nosey – I wanted to know what they were talking about.

I also heard Indian languages when Navajos and Pueblos came into our store to trade. And my first husband, whom I married in 1952, was a first-generation Italian whose folks spoke Italian. I discovered that I have an ear for language. It's easy for me to immerse myself in a new language – pretty soon even though I can't speak it, I'm understanding what people are saying. Maybe it's a terror of not knowing what's going on – to such an extent that my whole body goes into overdrive and says, *tell me what's happening.*

I also grew up with several very different musical traditions. Sometimes, when I'm meditating on a particular subject for a poem, I'll notice a drumbeat in the rhythm of my thoughts. It will be incorporated in the enunciation, the syllabics, the way I choose words. Or I'll hear that goatskin drum Mediterranean people play, or the *oud,* the little stringed instrument I grew up with, which is a very different, much more passionate, very adrenaline-raising kind of music. Or finger cymbals. And then, growing up in the West, I was raised on cowboy music. I was a horsewoman – I rode horses, I roped, branded.

I think the closest I come to integrating these aspects of language and music consistently turns out to be in the *she) poems*. The *she) poems* began to come out in the late '60's, early '70's, as the voice of an "observer" recording my life through the eyes of this other woman who is living an incredible life. It's as if one part of me is standing aside, observing what the other experiences. And yet, they're both me. Different rhythms move through the poems, but they have to fit, like a puzzle or gloves. The challenge has been to balance and harmonize all of it so that it is one voice. I had to turn sixty to really make it work.

The poems came out in short and then longer bits over a period of twenty years. They dried up during years when there was a lot of upheaval in my life. Then, in 1984, on my first trip to Europe, I returned to them again – I did the journey sections during three months there, the sections about my discovery of Ludwig and his castles, of discovering a past life in Germany.

But then, after I moved here to the Missouri farm in 1989, I wasn't able to write. After working for two years at beginning to renovate our Victorian farmhouse, I realized I was totally cut off from everything and everyone I knew. I knew no one in Missouri – I was sixty miles away from a community where I knew one person, my mother-in-law. I needed dialogue and conversation, I needed feedback, interaction. I realized that I had to start something new for myself. So I got involved in the local art community and, drawing on my teaching background, started teaching classes on American Indian spiritual frameworks and culture at the junior college. And then the observer was watching again, seeing me living a new segment of my life. That's when it came together.

While I was in Europe again in the fall of '94, I started

writing more *she) poems,* whole big chunks. And when I came back, I really knew I had come home – a *new gladness/of coming home.* I had a home for the first time in many, many years.

Recently I re-edited the early parts, cleaned them up, changed them so they would fit with all the rest. When I say "cleaned," I mean the cleanliness of image, the blending of image with abstract, intellectual reflections which are also part of who we are. She) is living all those experiences. And she's reflecting. Because she's also an academic, a scholar, she uses analytical language. And the journaling voice, which is another aspect of women's writing, finds its way in.

I'm aware of the long way I've come in my writing. When you start you don't know what you're doing, you're insecure, unsure. Every word that you put down you throw away, then you pull another and throw that away. And you defend a piece of junk because it's your precious words. Early on I was writing "poetry-ese," but I couldn't understand why people were calling it that. Big heavy duty poets would say, *that's not poetry.* Or my sister, who has an MFA in litera-ture, would say, *that's not poetry.* Well, how do you know what's poetry? I would struggle with that when I was first writing, long before the *she) poems,* and ask, what's the difference between good and bad.

I think it was, again, a matter of my never quite feeling good enough. I felt that because I came from a multicultural background, I wasn't really immersed in the English lan-guage. When you have so many languages around you, float-ing in your consciousness, you never get to the inference level, the deep empathic and telepathic level of a language. The only one you have that in is your native language and which one is my native language – none of them really.

So I forced myself into English, into all of its levels. I immersed myself in the literature. Then, by osmosis, I began to pick up the inferences. Still, I feel that English is one of the most difficult languages on the planet in which to express your fullest passion. You have to fight, you have to work so hard. I know Spanish well and I know that in Spanish your passion is right there – on the edge, immediate. In regard to the Indian languages that I come from, though Indians are not overly passionate people, when they are, the words are there immediately. English is a watered-down language. You just have to describe and describe and describe to communicate one bloody moment of passion.

Eventually there came a point when I understood that I had mastered certain skills. There's a surety, knowing that you've acquired skills, that you've honed them. When you pick up a pen you know right away, for the most part, if it's going to be good work. When it's not, you throw it away. Of course, you always continue to refine. And there's always new information, another perspective, another way of seeing. There's always growth that can take place.

At the time of the *she) poems'* first emergence, I felt there was an audience that wanted and needed to hear what I had to say – as I need and want what other people have to say. I say "emergence" because it's a word that means a lot in the Laguna tradition – we emerged from the Fourth World into the present world. We emerge into sunlight, into daylight, into full flower, into full bloom, which is happening for women around the world. I feel very much a part of that.

The *she) poems* were an attempt to speak to multicultural women, to mothers, wives, mistresses, to aspects of womanhood, girlhood, childhood that reside in any individual woman. I know, if it's like that in me, it's got to be like that in other women.

Many voices of women speak in the *she) poems.* One of them, ironically, is almost a male voice. I have a female body, but many times I'm both male and female, I can perceive both. I grew up in a very "macho" man's world in the country, in the ranching business. At one point I hated being a female because I wasn't allowed to do the heavy things. Then I discovered I could, and was left alone to do what I wanted to do. I am a domineering person in many respects, I know how to be a general – I'm a Capricorn, what can I say! I know how to be a leader and to direct people as a manager or chairwoman. In this culture that's a very male characteristic. I used to have to hide it because it was unacceptable in white culture, but it's not unacceptable in Indian culture. Laguna women are very strong, it's a matriarchy, a woman-centered culture.

My mother, however, did the opposite from what her mother did. She shifted to being the one that was more outwardly dependent on her mate than my grandmother was. She was almost a half-breed and it's painful being a half-breed, because the tribe punishes you and the white culture punishes you – neither group lets you be who you are. Everybody reminds you that you are the product of miscegenation, so if you can pass, hide it. But I never wanted to live like that. I wanted to live out in the open, so that whatever I've done, if you find out about it, it's okay.

And then there's the voice of the mother, thinking about my kids. I've been a welfare mother. I lived on food stamps for a short time. I used to buy twenty-five pound lots of oats and then cornmeal from a natural foods warehouse – that's the story behind *she) noticed moths/springing full grown*....

There's the voice of the grandmother. And the woman of color, an Indian woman – the responsibility of being an elder, accepting that cloak; it's a heavy responsibility. If I've done anything in my life, I've run away from that responsibility a goodly portion of my life. But when you are tribally connected, you are connected for life. Being an elder means you have responsibilities for the ongoing education of the children, and that's your contribution to the tribe, making sure that the children have an historical continuity even if you live away from the tribe. I have learned to accept that now I'm the carrier of history, now this information must go out to the children. The *she) poems* carry some history and information that's going to children generations down the line. I don't write for the present, I write for the future. I've always known that.

Acknowledgements

Nellie Wong

Thanks to the editors of the following publications in which some of these poems first appeared: *Berkeley Fiction Review, Freedom Socialist Newspaper* and *Long Shot*.

Florence Weinberger

Hiding was previously published in *Lifecycles, V.2: Jewish Women on Biblical Themes in Contemporary Life,* Debra Orenstein & Jane Rachel Litman, eds. (Woodstock, Vt.: Jewish Lights Publishing, 1997). Permission granted by Jewish Lights Publishing.

From Where the Feet Grow, Apple and *American Beauty* were originally published in *The Invisible Telling Its Shape,* poems by Florence Weinberger, (Fithian Press, 1997).

Several poems in this work were originally published in the following publications: *Calyx, Poetry/LA, The Raven Chronicles, Ghosts of the Holocaust: An Anthology of Poetry by the Second Generation. Mame Loshen, the Mother Tongue* was reprinted in *Truth and Lies That Press for Life* and *Grand Passion: The Poets of Los Angeles and Beyond. Survivor* was reprinted in *Images from the Holocaust* and *Blood to Remember: American Poets on the Holocaust.*

Pearl Garrett Crayton

How Deep the Feeling Go first appeared, as first prize winner, in the 1995 *Chapbook of the Deep South Writers Conference.* The poem *Black Cat* first appeared in *Reed Magazine,* 1991. *Driving* was first published as a "distinguished work" in the 1999 *Detroit Black Writers Guild Chapbook.*

Joan Swift

The poems *Your Hands, My Scream, The Phone Calls, Exchange* and *The Lineup* are reprinted from *Parts of Speech* with the permission of Confluence Press © Joan Swift 1980. The poems *Ravine, Coroner, Her Husband, Victim, Beside her Husband, Her Husband, to Himself, His Mother, His Sister, D'Lo, de l'Eau, Another Witness, Detective* and *Prisoner* are reprinted from *The Dark Path of Our Names* © Joan Swift 1985 with the permission of Dragon Gate, Inc.

The quotation from William Stafford's poem, *Thinking for Berky,* was published in *Traveling Through the Dark,* Harper & Row, © William Stafford 1962.

The quotation in Spanish appearing in *Why She Wants to be Sand* is from César Vallejo's XLV, translated by James Wright and published in *Neruda and Vallejo: Selected Poems,* edited by Robert Bly and published by Beacon Press. © Robert Bly 1971. © The Sixties Press 1962, 1967.

This manuscript was completed with support from the National Endowment for the Arts.

The poems in the section entitled *1970,* with the exception of *Perjury,* appeared in *Parts of Speech,* published by Confluence Press, Lewiston Idaho, © Joan Swift 1978. Those in the section entitled *1983* were published in *The Dark Path of Our Names,* Dragon Gate, © Joan Swift 1985. I have made some minor changes in the poem entitled *His Mother.*

The poem on page 105 beginning "Sister victim, I could have told you storms…" first appeared as part of a seven-sonnet sequence entitled *A Crown* which won second prize in the Ann Stanford Memorial Award, *The Southern California Anthology,* Fall 1988. *Nightjar* was first published in *Poetry Northwest,* Summer 1992.

My thanks still to Senior Deputy District Attorney Rockne Harmon of the Alameda County District Attorney's Office in California, as well as to Inspector Art Guzman, without whose help many of these poems could not have been written.

I am also grateful to the National Endowment for the Arts, Ingram Merrill Foundation, and the Washington State Arts Commission for their support during the writing of most of these poems.

Also available from Chicory Blue Press

The Crimson Edge: Older Women Writing, Volume One, edited by Sondra Zeidenstein. "A revolutionary book." – Carolyn G. Heilbrun.

A Wider Giving: Women Writing after a Long Silence, edited by Sondra Zeidenstein. "A masterly achievement." – May Sarton.

A Detail in that Story, poems by Sondra Zeidenstein. "One of the best and most honest books I've read this year." – Sapphire.

Memoir, poems by Honor Moore. "It is not only beautiful work, it is brave." – Carolyn Forché.

Heart of the Flower: Poems for the Sensuous Gardener, edited by Sondra Zeidenstein. "This is an anthology of pure delight." – Gerald Stern.

....

Order from:

Chicory Blue Press, Inc.
795 East Street North
Goshen, CT 06756
(860) 491-2271

Please send me the following books:

_____ copies of *The Crimson Edge, Volume Two* at $17.95

_____ copies of *The Crimson Edge, Volume One* at $16.95

_____ copies of *A Wider Giving* at $14.95

_____ copies of *A Detail in that Story* at $12.95

_____ copies of *Memoir* at $11.95

_____ copies of *Heart of the Flower* at $13.95

Name _____

Address _____

_____

Connecticut residents, please add sales tax.

Shipping: Add $3.20 for the first book and $.50 for each additional book.